Contents

Tales of the Sword ....
Wolf Killer 2
The Bloody Hill at Senlac 38
Wulfstan: the making of a Varangian... 70
The Hostile Land... 121
Other books by Griff Hosker... 179

Tales of the Sword

By
Griff Hosker

Published by Sword Books Ltd 2020

Copyright ©Griff Hosker First Edition

The author has asserted their moral right under the Copyright, Designs and Patents Act, 1988, to be identified as the author of this work.
All Rights reserved. No part of this publication may be reproduced, copied, stored in a retrieval system, or transmitted, in any form or by any means, without the prior written consent of the copyright holder, nor be otherwise circulated in any form of binding or cover other than that in which it is published and without a similar condition being imposed on the subsequent purchaser.
A CIP catalogue record for this title is available from the British Library.

Foreword

This is a series of stories culled from the pages of the notes from my novels. There is Wolf Killer from the Dragonheart books. I killed off Wolf Killer too early in the series because I felt he was taking away from the real story, that of his father. Then there is Wolf who comes from the Housecarl series and his story enables me to tell the tale of the Battle of Hastings. There are characters I sketched out and did not fully develop, like Robert of St. Michel from the Anarchy series of novels. Wulfstan only appeared in the first Anarchy novel but I wanted to fill in the back story of how men joined the Varangian Guard and why. This compilation is one of, what might become, a number. We shall see. I hope you enjoy this sample of my work.

Volume 2 should be out towards the end of the year and will encompass the modern era from the Napoleonic Series to World War 2.

Wolf Killer

My name is Wolf Killer but I was born with the name Arturus. I am the son of the legendary warrior, Dragonheart, and there was a time when my father and I did not get along. It was a curse caused the rift. I had caused the curse and so I never spoke to my father about it. Perhaps I should have. When we look back on events, we see them so clearly and our course of action becomes so obvious that we wonder why we did what we did. I am beginning the tale at the end and that is never a good place for the end is when you know all and see things clearly when, at the time they are happening, they are hidden in a fog, a little like my words.

It was hard growing up with a father like Dragonheart. I knew of none in our clan who did not simply like him but almost adored him; to them, he could do no wrong. He had his enemies, of course, but they were Danes and Saxons who were nithings and lived beyond our land, the Land of the Wolf. I became an Ulfheonar like him and I even killed my first wolf when I was little more than a boy. This was a feat which was sung about by Haaken the Bold who normally sang about the Dragonheart. I was always trying to catch up with my father. Moreover, I had a flaw within me. I saw it and I knew that my wife, Elfrida, did too. I hoped that my father, Dragonheart, did not but I wondered if he would see the inherent weakness that lay deep within me. I was afraid to fail and any fear was a weakness. I wonder now if my mother's death had caused the division. Of course, I did not like Brigid, his new wife, for she was a follower of the White Christ and although she appeared to accept our way of life, I was suspicious of her. That helped to drive me away from my father's home and I wonder now what would have happened had I stayed by the Water under the gaze of the mountain that was Old Olaf.

I was, of course, happy at Elfridaby. I had my wife and two young sons as well as my hall and hearthweru, the Wild Boars. I had raided Neustria with Asbjorn the Strong and Eystein the Rock. We had lost men but brought back great quantities of treasure. I was not short of coins for my father always gave me a share of his treasure when he raided yet I resented it for it seemed as though I could not take my own. Now that I had a large amount of treasure, I would make Elfridaby as strong as Cyninges-tūn. We would have a harder task for I did not have the Water for defence. I had a boggy piece of ground and a small river but I had seen enough Roman walls to know how to use nature to help defend my hall.

Garth, my youngest son, was little more than a babe who had just begun to crawl, toddle, climb and, generally, make his mother's life hectic. However, Ragnar, the elder of the two, was big enough to be able to help me and my warriors as we toiled digging ditches and hewing trees to make a palisade. Siggi Flat Nose was the leader of my hearthweru and he ensured that all the men worked as hard as he did. It meant the work moved on at a rapid pace so that at the end of each day we could see the progress that we had made. It made the food each night taste all the better and the ale we drank all the sweeter.

The fact that I had taken a wife and children encouraged my men to do the same. Neustria was the first raid for some years and the young men who had first been the Wild Boars were now men grown and they had planted their seed in the maids. Not all of the women they took as wives were of our clan. We had taken slaves. My father had begun life as a slave and slavery was not the end of the world as my father had proved, for Dragonheart, this had been a beginning. I gave those who married a farm for, like my father, I knew that a man who had ties to the land would fight all the harder to defend it and I would have a barrier around my hall. We also attracted others who journeyed to my land which was fertile and easy to farm. Cyninges-tūn was surrounded by a ring of peaks. There was not as much land for farming until one reached Windar's Mere or the Rye Dale. Here the land was rolling and the hills and peaks lay to the north and west of us. Sigtrygg, further south, also enjoyed more attractive farmland. So it was that young men, some with families and some without, came to ask me for permission to farm. None were Saxons for the Mercians feared our pagan ways. Each man who came was examined by Siggi and me. We listened to their words and looked in their eyes. We looked for the hidden cross of the White Christ. Any who did not meet with our approval was sent hence. More than half of those who came were sent away.

One of the first things we did with the new men was to train them to fight in our shield wall. Once a week we would gather at Elfridaby, on the raised, dry ground where we grazed cattle, sheep and pigs. The boys would drive the animals from the grazing into the pen we had constructed and then my men and boys would practise the art of war. The youngest boys, like Ragnar, had slingshots. The ones who were a little older and had more strength used bows. All of the rest had a shield and a spear. We would practise our formations. My men would form up in two lines with my hearthweru in the centre of the first line. We had, generally, mail and a helmet. Also in the front rank, would be the men who had a helmet and some sort of mail. Often this would be just a vest or a hide jerkin with pieces of metal sewn on. The rest would be the ones who often only had a spear, shield and a sword. The slingers and archers would stand before us. We taught them all how to open ranks to allow our boys to retreat through our ranks and we practised changing into a wedge. As Jarl, I would be the tip of the wedge. Siggi would stand behind me to my right and Faramir the Fair would be to his left for they were my best two warriors. The front ten were my hearthweru. We would bang our shields and chant; I had no Haaken One Eye to compose sagas and my chants were quite simple. We used them to control our speed and to keep us all in step. We would practise thrusting with our spears at imaginary enemies. When we had finished with the work on our formation, we would take wooden practice swords and spar while the slingers and archers practised hitting targets. They knew the range of their weapons and tried to be as accurate as possible.

My wife was not a volva like my sister but, even though she was a Saxon, she had some powers. She had been abducted, along with my son, by the witch Angharad and taken to Ynys Môn. Since then she had kept her powers hidden. One evening after I had had another successful day working on my walls, my wife seemed distracted. It was not Garth for he had eaten well and was now being rocked to sleep by Bergljót, a thrall. My wife and I were close; I think we were closer than my father was to Brigid. I sensed that something was wrong.

"What worries you, my love? Are you ill?" Warriors feared nothing save ailments striking their families for we could not fight disease and the Sisters!

She smiled and patted the back of my hand, "It is probably nothing but…"

"But what? Speak for if there is aught which disturbs you then I should know." I began to fear that it was something serious.

She sighed, "For the past month I have been aware of some threat here in Elfridaby. I could not put my finger on it but it seemed to me that there was some power at work."

"A witch?"

Shaking her head, she said, "Not here but close. No, it was not a witch but …" she shook her head, "it is hard to explain to a warrior. Kara and her women would understand. There is harmony in the land for all of the people work together. Until a month since we had that harmony but for the last moon, I have sensed a disturbance." She smiled, "You know when there is an itch you wish to scratch but cannot find it?" I nodded. "It is like that."

I felt helpless for I could do nothing about such things; I was a warrior. "Let me know when you sense anything. Perhaps I should build a steam hut so that you can dream as Kara and Aiden do."

"That might help but I do not have your sister's powers. I will speak with the other volva in the village and ask them to spin with me. Sometimes the collective minds of women can be a great force."

The seed was planted in my mind. Over the last two months or so five warriors had come to join us. I had seen nothing untoward in any of them and, indeed, they had all fitted in well. They all lived in my warrior hall with the hearthweru who were unmarried. The next day as we worked on a wooden tower we were building at the south-eastern corner, I watched the five who had recently arrived. Sven Broad Shoulders and Folki Folkisson were the eldest of them all. They looked to have seen twenty summers. The other three were little more than youths who wished to be warriors. Dreng the Dane, Bjorn Dog Tooth and Vermund Larsson had all arrived together and it was those three who seemed to me the ones whose story, now that my wife had set me thinking, I mistrusted the most. They had come from the land to the south and east. Their story was a plausible one. Two had lived south of Loidis and their village had been attacked by Mercian raiders. The two of them had been the only ones to escape the slaughter for they had been watching the sheep on the fells. They had Mercian weapons they said that they had taken from some of the Mercians they had caught. They met up with the third, Bjorn Dog Tooth who had also been orphaned and they became shield brothers. At the time I had believed them but now I began to doubt myself.

Sven Broad Shoulders had come from Jorvik and hated, so he said, the Danes. His father had been killed in a blood feud and the jarl had banished Sven. Sven was angry for he knew it was all false. They had wanted his father's farm and this way they got it. Folki Folkisson was the most intriguing, He said that he had sailed with Hrolf the Horseman and when he had heard of the Land of the Wolf, he had been curious enough to wish to travel to see it. I had taken both of these stories at face value but now I began to think of reasons to suspect them. Folki had never even tried to get to Cyninges-tūn and if he had truly wished to see the heart of the Land of the Wolf then he would have gone there. Jorvik was a cesspit of Danes and Saxons who hated us. Any man who came from there was suspicious but there was something about Sven that I liked. I had made mistakes before and so I determined to watch them all closely.

It was Siggi who discovered the signs of a spy. He and some of my hearthweru were hunting in the woods to the south-west of us. As yet it was still wild and there were not even trails there, except for the ones made by animals. Siggi spotted the marks left by a sealskin boot. Had we not had recent rain then he would not have seen it but he did and knew it was not one of ours for none had been in the woods for a month. I was fortunate that he mentioned it to me when he returned. He was surprised at my reaction. "Is there something I should know, Wolf Killer?"

I nodded and led him to the gatehouse wall which was empty. I told him of my wife's premonition, and he said, "So this may be the cause of the unrest in your wife's mind? Either a traitor in our camp or a spy in the woods?"

I had not thought of that and I wondered if I had misjudged my new men.

Stroking his plaited beard, he said, "If you wished to ensure that it cannot be one of the five then throw them from your land or have them killed."

I thought that a little draconian and shook my head, "It would break my wife's heart to think of someone dying because she had a strange feeling and I do not think I could live with either killing or evicting four honest men."

"There may be more than one spy."

I shook my head, "You are filling my mind with joy, Siggi Flat Nose! That single snake which wriggled through my dreams will now become a nest." I wondered what my father would do. Then it came to me; he would use his head. "We can kill two birds with one stone. If there is a spy in the woods and one of our people is talking to him then let us flush him out. The next time we have all of the clan for training then let us go to the woods and form a line of beaters and drive the man into a trap. His accomplice or accomplices may give themselves away and, at the very least, we can ensure that we have no spies watching us."

It was two days later when our bondi farmers and warriors gathered at my hall for their training. This was the one day of the week that they all enjoyed. Most brought their families and the women would gather with their children to exchange ideas about food, spinning and the ailments which were circulating amongst their families. The men liked the fact that they could fight or train to fight. There would rarely be blood but in the sparring, many of my warriors enjoyed the challenge of defeating one of my hearthweru who were equally keen to avoid an ignominious defeat. It made for a lively and entertaining time.

I addressed them all, "Today, we are training you all for different skills than normal." I could see that I had them intrigued, "As you know my father and I are both Ulfheonar and one of the skills we employ is the ability to hide in plain sight. I would not expect you to do that but we have discovered that someone, not of this clan, has passed close by our land. Siggi and I believe that he is still around. I do not know about you but I do not like the idea of someone lurking close by. Today we will hunt but it will not be the game which inhabit the wood of Hesel. We will hunt a man." My Ulfheonar had been told of the possible traitor and I did not need to look at the five suspects for my men were already doing just that. "Siggi and I will join the beaters and the rest of my hearthweru will ride to the far side of the wood in case our unwanted guest tries to escape. You will not need your helmets nor your shields. Take spears, bows and swords. If we find this person, I want to question him. There may well be an innocent reason for all of this but, equally, there may be something sinister! This is my valley and I will protect it against all enemies."

This was the moment when the spy in my camp, if he was inexperienced, might run. No one moved.

"Hearthweru ride!" As they galloped off, I shouted, "Siggi will assign your positions!"

Siggi made it look partially random but he had each of the five separated from the others and flanked by two men we knew to be beyond reproach. I took the right-hand side and Siggi the left. Ragnar stood with me. He had no idea of the threat but thought it a great game. He had with him his sling and I just said, "Stay close to me, no matter what happens."

"Aye, father!"

I still hoped, as we set off towards the wood, that I was wrong and that we would find just a spy and that had been the disturbance my wife had felt. My hearthweru were taking a long loop around the wood and they would be in position before we started our march through the wood. There had been a Roman fort close by and the Romans had copsed the wood at some time in the distant past; we still used it to collect wood for the winter. The result was a light and airy place which the deer enjoyed for the wolves had long since retreated north of Úlfarrberg. There were brambles and weeds but the animals had grazed them so that their paths were still usable. They were not human paths and led to places of shelter and water. Whoever was in the wood would be close by water and would have had to take an animal trail to get there. When we reached the wood, I used hand signals to position the men. We had just five paces between us. I handed my spear to Ragnar and took out my sword. "Stand behind me and hand me my spear if I need it."

"Aye, father." I heard the nervous tension in his voice. We were hunting the most dangerous of prey, man! I had no path before me and would have to clear one. When Siggi raised his spear, I signalled with my sword for us to move forward. I hacked through the brambles and, taking out my seax, hacked at my left to move the spiky plant away from Ragnar. A thorn could take out an eye. I was pleased that even the boys kept silent. We were making enough noise as it was for each sword or seax slash through the foliage seemed inordinately loud. Our prey, however, would have no idea how many men sought him. As my line of men moved inexorably towards the centre, I began to picture the man. Unless he had fled before we began the hunt, he would know that men were approaching from the northeast. Logically he would run south and west but, if he was clever, he would head south and east or north and west. That was why Snorri and I were positioned as we were. If he chose to be clever then he would have to face one of us.

It was Sven Broad Shoulders who shouted to let us know he had found the camp. I wondered if the cry was to warn his ally. I shouted, "Hold your positions! Ragnar, stand here. Olvir, watch my son."

"Aye, jarl!"

I walked along my line until I reached Sven. He pointed to the ground, "See, Jarl Wolf Killer, here he made his fire. You can feel that the coals are still warm." He pointed to a spot between the fire and the water, "And you can see there where he emptied his bowels." He shook his head, "It is a poor warrior who shits so close to his bed!"

"You have done well." I headed back to Ragnar and as I went, I shouted, "Watch for his tracks. We have not passed him and he must be south and west of us."

As I walked back to my position, I looked at the faces of the five men we suspected and none of them gave anything away. They all appeared to have the same expression as my other men, the ones I knew I could trust. Was I wrong? Our noise startled some of the animals in the woods and I just hoped that they would not enable our prey to escape. I heard a cry from ahead and I shouted, "Hold the line! Our men are mounted! He will not escape." I looked for the five men. If they disobeyed and broke then it would be a clear admission of guilt. None did and, once again, I was disappointed.

When we reached my Ulfheonar I saw that they could not hold my gaze, "Well?"

Snorri Long Walker spoke, "He is dead, Wolf Killer."

My eyes narrowed and I sheathed my sword. I was angry and the last thing I needed was a weapon in my hand. "I wanted him alive."

Snorri nodded miserably. "Deer emerged first and we are just men, Jarl. Our eyes went to the deer and he leapt at me with his sword. I just reacted as I have been trained to do. I had slain him before I knew." I was about to shout when I saw that his left arm was badly gashed. It showed how close he had come to a serious wound.

I nodded, "We will speak of this later. Have your arm bound and Siggi and I will examine the body."

Siggi turned over the body. Snorri had slain him with a slash to the throat. He was not a Christian for he had about his neck Thor's Hammer. There was something about his face which looked familiar but I could not tell what for his face was contorted. He had a beard and long hair but neither had been washed for some time and were matted. The sealskin boots confirmed that he was a Viking as did his leather byrnie. He had no clan markings and, in his purse, he had a collection of small coins but they came not only from Jorvik but Wessex, Frisia and Mercia. Any warrior might have a similar collection of coins. He had a sword but it was not a long one and he had a dagger. He had no shield. How had he got here? If he had walked then where had he come from? Finding the man had merely posed more questions and answered none.

My hearthweru carried the body back to the stad. We would place his head on the gatepost as a warning to others. I still hoped that, if he had an accomplice, he would react. If I had a galdramenn like Aiden or a volva like Kara then my life would have been so much simpler for they would have been able to sniff out the traitor. My men, in contrast, were elated. They had helped to catch a spy and an enemy. I think that most of them could not understand my anger which, although I had not voiced it, was clear from my manner and my actions.

Ragnar asked as we headed towards my newly dug ditches and walls, "Why are you not happy, father? The spy has been caught and whatever he was doing has been stopped. You should be happy."

I could not tell him that I still suspected one of my men and that I was no closer to discovering his identity. "I just do not like the thought of enemies hiding close by!" My wife was the first person I sought once I was in my hall and after I had sent Ragnar to put my war gear in its chest, I asked her, "Do you still have the same feelings you had?"

She smiled, "You know when you are on the beach, close to the sea?" I nodded, "The waves come and they go. Sometimes it is a larger wave. That is what it is like for me. The feeling of danger is not there all the time. Today, while you were gone, I did not feel it but, this afternoon I sensed it a little more."

I smiled and kissed her, "Then I have my answer for we killed the spy at noon. One of my new men is still a threat."

My father would not have said what I said in the manner in which I said it. I was loud and it was in public. We had thralls and they might have heard the words. As I said, when I began my tale, looking back always give one perfect vision. At the time I was in a fog. We ate as normal and I went to speak with Snorri after I had eaten. He was in the warrior hall and his arm had been treated and stitched. The others, the five new men and three of my hearthweru gave us space to speak.

"How is the arm?"

"I have had worse, Jarl, and it is my shield arm. I am sorry, I would have done anything to have followed your orders."

I had been thinking about this and I realised I had done him a disservice. "When you looked at the deer, had you seen him before they were spooked?"

"No, Jarl, and I have good eyes. He must have been well hidden."

"Or he had the skills of an Ulfheonar. You have fast reactions and yet this man almost slew you. Had he possessed a longer sword then he might have succeeded. Your horses, were they in sight?"

"Aye, Jarl. They were just five paces from us for we did not know if we might need them in a hurry."

"Then he was trying to get to a horse and had he succeeded then we would still have to fear his presence. I am sorry for the way I spoke with you. It was wrong of me."

"No, Jarl, I am in the wrong and I will atone."

I stood and said, "Goodnight and tomorrow we finish the work on the walls. The day after we will try to see if we can discover whence came this spy!"

I felt better, somehow, for I was looking at the beaker as half empty when it was half full. We had rid ourselves of a spy and we would find his accomplice, eventually.

I was awoken before dawn by Siggi. I left my wife as she woke and went into the hall to speak to him, "Jarl, I have dire news, when I went to make water this morning, I found the body of Dreng the Dane. His throat had been cut and Bjorn Dog Tooth and Vermund Larsson have both gone. How they got by me I shall never know; perhaps I had too much ale and mead last night."

"Get the hearthweru and saddle the horses. I will meet you outside." I turned to Elfrida, who had appeared in the doorway, "I must leave you to hunt down these dogs who have crept into my home and have betrayed me."

"Take care! Your life is not worth that of such snakes."

I dressed quickly but I donned my short mail byrnie. If I was riding then my long one would slow us down and impede my movements. By the time I reached the stables, it was dawn and men were waking. I waved over Snorri whose arm was in a sling. "We go hunting two killers. With your wound, you cannot come and so I leave you to watch over my family, my hall and my stad."

He nodded, grimly, "This time I swear on all that I hold dear that I shall not let you down."

Ragnar had donned his hide jerkin and I said, "And where are you going?"

"I go to hunt the killers with you."

"No, you do not! You watch your mother and guard her. I have my hearthweru and they will be enough to do the deed." He saw in my eyes that I would brook no dissension and he nodded. There would be just ten of us but that would be more than enough. Siggi handed me my shield and I slipped it over my back. I tied my spear to the saddle and my helmet to my spear. Leif Leifsson brought each of us a skin filled with ale. I hoped we would not need food but, if it took longer than I expected then we would forage. We had to move swiftly. I saw that Dreng's body had been covered by his cloak and, as I mounted, I said, "Snorri, have him buried, I did him a disservice for I thought he was a spy."

Faramir the Fair pointed to the south and east, beyond the open gate. "I found prints heading that way."

He hesitated and I said, "Spit it out! I will not bite off your head!"

"One set of prints were deeper than the other and yet both men appeared to be the same size. I saw them in the dew."

I saw what he meant, "Then one was burdened and the other was not!"

That was a puzzle. If they had both left and killed Dreng why were they not equally burdened? The answer became clear just two hundred paces from the walls of Elfridaby behind a small hut used to store tools. The ground fell away after the hut. We found Vermund Larsson who had a wound to his stomach. The blood trail was clear and he had been stabbed before dragging himself to the grub hut. He was dying and had already bled a great deal. I thought he must be dead but, when I knelt over him, he opened his eyes and spoke. His voice was hard to hear and I had to lean in closely to hear him, "I am sorry, Jarl. I tried to stop him when he followed Dreng but I was slow."

I took out my sword and placed it in his hands, "Speak while you can, Vermund, so that we can wreak vengeance on this murderer."

When he spoke, his voice was laboured. "We met Bjorn Dog Tooth in an inn in Jorvik. He had heard us talk of wishing to come to the Land of the Wolf and asked if he could come with us. We thought three would be safer than two and took him. It was only today when we captured the spy that we began to suspect Bjorn for when we had met him, he had been speaking with the man Snorri killed."

"Then why did you not speak?"

He coughed and blood came from his mouth, he did not have long for this earth, "We were going to. In fact, our plan was for me to keep him occupied while Dreng sought you out to tell you. He must have heard what we planned or suspected us. He dropped the dice on the floor and when I bent to pick it up, he slipped out."

His eyes closed as a shock of pain raced through him. He did not have long left to live and I could piece together the events of this night. What was more important was where he would have fled. "Where was his home?"

He opened his eyes and his voice was even weaker than it had been. "I think it was close to Loidis, north I think." He lowered his voice so that it was barely a rasp. "His mother is a witch and Bjorn is a Dane. Dreng said that…" His eyes closed but he had died with his hands on my sword and he would be in Valhalla. He had been brave but he and Dreng had been foolish. Bjorn Dog Tooth was a clever and cunning man. They had been duped.

I stood. "So Dreng tried to come to me and he was killed by Bjorn. It explains why he was heavier than Vermund here, Vermund had neither sword nor hide. Bjorn was armed; if either of them had come to me then we would know whence came this danger. Karl, take his body back and ask Snorri to bury him, fetch food for we ride to Loidis. You can catch us up; we will leave a sign for you."

As we rode Siggi spoke with me, "He was a tough man, Jarl, and would have made a good warrior. He took some time to die."

"So, when did Dreng try to come and speak with me?"

"Sometime in the evening, Jarl, after they had eaten but when the other warriors had gone to their beds and were sleeping."

"Then he has almost a whole night's start."

"He is on foot."

I pointed to the distant hills which marked the natural border between east and west. "And once he gets there then there are many trails he can take. We could spend days finding the right one."

Siggi shrugged, "Then do not follow the trail. We know where he is heading, Loidis or somewhere close to that settlement. We get there and seek him out. He did not give us a false name for Vermund and Dreng used it all the time. We seek those who knew him."

Siggi was wise and in all matters which were military, I would heed him. We kept following the trail for Bjorn Dog Tooth would have taken the most direct route travelling, as he had, in the night. Perhaps he thought that Vermund would die as quickly as Dreng and that we would not know where he had gone but it made sense for him to flee as fast as possible. As Vermund had shown I had trained men who were tough.

We were on horses but soon it would make little difference if we rode or walked, for the terrain was rough and we would travel at the same speed. He would be tired and we would not but that would be all. The land around Loidis had been a Kingdom in its own right at some point in the dim and distant past, Elmet had then been devoured by Northumbria. King Eanred was too busy in the north dealing with the Scots and the Picts and that explained why the Danes, while they did not rule the land, controlled it. The eorledmen who had been given the responsibility of keeping Jorvik a Saxon stronghold had failed and the Danes were spreading their tentacles across the land. There was hope that we might find him, however, for the Danes had no leader, as such. They had many clans and they often worked against each other. There was the Clan of the Skull Takers, The Blood Letters, and others with less violent names, The Clan of the Weasel, The Deer Hunters and many others. We had met some and defeated them when they had banded together to take the Land of the Wolf from us. What we did not know was Bjorn Dog Tooth's clan. Had Vermund told us then that might have made life easier. I had an idea that it was a clan, as yet unknown to us. His name, Dog Tooth, made me think that it was part of the clan name for he had not looked as though he was named for his looks. It was little enough to go on but it was a start.

    The old road Bjorn took passed within twenty miles of Sigtrygg's stad but I would not ask another jarl to help me on this quest. I had brought the snake into my clan and I would remedy my mistake. My Wild Boars would become warriors on this quest, or die trying. We had more than seventy miles to go and we kept up a steady pace. Karl Karlsson caught up with us ten miles from Elfridaby. He had a spare horse and it had food upon it. I knew why he had brought a horse for a long journey might see a horse injured. As we headed south and east, I was silent. I had been taught well and I was looking at the land to look for potential ambush sites and places where there might be danger. I stored that information. My head was filled with information and while much of it might never be needed when we did need it then it might save our lives.

    It was getting on to dark when we reached a small Saxon village. There were few Saxons living in this part of the world and any who lived here, I knew, would be tough and able to defend themselves. I had my men take off their helmets as we approached and we kept our hands from our weapons. From the number of huts, I knew that there could only be ten men at the most in the village and my handful were more than capable of dealing with them but my father had taught me that you did not invoke a battle without a good reason. Elfrida was Saxon and I had a good command of the language. When we reined in, we were surrounded by the menfolk. The women, old and children remained hidden in the round huts. The weapons which were held did not appear threatening. Six of them had swords and I knew that they would be good swords but the rest held spears, billhooks and wood axes.

An older man stepped forward, "What brings Vikings to Helgeflet? We have little here to take."

I dismounted for I knew how intimidating it is to speak to someone who towers above you. I kept my hand from my sword but I saw the man's eyes take in my mail and my sword in its richly decorated scabbard, "I am Wolf Killer of Elfridaby, the son of Dragonheart." When the men's eyes all widened, I knew that they had heard of us. "We are hunting a murderer. He is a Dane called Bjorn Dog Tooth and he killed two of my men. We have followed his trail. Have you seen him?"

The headman looked to a young man next to him and then back at me, "I am Edgar of Helgeflet. My son, Ethelred, told me of a Viking he had seen skirting the village. By the time we had gathered men to find him he had disappeared."

I nodded, "And when was this?"

His son said, querulously, "It was when the sun was two hands past noon, lord."

I saw his father frown at the use of the word, lord. Edgar was a proud Saxon who did not like to defer to a Viking. "And this is the road to Loidis?"

Edgar spoke, "Eventually, but the road becomes harder towards Shipton. If your man has tried to cross that valley, he will find men who defend their homes. We are few in number but they have many sheep around Shipton and it is a prosperous place. We could not bar you the road nor this murderer but they could."

I smiled at his bravado. He was clinging to the idea that these Saxons could stop us. We had defeated the men of Northumbria and of Mercia, not to mention Wessex. I doubted if sheep farmers, no matter how numerous, could cause us a problem but I nodded and said, seriously, "And we mean no harm. Thank you for your advice. With your permission, we will camp upstream of you. We are tired. We have our own food and I swear that you will come to no harm."

He said, "This stream is a holy one and we are protected by it. I do not fear you." His eyes showed the lie but I nodded. "You may camp but do not make water in the stream or empty your bowels for if you do you will be cursed."

I hid my smile for what he really meant was they did not wish their water polluting. "We are the Clan of the Wolf and we do not squat like animals over water. Your stream will be safe from us as will you."

We made our camp and lit a fire but I also had my men make a few traps around the camp. It was partly in case the Saxons decided to be suicidally brave and try to kill us while we slept but it was mainly in case Bjorn had been cunning and not fled but hidden so that he could steal a horse. I was relieved when we woke after an undisturbed sleep. The fire had died and it was not even dawn when I rose. Siggi and I were the eldest and we both slept less than my young hearthweru. We made water and roused the others. We ate as we rode and as we headed south and east, I reflected that I would soon suffer from the saddle. I had not ridden as far in a long time.

Shipton was, indeed, a prosperous place and had a wall around it. Perhaps we were seen from afar and they had barred their gate against us. I kept my hands from my weapons as we approached the walls. Men appeared on the fighting platform of the palisade. My warrior's eye took in the fact that the wall was little taller than the height of a man on a horse. If the clan had wanted then we could have taken it easily. Strung bows with nocked arrows were aimed at us. I spread my arms and said, "I come in peace. I am Wolf Killer of Elfridaby, the son of Dragonheart and I seek a murderer."

A Saxon with a helmet who looked like the leader spoke, "Is he a Viking like you?"

"He is a Dane, aye. Have you seen him?"

He nodded, "Last night we admitted him for he was alone and he rewarded us by slitting the throats of two men and stealing a horse."

"Then know that he will be punished and I will return your horse when we find him."

He looked surprised, "Why?"

"I have no cause to fight you, Saxon. This burgh is far from my home and unless you are foolish enough to try to make war on the Dragonheart then we will never need to fight you. Describe the horse for it will help us to find this murderer." I saw the look of doubt pass across his face. "What have you got to lose? If you tell us then we move on and find him, kill him and bring the horse back here. If you do not tell us then we moved on, kill him and keep the horse for ourselves!"

The Saxon nodded, "It is a chestnut horse with two white socks and a white blaze." He shook his head, "It is my horse."

"Then we shall fetch it back."

We kept heading south and east but we now had information which would help us to narrow down the search. We had entered the land of the Danish settlers. It meant we understood the people more. The Saxons were Christians and you never knew how they would react. A Dane or a Norse was different. We struck lucky at a farm just ten miles from Shipton. We stopped for water and, after I had told him who I was and what we were doing, the Dane who farmed there, Gandálfr Larsson, told us of the man on the horse. "He was heading for Orsna Ford. It used to be a collection of huts twenty years since farmed by a few Saxons. They were good people and prospered for the village is built across the road constructed by the ancient people, the folk of Elmet, to travel from the valleys north of here to Loidis. Then this new clan arrived and, gradually, the Saxons left and they grew. They have a palisade around their walls."

"Do you have much to do with them?"

"Very little but I recognised the man on the horse. He is the son of the chief of the clan. He and his father came to ask me if I would sell my land when they arrived a couple of years ago. I sent him packing. I am a Dane but I know a bad Viking when I see one and I did not like this one. He even threatened me with a witch." He laughed. "My wife is a volva and I have seven strong sons. I bow my knee to no one." He looked at my men, "Your lads look handy but if you have no volva then have a care. Witches are tricky creatures." He took from beneath his tunic a piece of woven wool. "My wife weaves a spell once a week for me and it keeps me safe!"

I liked the farmer. I think that if I had had his farm I would have behaved in the same way. Knowing that our prey was close we moved more cautiously for the ford was less than fifteen miles from the Danes' farm. We stopped before dark and found a small stream which ran north to south. The farmer had told us that the village owed its existence to a ford in a stream, hence its name, ford of the horse. It was a place where the horses and carts used by merchants could cross the river. As we could easily walk across the stream, we knew that the village had to be downstream and as our prey had reached his home then there was little to be gained from rushing in. This time, when we camped, we surrounded ourselves with snares and we hid our camp in a dell. Lighting no fire meant a cold fare but we did not mind. We were warriors. With Faramir the Fair on watch, the rest of us sat and spoke, albeit quietly.

Karl Karlsson said, "We have been lucky to find his trail, Jarl. Perhaps too lucky. How do we know that he did not put that farmer up to his story? This could be a trap to lure us to our deaths. The Danes wish harm to you and your father. I have asked myself why they should send two spies. One reason is that they were preparing to attack us."

"You are probably right about that. Sending spies would show them our weaknesses. When they have come before they have been as blind men feeling their way in the dark. But I believe that you are wrong about the farmer. I looked into his eyes and I saw the truth. I believe that the Weird Sisters have sent us here and they have given us the clues. They do not like murder unless it serves their purposes."

Karl was persistent, "But the witch?"

"Kara, my sister, is a witch. I know their power and their limitations. I do not fear the witch but I will respect her. The Sisters are using us to punish the murderer."

"And do you have a plan, Jarl?" Siggi shook his head in irritation at Karl's persistent questions.

I nodded, "I am Ulfheonar and I will scout out the village."

Siggi's face darkened, "That is a risk, Jarl."

"Life is a risk but as it is me who is taking it then it is less so. I trained with the best and I have hunted with the Ulfheonar. I know how to hide in plain sight. This Bjorn Dog Tooth is not worth another man's death but we need to send a message to this clan and their masters, that men who tangle with us risk their death."

Erik Red Hair, who was one of my younger hearthweru asked, "Their masters, Jarl?"

"This clan is too small to take on Dragonheart and the Clan of the Wolf. The farmer hinted that these were a small clan and what better way to gain power and become powerful than allying yourself with someone who has the strength to give you what you desire. It could be the Danes but, equally, it could be Egbert. We may not discover that yet but we can send a message." I stretched, Siggi, take command of the camp. I will need my wits about me and so I shall sleep."

I laid my cloak on the ground and placed my sword in easy reach. Pulling my bearskin cloak over my body I reached into the leather satchel I always carried with me and took out the piece of woven material my mother had given me when I was young. There had been much danger on Man and she had given both Kara and me a woven spell she had spun to keep us safe. Kara no longer needed hers for she was a volva more powerful than my mother had been. I silently invoked my mother's help. It did not do to overuse the spell and so I only ever used it when I felt I might be in danger. Had there not been a witch then I would not have done so. Once I had asked my mother to help me, I felt at peace. I secreted the spell back in the satchel and dropped into a deep and dreamless sleep. I had my hearthweru to watch over me and I was as safe in their protection as in the Emperor's palace in Miklagård!

I woke before dawn and saw the reassuring shadows of two of my hearth weru. I made water and then went to the stream to wet and wash my face. I had taken off my byrnie the night before and I would leave it at the camp with my men. I would also leave my sword. The scabbard and the fine quality of the blade would trumpet to the world that I was an important warrior. I would use the seax in my belt and the one hidden in my boot if I had to defend myself. By the time I was ready to eat the camp had awoken. Siggi came over to me as I ate some food and drank some of the ale from my skin.

"Tell me your plan, Jarl, so that if aught goes awry I can find a solution to the problem."

He was ever practical and even though he disapproved of my action he would do all that he could, including giving his life, to see that I was safely returned to Elfrida. "The farmer told us that people pass along the ancient road to cross the stream at the horse ford. I intend to hide close to the road and when a suitably large enough group of travellers heads south then I will join them. I will go no closer to the walls than I need to. I am Ulfheonar and I was trained to look for weaknesses and numbers. I can do both very quickly and when I have crossed the river then I will find another way back to the camp. I will head up the opposite bank to here for I know we can cross it on foot at this point."

He seemed mollified by my plan. I suspect he thought I would be foolish enough to head into the village and boldly look at their defences. That would have been the act of a rash young warrior. The Ulfheonar and my father had shown me that my mind was stronger than my heart! "We will keep a good watch here and I will send Rolf across the river with his bow to keep watch there, in case you are pursued."

"If I am pursued then we have failed."

He nodded, "May the Allfather be with you."

I pulled the hood of my cloak over my head and, as I headed through the woods for the ancient road I sought a stick. I found a piece of blackthorn which had been broken from a tree. I reached a point where I could stay hidden but still see the road. The old road was not Roman and so it was not unnaturally straight. It twisted around the bump in the land upon which I squatted. I took out my seax and shaped the blackthorn staff a little. It was still a little after dawn and I did not expect too many travellers yet to be on the road. Loidis had a market and farmers from the valleys north and west of me would be bringing their goods to sell. I let a merchant and his two horses, with a thrall in tow, pass me for they were not what I sought. I waited until a shepherd and his son came down the road with their dog and a small flock of sheep. They seemed to me to be perfect. I headed across the small knoll to the road they would travel and I stood simulating making water. I had my back to them and I heard the sheep first. I feigned finishing and turned, just as they came into sight. They were Saxons and so I used Saxon to speak to them.

"Well met, my friend." My hood was over my head and the colour of my hair and beard hard to see. I leaned heavily on the blackthorn staff.

The Saxon's eyes narrowed. "And to you. We did not see you before, old man."

I shook my head, "I left my home," I waved vaguely towards Shipton, "before dawn. I have an old man's bladder. Do you go to Loidis for I am thither bound?"

"Aye."

"Could I walk a little way with you for I miss the company."

I saw him looking around to see if I had others with me. Seeing none he nodded, "Aye, I am Aethelward of Inhrypum and this is my son, Harold."

I walked towards him and I stooped to disguise my size and to accentuate what appeared to be my infirmity, I limped. "I am Edgar of Prestune." I saw that the dog had continued to harry the sheep while we waited, "A good dog."

"Aye we could not manage without him and you may well be of assistance as this flock is the most troublesome I have ever had. I shall be glad to be rid of them. Dog, on!" The sheepdog started them again and I stood to one side of the shepherd.

"You are selling them at Loidis market?"

He nodded, "Aye, and then moving north. There are too many Danes around here. I will cross the great river to the north and find a farm closer to Dunelm. I have heard of some families who have been driven from their homes by Danes and King Eanred seems incapable of stopping them. What is it like around Prestune? I hear there are Norse close to there."

"They let us live. Norse are not Danes."

"Aye, you have the right of it."

We continued to head down the road which sloped gently towards the ford. I used my stick to affect the actions of a man who was much older than I was. "How will you get them across the horse ford?"

"The dog is a good swimmer and the sheep stay together when they cross. There is a Dane there who charges a silver penny for travellers to cross. He is a robbing bastard!"

I said, "For your company, I will pay the coin for the ferry."

"That is generous." He continued, "You did not say why you are going to Loidis."

I handed him the coin which he took, gratefully. "I do not. I am heading for the Roman Road south. I am on a pilgrimage. The plague took my family and I sold my farm so that I may travel to Lindune and pray at the church of St Paul of the Bail. I would have gone to Rome but I am not sure I would be able to manage that journey." I made the sign of the cross as I had seen the followers of the White Christ do. I had heard of the church from Uhtric, my father's thrall. The story and the signing of the cross seemed to convince the Saxon that I was harmless and our conversation became more convivial. It was in the fourth hour of the day when we reached the ford. My men and I could have done the journey in a quarter of the time. I saw the merchant I had spied earlier sitting in the boat and being rowed across as his thrall swam with the two horses. The water was not wide and the boatman did the journey so quickly that I agreed with Aethelward's assessment of him.

The merchant waited on the boat until his horses and goods had arrived safely on the other bank and that afforded me the opportunity to study the palisaded walls. There was a pair of longhouses inside and they had a stout gatehouse. I could not see all the way in but it seemed to me that there was just one entrance close to the ford. Two warriors lounged at the gate but neither wore mail. The walls were as high as a man and would pose no obstacle to my men. As the boat headed back to us Aethelward set his dog to drive the sheep across the river and his son took off his boots and tunic to swim naked across the narrow stretch of water. Aethelward picked them up. As the small, raft-like boat came back for us I heard the tramp of feet. Men marched from the settlement. At first, I feared that I had been recognised and then dismissed it for they headed to the flat area between the road and the settlement. They were going to practise just as my clan did. I recognised Bjorn Dog Tooth and observed that he now wore a mail shirt and had a good helmet and sword. It confirmed that which I knew already, he was a spy. I saw his father, the hersir and he had a full mail byrnie. There were just twenty men in total and eight boys.

As the boat nudged next to us, I kept my eyes on the men to see how good they were and I leaned heavily on my staff. I heard Aethelward say, "Here is the coin."

"There are two of you. It should be two coins."

"You are a robber and a villain. Rather than pay you twice we would swim across!" He did not know if I could swim, of course, and it was a ploy, which worked.

"There is no need for offence. I will take you for your friend looks old."

We climbed in the boat and I said, "Do your warriors practise often?"

"Just on Woden's Day." As he poled us across, he grinned, "There is a lord sent word from Jorvik that the clan might go to war with him and we would be rewarded."

We nudged ashore and Aethelward stepped out and helped me ashore. I said, innocently, "A Saxon lord?"

Laughing he shook his head and began to pole back across the stream, "No, a Dane, Ragnar Ruriksson. He has already paid us silver. See our hersir's mail coat, it is the first sign of our newly found fortune! Our clan will become bigger." He began to pole the boat back to the other bank.

As Aethelward's son dressed the shepherd said, "And this is why we leave for the north. Jorvik is Saxon no longer. The Danes rule it. They will encourage small clans like this one. I am not a man who likes to gamble but I would bet my flock that when this Ragnar Ruriksson is ready, he will sweep the last of us from this land. You will be safe in your church but I would not return to Prestune."

I said nothing for I had worked out a way to leave him without his becoming suspicious. As the road climbed towards Loidis we took a break to rest the animals. I said, "You know, friend, I think that meeting you was the best thing to happen to me. I think I will return to Prestune and warn those of my village of the dangers. Perhaps God intended me to meet with you so that I could hear of the threat from the pagans."

"You will be safer in the church!"

"Sometimes a man has to think of his people and not himself. Go with God!"

"And you too."

I shuffled back down the slope and, as soon as I was out of sight, I left the road and struck out north. The ground was undulating with shrubs and scrubby trees. I soon disappeared from the sight of the road and I was able to run. I headed north and then turned north and west. I ran for an hour until I found the stream. I was fairly certain that I was north of Orsna Ford but I advanced cautiously sniffing the air as I went. I smelled no danger and when I reached the stream, I waded across it. This was not my land and I was uncertain of where I was in relation to the camp. I headed due west for I knew that the road paralleled it and I would have a better idea of gauging my position from it.

I found myself just south of the bend where I had met the shepherd. The pellets left by the sheep where we had spoken confirmed it. I struck out for the camp. I took pleasure in sneaking up on Karl Karlsson so that when I tapped him on the shoulder with my staff he started.

"Jarl, I could have slain you!"

I laughed, "With your hand on your spear and your thoughts back in Elfridaby? I think not. Come, as a sentry you are of little use and I do not think that we will be disturbed."

Thanks to Karl's misplaced feet the others were ready when we reached them. Siggi asked, "Well?"

I sat down and picked up the ale skin. I drank deeply. The shepherd had had only water and sheep's milk. Neither had satisfied me. Wiping the beer from my mouth I said, "They have just twenty men and some boys inside their burgh. The wall is as high as a tall man and there is but one gate in and out. I have seen Bjorn and he and his father appear to own the only two mail shirts in the village. They serve a Dane called Ragnar Ruriksson although he does not appear to be near." I was really speaking with Siggi who understood my mind better than any. "I think this Dane is laying the groundwork for an attack on us or the land of the Wolf. I do not think it is imminent because they only sent two young men to spy for them. This clan look to be poorly prepared to take on the Clan of the Wolf. Perhaps that is why they sent spies first and we may be able to nip this threat in the bud."

"Then what do we do?"

"That which I said we would. Tonight, we scale their walls and enter their two longhouses. I am guessing they will have no more than two sentries, so that when we have slain them, we will each have to slay two men each. They will be abed and have no mail. We will have surprise on our side. If we can we take Bjorn back so that we can question him then that will be a good thing but I do not want to lose any men."

Siggi nodded, "Our horses?"

"We leave them tethered nearby. We will use the stream to approach the village for the water bubbles there and the bottom is sandy." When I had returned, I had scouted out the river at various places. "Rest while you can." My men nodded and went to prepare their war gear; they were warriors.

Siggi brought over my mail shirt, helmet, shield and sword. "And the women?"

"We let them live."

"Even the witch?"

My hand went to my satchel. I had forgotten her. "I would not be a witch killer for the Sisters do not like that but if we have to then she shall die."

"Wolf Killer, you risk a curse."

"Perhaps not." I prayed to the Allfather that my mother's spell would save me.

I rose at dusk and donned my byrnie. My sword and daggers were still sharp. I slung my shield across my back and saddled my horse. I led my animal and war gear into the undergrowth for this was a ritual I liked to do alone. It was preparation for war! I would not need my spear for this would be sword work. I knew that I was more confident with my sword than my men and that included Siggi. We had all fought before at night but night was the time of the Ulfheonar and we knew how to use shadows and fear to gain an advantage. I took out the red cochineal and put it upon my face. I had an open helmet and the sight would be a terrifying one. I left two patches of bare skin beneath my eyes. Elfrida had told me that the effect of the pale skin amongst the red made it look as though there were daggers coming from my eyes. I hoped that the village would be asleep and that seeing me in the half-light from the longhouse fire would make them think that I was a demon. Finally, I smeared the last of the cochineal on the backs of my hands. It would make them look as though I had bathed in blood. I donned my helmet and my bearskin over my helmet and my back. I was an Ulfheonar once more and I led my horse back to the others. I saw two of them start and clutch at Thor's hammer when they saw my face.

Siggi just nodded approvingly, "Jarl, you could do this alone for you are Ulfheonar!"

I could play this game too, "Perhaps I should. If you would wait here…"

Siggi shook his head, "No, Wolf Killer, we are hearth weru and we follow you wherever you lead."

"Then let us mount and make our way to Orsna Ford. From now on until we have slain all of the men there will be no words. Watch my hands and my signals!" One important lesson learned when I had served with my father's Ulfheonar was that you had to train men to know what you meant without words. When we practised war, we practised signals. They would know what I intended from my hands and my sword. I led us down the stream. The wind was from the south and brought me the smell of woodsmoke. Sparks from the turfed tops of the longhouse confirmed where the village lay. As we were upstream from the ford, I knew that we could leave the horses on the bank of the river. As the smell of human and animal habitation grew so I sought somewhere to climb from the river.

I heard voices ahead in the dark which told me that we were getting closer to them and I swept my arm to the left. Whatever lay close would have to do as a place to leave our horses for I did not wish to risk alerting the villagers. The fear of the witch still nagged at me. My horse struggled to make the top of the bank but, once I was there, I saw that there was a stand of willows. The many branches of the water greedy tree would be perfect to tether our horses. I dismounted and went to my saddlebag. I did not use my reins to tether the horse; instead, I tied a piece of rope, the length of a man, to his bridle. That way he could graze the grass and, if he needed, drink from the river. Siggi emulated me as did the others who had had the foresight to bring a rope. I realised then that I had much training to do if my Wild Boars were to become the equal of my father's men.

It took time to settle the horses and for my men to gather their weapons. There was no hurry for the voices had told me that there were still men awake and I needed them all asleep before we closed with the walls. I especially wanted the witch to be asleep. I led them, when they were ready, down the trail which twisted along the river. I had trained them to follow in my footsteps and I chose each step carefully. I heard voices again and I stopped so that I could listen. I had deliberately brought my open-faced round helmet so that my ears could be used to their best effect. I smelled the men who watched on the walls; it was a mixture of sweat, the urine on their breeches and ale. We liked to bathe; this clan, patently, did not. I realised that the sound was coming from the walls and was the sound of the sentries. I made the sign for the others to wait and then shifted, like the shadow of a breeze blown tree towards the wall. There is an art to walking in plain sight and not being seen. Every Ulfheonar knew how to do this and it was second nature to me. I saw as I neared the gatehouse that there were three men on the fighting platform. I knew that the phrase fighting platform flattered it for the wooden walkway was just the ditch into which they had planted their palisade and a series of planks along which they could walk. It was just the length of a long sword from the ground. The gatehouse was marked by a roof to afford some protection from arrows should they be attacked. I could not make out the words but I did not need to.

Having worked out where the sentries were, I knew where we could enter the burgh. Returning to my men I led them east, well away from the wall. I was relieved to hear silence from within. Silence, that is, punctuated by snores and the sound of snuffling. I did not hear the sound of growling dogs and that was a relief. As we passed the corner of the north wall, I heard the sound of a horse and knew we had passed the stables. When we reached the east wall, I closed with it and pointed to Lars and Faramir the Fair. They took Lars' shield and held it. I made the sign for Siggi and Rolf to come with me, walk along the north wall and kill the sentries. I made the sign for Petr and Bergil to walk along the south wall and help us. The rest would follow when they could. I waited until I heard the voices begin to speak on the far wall, which housed the gate. Then I stepped onto the shield and my two men boosted me so that I could slip over the wall. Drawing my sword, I moved along the fighting platform using a crouching run. It meant I was below the top of the palisade. The nature of sentry duty is that you are looking for danger from without and not within, Good sentries would have walked the perimeter of the walls regularly but these had not moved since I had first spied them.

I was gratified that I heard no steps behind me. It meant my men were moving as silently as I was. I used a sliding action with my boots so that I did not stamp on the wood. When I glanced over to the side, I saw that my men had heeded their training well. They were shadows which seemed to move imperceptibly. We were helped by the fact that the sentries were looking west and laughing at something one had said. The danger would be when we struck at them. There was a good chance that, unless we were very lucky, one would cry out and awaken the men of the burgh.

The corner of the wall was just twenty paces from the gatehouse and would be the trickiest to navigate quietly. What helped us was that they had built a shelter over the fighting platform to protect the warriors there. I slipped my seax into my left hand as I edged slowly down the fighting platform. The three sentries had their heads together. Whilst the night was not cold, it was cool and they were huddled together for there was no brazier on the wooden wall. I had to assume that I would be alone when I struck and I had to try to kill, or at the very least, silence, the three men. It seemed impossible. If there was noise then the burgh would be awakened and I would lose men. Out of the corner of my eye, I caught a movement in the eastern part of the settlement. Some of my men were descending to watch the warrior hall. It was Lars and Faramir the Fair and it made me happier for if there was noise then they would be able to deal with it.

As I stared at the three men, I saw that their arms were resting upon the palisade. I took another step and was so close that I could make out their words. They were speaking of a tavern in Loidis and the Saxon whores they had enjoyed. They were boasting of their prowess in bed and the size of their manhoods. It explained the laughter. I used the sudden braying laugh of one of them to step forward and ram my sword under the arm of the nearest Dane and up into his throat. He died instantly and tumbled over the palisade, landing with a dull thud. I had kept moving and my seax slashed across the throat of the second Dane. I saw the mouth of the third Dane open and then Bergil's blade emerged from his chest. The two men we had just slain slumped to the top of the earth mound upon which the palisade was built.

    Sheathing my seax, I clambered down the steps to the gate. I gestured for Siggi and Rolf to open it in case we needed a quick departure. I hurried to the two longhouses. One would be the hall of the Hersir and his family while the other would have the warriors and their families. I saw that Lars, Leif Leifsson and Faramir the Fair were outside the warrior hall and I signalled for Bergil, Petr and Karl to join them. That left my men and me with the hersir. I knew that his hearthweru would also be in this hall. While Bergil and the others might have more men to deal with they would be the poorest of the clan.

    When Siggi, Erik Red Beard and Rolf joined me, I went to the door of the larger longhouse. I knew it was the hersir's from the skulls of the dog which hung from two wooden frames on either side of it. Below the skulls were hanks of hair. They had been taken, I did not doubt, from the heads of enemies. They had to be the symbols of the clan of the dog and it explained Dog Tooth's name. Inside I could hear the sounds of snoring and also the unmistakable sound of coupling. Someone was awake and that complicated matters. I had lived in a longhouse and knew their layout. There would be a fire in the centre. The hersir and his family would occupy one end while his hearthweru would be close to the door. The side furthest from the hersir would be where the servants and thralls slept. That would be the most crowded part of the longhouse. The door would not be barred and the handle was a simple latch. I looked over to Bergil and nodded. With my left hand, I lifted the latch and then pushed the door open with the tip of my sword. After the dark of the outside the glow from the fire lit up the interior and the warmth hit me as I stepped inside. A quick glance told me that the hersir and his family were to my right behind the curtain, for to the left, at the far end, there were many asleep. As luck would have it the couple who were making love were close to the door. When the woman saw the red-painted wolf standing in the doorway with a sword in his hand she screamed and, as the man lifted his head, I kicked him hard under the chin. His head snapped back and he lay still.

    I leapt over his body and headed for the curtain which I knew would be the sleeping chamber of the hersir. I could leave my men behind me to deal with any warriors. It was Bjorn Dog Tooth and his father that I needed to deal with. I needed to take the head from this clan so that they could not come back to haunt us. I now knew that this clan was just part of a larger alliance. One warrior, a hearthweru by the tattooed markings on his body, leapt at me with a sword. As I parried away the weak blow, I drew my seax and rammed it between the ribs of his naked body. I twisted the blade and tore it out sideways so that it ripped a hole in his side. I think he was dead before his body struck the ground. The longhouse was now filled with screams and shouts. The noises were punctuated by the sound of steel on steel and the sound of blades striking bones and bodies.

Bjorn Dog Tooth saw me as I spied him. He was to my right. Rolf raced to my left side as a naked warrior stood brandishing an axe. Siggi Flat Nose and Erik Red Beard would be behind me dealing with the other hearthweru who were closer to the door. I faced Bjorn Dog Tooth and he screamed at me, "You should not have come, Wolf Killer, for you will die here rather than in your hall!"

It was laughable for although he had a pair of breeks on and held a sword and a seax, his pale naked body was underdeveloped. My son, Ragnar, could have beaten him. It also made me smile for I saw, in his eyes, terror, despite the bravado of his words.

"I am here to ensure that Vermund and Dreng are avenged and that you do not go to Valhalla and then we shall end the days of the Clan of the Dog!"

I knew he was afraid for he began to back off and look for support. Two men came at me from my side but Siggi and Erik tore into them with flailing blades. I felt something thud into the shield which lay beneath my cloak. It would take an extremely lucky strike to hurt my back. I swung my sword at Bjorn. I could not bring it over my head for Bjorn was below the sloping roof of the longhouse. He tried to block it with his seax but he was weak compared with me and he barely slowed it. The end of my sword sliced into his leg and blood began to seep from the wound. A woman rose from my left and lunged at me with a seax. She tried to stab with the weapon which was a mistake as a Saxon seax is a slashing weapon. It scratched down my mail and I punched her in the face with my left fist. She crumpled to the floor. Her attack encouraged Bjorn Dog Tooth who lunged with his sword at my face. I parried with my own and then brought my seax around to slice across his bare chest. My seax was sharp enough to use to shave and it cut deeply. He stepped back again and fell over the body of a warrior killed by one of my other men. As he fell, I stepped forward and hacked at his wrist. I severed the bone and the hand holding the sword fell to the earthen floor of the longhouse. His lifeblood was ebbing away from him. Sheathing my seax I took the sword from the lifeless fingers and leaned over him. "Now you will never see Valhalla!" Using his own sword, I pinned his body to the earthen floor by stabbing him through the neck. Drawing my seax once more I looked for more enemies.

I turned and saw that the hersir had managed to don a mail shirt over his breeks and he held his sword and seax. The last of the warriors were fighting with my men and I saw Rolf approaching the hersir. Rolf was good but he was young and, as I headed across the longhouse, I saw the hersir's wife and my blood chilled. She was a witch and she was weaving a spell even as we fought. Rolf's sword and that of the hersir clashed and I forced my way across the longhouse. I heard the chant from the witch as I neared them, *"I curse you and your offspring. I curse your family and your clan. I curse you for all eternity."* Her voice was in the chillingly hypnotic chant of a witch. It was the sort of voice which unmanned a warrior and could kill as quickly as a sword.

Rolf suddenly stopped fighting and the hersir's sword swept sideways to bite into the side of his head. I knew that Rolf was dead before he hit the ground. I screamed, "No!" and ran at the hersir. He would now face not just a warrior but a Jarl and an Ulfheonar. My first blow was so hard that it forced him to step to the side and exposed the witch who was still weaving.

She grinned at me and began to chant, *"Wolf Killer will die, with all of his men and the Dragonheart will mourn his whole long life."*

The hersir regained his feet and brought his sword around to backhand me but I easily blocked it with my seax.

"The witch can save her father but I curse Wolf Killer to an early death."

The hersir's sword came at me again. The witch was a distraction and her chants and her spell were aiding her husband. I managed to block the hersir's sword but so long as the witch lived, he had a good chance of winning.

"I curse Wolf Killer who shall die with his son, and his wife will…"

She got no further for I took two steps towards her and swung my sword in a long arc which hacked through her neck as though it was made of butter. I heard the hersir scream, "No!" and I felt his sword hack at my back. My wolf cloak and shield saved me. I was propelled forward but no hurt was done and I whirled around and ran at the hersir. He had thought his blow had ended the combat and I saw the shock in his eyes as my angry eyes ran at him. He blocked the strike from my sword with his own sword and seax but he could do nothing about the seax which ripped across his thigh. It was the same wound I had given to his son. It was a wound which would weaken the Dane but I intended to end this quickly. I had lost one man and that was one more man than I had expected to lose. The witch had cost us dear and I was now cursed!

The hersir must have known that his end was nigh "You may have won this day, Wolf Killer, but there are enemies gathering who will ensure that you and the Dragonheart will be long forgotten when we take your land. My brother and his clan will avenge my death!"

"You have spoken enough, Dane!" I slashed with my seax at his unprotected throat and his seax and sword came to block the strike for he had seen how quick were my hands. I drove the sword through his mail links and into his chest. Once the metal resistance was broken the sword slid up and through his flesh; it ripped through his heart and came out of his shoulder. I was aware that the longhouse was now silent. As I pulled my sword from his body I turned and saw that Siggi and Erik were the only two warriors left alive in the longhouse. The women, children and thralls had fled for only a fool would have stayed in a longhouse with Vikings who were intent upon death.

"We were watching your back, Jarl. The others are driving the women and the children hence."

I nodded, "Rolf was cursed but he died with his sword in his hand. This shall be his funeral pyre. We will find the stolen horse and then burn this to the ground!"

"Is that wise, Jarl, for we are in the land of the Danes and they will investigate?"

I was angry for Rolf had died and I felt to blame, "I care not. We cannot bury him for the Danes would dig him up and abuse his body. This way we burn all." I knelt down and picked up the piece of weaving still clutched in the dead witch's hand. "Including this curse!"

Both men clutched their hammers as they had not heard the curse. Siggi understood now and he nodded. "Erik Red Beard, find the treasure of this clan for it shall be weregeld for our brother in arms!"

I left the charnel house which was the longhouse. We had been few in number but we had been better warriors than the Danes and they had paid the price. Some of their women had died. That was inevitable. It had been dark and we had been fighting for our lives. As I emerged, I saw that the rest of my men had survived. I shouted, "Faramir the Fair, see if you can find the horse. The rest of you burn the warrior hall and set fire to the palisade. The wind is from the east. Start the fire there."

I went to the trough which had the water the women used to wash the vegetables and, taking off my helmet, I doused my face in it. I wanted to cleanse myself and I was unconcerned that my face was still red. Had my father led this raid then none would have died and he would not have been cursed. I still had much to learn. My father had forgotten more about fighting than I would ever learn. I knew, at that moment, that I should have stayed closer to him but I had thought I knew it all and I had left him to become a new Dragonheart. The witch's curse rang in my ears. I would die young but not my father. One of my sons was cursed but which one?

Bergil came to me as I shook my head like a wet dog, "Wolf Killer, the women are all fled and they took the road to Loidis."

I nodded for I knew what it meant, "They will be there by dawn and then the Danes will follow us."

"Aye, Jarl."

"Let us hurry!" Faramir and Leif came leading not one but three horses. I recognised the horse stolen from Shipton. "Load the horses with the treasure."

The warrior hall suddenly erupted into flames. My men must have found pig fat to accelerate the fire. Now that the horses had been taken the stable was fired and the straw and animal waste made the flames there soar into the night sky. Smoke and soot filled the air and the wind blew it towards us. Siggi and Petr came with two chests. "This was a rich clan, Wolf Killer!"

I nodded dully for the treasure meant nothing to me. Flames began to lick around the door of the hersir's longhouse. "Let us go. Our men have been avenged!" Rolf's body would be burned and he would be in Valhalla. Bjorn Dog Tooth would not and the murderer would wander through the vast emptiness of nothingness for all time. I was the last to leave the burning Danish settlement. Siggi was right it would be a beacon to tell all the Danes who lived close by that they had been raided. The women and children, not to mention the old men who had escaped would tell the jarl at Loidis that it was Vikings led by Wolf Killer. They would seek vengeance and we had seventy miles to travel before we reached the safety of our own land. We would head for Sigtrygg's stad and that would cut almost fifteen miles from our journey.

We reached our horses just before dawn and we quickly mounted them. I hung my helmet from my spear and used the bearskin to cover my saddle. We had more spare horses now and having rested them for a day we could make good time. We were vigilant as we rode but having seen few Danes on our way to Orsna Ford I was confident that we would be safe until the warriors from Loidis caught up with us.

We stopped at the farm of Gandálfr Larsson and he nodded his approval. "You have done what needed to be done, Jarl, but they will come after you."

"I know and if they come here then tell them that I have returned home."

He laughed, "That will be a chase and I would love to be a hawk and see it unfold. May the Allfather be with you."

We reached Shipton just a couple of hours later. Our horses were ready for a rest and we reined in before the gates which were, inevitably, closed. I turned to Siggi while holding on to the reins of the horse we had recaptured. "Take the other horses to the river and water them." I walked towards the wall with the Saxon's horse.

Seeing my men head away the Saxons thought it safe enough to open the gate. The Saxon leader walked towards me. He wore no helmet and I saw that he was of an age with Aiden. He smiled, "I am Beorhtric the Thegn of Shipton and I confess that I am surprised for you kept your word."

I handed him the reins, "Then know that a true Viking will never be forsworn. Danes?" I shrugged. "I am also here to warn you that we killed all of the warriors and destroyed the settlement at Orsna Ford."

His eyes widened, "With this handful of men?"

"The clan was well named for they were dogs and we are the wolf! I would keep your gates barred for they will come after us. Tell them where we went for this is not your fight."

He nodded, "You are a strange Viking."

"I was raised by the greatest Viking of them all, Dragonheart! They will ask where we went." I pointed north and west. "We take the road home!"

We gave the same message to Edgar when we reached Helgeflet who nodded, "Thank you, Wolf Killer. You are welcome to rest here within my walls." He had changed his attitude towards Vikings and, I daresay, that was because of the respect we had shown him.

"No, we will push on. They will come for us but I hope to bloody their noses before they can hurt us."

As we rode north Siggi confided his fears to me, "Are you sure that we can do this, Wolf Killer? Would it not be better to ride these horses to death and reach Sigtrygg's stad?"

"It might be but," I pointed to the west where the sun was setting, "we will need to camp soon and I recall a place where we could not only camp but, when the Danes come, then hurt them."

"It would take a prodigious ride to catch up with us already, Wolf Killer, for we have ridden further this day than I have ever ridden before. I can see that I need a bearskin to cover my saddle."

"Did you not hear the words of the hersir? The clan was part of a larger family and Loidis was their centre. We found horses at Orsna Ford and that was a small clan. Do you not think that the lord of Loidis will have many more horses? He will have mailed and armed men and he will wish to capture or kill the son of the Dragonheart. I know this is my fault for I have stuck out our necks and they are in danger but I have a solution. Trust me, Siggi Flat Nose."

"I always do, Wolf Killer, but I am not Ulfheonar and I have doubts. We have few men."

I nodded, "But they are our men and they are the Wild Boars." I did not tell him that I wanted to be awake at night and not risk sleep for the witch's curse echoed around my head. My sister and my father could cope with the dreamworld but I had never been comfortable there. For me, it was a dangerous place.

We reached the place I had seen on the way south just after dark. We had ridden the horses too far and had we tried to go further we risked doing them irreparable harm. Dismounting I said, "I know you are tired and need hot food and sleep but you shall have neither until we have made this a place of death for those who follow us. I have chosen this place for it affords us the opportunity to end this chase. The Danes will pursue us, even to the borders of our land and beyond. I am a prize without compare and we have hurt them." They nodded and I pointed to the road. "We have just climbed this slope and it wearied us. This is where we will stop them. Tonight, we cut brambles and ivy to make the trees which line the side of the old road impenetrable. We embed our spare spears to stop their horses charging at us. They will ride over the hill tomorrow expecting to catch sight of our sign in the distance. They will have followed the trail of our horse dung all the way from Orsna Ford. We will make a wedge here and when they rise, we will charge them and their horses. Siggi can use his axe to hew the heads of the horses and we use our spears to kill the Danes. Bergil will use Rolf's bow and use his arrows to kill those at the back."

Karl was his normal pessimistic self, "And what if there are too many of them?"

I laughed, "Then we will all have more Danes to kill but I do not think that there will be many. If they catch up with us then they are riding good horses and are good horsemen. I believe that it will be no more than twenty men and I will be surprised if it is even that number. You have complained all the way back about your sore backside, Karl, and you are hearthweru. These Danes will not be used to riding and, more importantly, until they see us, they will have their weapons sheathed. They may not wear their helmets. We strike so hard and fast that the battle will be over before it has begun. When all is done then we can sleep knowing that we are safe."

It took just a couple of hours to complete our work. I had the men take the horses half a mile up the road to tether them so that they would not alert the Danish horses. Siggi and I took some of the fresh horse dung and walked down the road and the slope. We dropped the dung on the road. The Danes would stop to see how fresh it was. By the time they found it the dung would be cold and dry; that would make them approach the rise confidently knowing that we had passed this way half a day earlier. I turned to look at the ambush as we walked back up the road. It was dark and it was not a true picture but it appeared to look harmless.

"And what if you are wrong, Wolf Killer, and they do not pursue us?"

"Then, at noon, we mount our horses and head home. If they do come and we fail then the survivors can ride to Sigtrygg. My father shall deal with the Danes then." We walked back to the others and I said, "Get some sleep and I will watch."

"We can all watch!"

"No Erik Red Beard, my mind is a whirling maelstrom and sleep will be hard to come. I am Ulfheonar and night is my friend. It is my command!"

They obeyed me and I leaned with my back against the hornbeam at the top of the rise so that I could look down the empty ancient road. I ran through the events of my life and how they had brought me to this point. The abduction from Man, the taking of Elfrida, Angharad the Witch; all of these threads had been spun by the Norns and, like my father, I was a plaything of the Three Sisters. What preyed the most on my mind was the witch's curse. I had killed her and that made me a witch killer. I did not regret that action but I knew it would have consequences. I desperately wished to get home for every moment spent with my family would now be even more important than before I had left on this quest. One of my sons and I would die. I had stopped the witch before she could curse my wife and my other son. The witch knew which son she had cursed but I did not. I know that I should have picked up the woven spell to show it to Kara. She might have been able to undo it but I had been angry and not used my mind. It was ever a fault in me and perhaps it would make me pay the ultimate price.

I quite enjoyed the solitude of a night watch. When I had been the youngest of my father's Ulfheonar it had often been my lot to have the loneliest of watches. I had taken it as an honour that warriors like Olaf Leather Neck, Haaken One Eye and Beorn the Scout had trusted me to keep them safe at night. The only disappointing part was that it was not a clear night and I could see neither the stars nor the moon. The night passed peacefully and when I saw false dawn in the east, I went up the road to see to the horses and to make water. When my men woke, I would send them to the same place too. As an Ulfheonar I had learned that some trackers could smell where men had made water. I doubted that the Danes had one such in their number but I would take no chances. I went to one of the water skins and used it to wet my head and freshen me up and then I returned to the others. I was slicing some pig meat to eat between the bread which Edgar of Helgeflet had given us when Siggi awoke. The bread was beginning to become stale and if we had had a fire then I would have toasted it. It would have to do as it was, Olaf Leather Neck was fond of saying, 'it fills a hole' and he was right. I sliced a piece from the loaf with my seax and bit some of the bread at the same time as the pig meat.

Siggi stretched, "Anything, Jarl?"

I shook my head. "Have the men make water up the road by the horses." He nodded his understanding and went around them to awaken them with the nudge of his sealskin boot. I had not taken my mail off yet there were still preparations to make. I took my whetstone from my satchel and put an edge, first on my sword and then on my seax. The second seax, in my boot, had not been used. When I was satisfied, I went to the barrier we had made next to the road. My men had done a good job and the ten paces leading to the brow and the ten paces on the other side were solid. Within a day or two, the brambles and ivy would show that they were dying but, for the moment they were still green. I stood behind the hornbeam and peered down the road. Ulfheonar were patient and I heard my men return from making water and begin to sharpen their own weapons. The sun had been up enough time for it to be three handspans above the horizon when I spied, in the distance, movement.

I turned and said, "Stand to, someone approaches. Leave space for me!"

They knew their business and Bergil took Rolf's bow and headed for the left side of the ambush. I peered down the road. I was not yet wearing my helmet and the cochineal had mixed with the soot from the fire to darken my face. I would not be seen unless I made a violent movement. That they were horsemen became clear for they moved rapidly down the road towards us. I also knew they were enemies for Saxons did not possess that number of horses. The Lord of Shipton had made that clear when he was so upset about the loss of one horse. I counted eighteen men and light reflected from their helmets and mail. When they stopped to examine the animal dung then I knew that they were looking for us and I took the opportunity to slip down and return to my men.

I took the spear from Siggi and said, "There are eighteen of them. They are mailed. Bergil, I want at least four to fall to your arrows. They cannot get at you and you will be honouring Rolf's memory if you do so."

I heard Bergil say, "I am not as good with a bow as was Rolf but today I will try to emulate my friend."

I picked up my shield and allowed the tip of my spear to touch the ground. It would not tire me as much. I heard their hooves as they thundered up the road. It was not a cobbled road and so the loud noise showed that they were galloping which was just what we wanted. I began to stamp my right foot and the others took it up so that we would all be in time. In a perfect world, we would have chanted but I did not want them alerted. This way, when I gave the command to charge, we would move on the same leg. It was a time when nerves could destroy a good plan. I had to listen for the horses and judge the moment to perfection. It would not be easy.

"Charge!"

We all stepped forward and I saw the helmet of the leading riders appear. I pulled back my arm and rammed forward even though there was no target. The speed of the horses and our movement brought my spear into the throat of the leading horse. Siggi was behind me and to my right. I was splattered by blood and brains from the horse whose head Siggi's axe sliced in two. The two dying horses moved apart and I tore the spearhead from the horse's throat. I saw a Dane look down at me with surprise on his face. Behind us, Karl and Petr were butchering the two Danes whose horses had been killed and I think the sight shocked him. It was the last thing that he saw for my spear hit him hard in the centre of his chest. He had a wooden saddle and was held in place. The head of the spear grated off his breastbone and then found a vital organ. As Erik Red Beard's spear stabbed another Dane through the leg and his horse's side Siggi's axe struck the chest of another Dane. We had had the easy part of the battle, for now they drew weapons. Five Danes were accounted for and I had to hope that Bergil had killed at least two. It made the odds a little better.

Close to us were three Danes on horses and they drew their swords and came directly at me. Bergil's arrow sprouted from the head of one of them and as a second struck my shield I speared the third in the gut. It was not a fatal wound and the Dane grabbed the spear from my hand. I let him have it for Siggi's axe took his horse's head and I was given the time to pull my sword. Erik's spear struck the leg of the Dane whose sword had hit my shield. As I punched with the boss of my shield at his horse's head, the horse reared and threw its rider into the brambles and ivy.

We had them for now the odds were almost even and as I saw another Bergil arrow hit a Dane I shouted, "Let us end this! Break ranks!"

In the wedge we were formidable but our striking power was only half what it could be. As soon as we broke then all of us ran at the Danes. They were now encumbered by their horses for the loose ones were desperate to get away from the smell of blood and death. The only way to go was through the other horses. My sword had yet to drink blood and when I swung it at the leg of the Dane who was trying to skewer Siggi I backhanded my sword and hacked through his leg. He began to fall from the horse and, in his desperation, he kept hold of the reins. All he succeeded in doing was pulling the horse on to him. He would have died from his wounds in any case but the weight of the horse crushed his bones and his internal organs. Faramir the Fair and my other men were now keen to get into the fight and they leapt over dead and dying men and horses to get at the Danes. Karl used a dead Dane to vault into the air and he knocked a Dane from his horse. The Dane landed in our bramble wall. Karl was a big and powerful man. When he brought his sword over his own head, he split the man's helmet and skull with one blow. It was the last act in the little battle on the nameless road in the middle of nowhere. Three men, one of them badly wounded, turned to run. An arrow from Bergil ensured that only one would be guaranteed to return to Loidis. I noticed that the three who fled had no mail. I did not blame them but I wondered if the Lord of Loidis would view their flight the same way.

I began to bang my shield with my sword, "Wild Boars! Wild Boars!" My men took it up and I saw, as we chanted, the elation on the faces for all had survived. Siggi and Erik both had wounds but they would not need a healer. We could stitch them and they would be a badge of courage.

I held up my sword, "Petr, Bergil, gather the horses. Karl, Lars and Leif begin to take the mail and weapons from the Danes. The rest let us see to our wounded. It was late afternoon when we headed for Sigtrygg's stad. The bodies were left where they lay. We cut a few hunks of meat from the dead horses and the rest were left to the carrion. The Lord of Loidis might come to recover his dead but I doubted it. We had avenged Dreng, Vermund and Rolf but at what cost? As the sun began to set, we spied the welcoming walls of Sigtrygg's stad and I brooded about the witch's curse. Should I have stayed in Elfridaby and let Bjorn Dog Tooth escape? I shook my head and laughed, making

Siggi stare. I did not explain. What was the point in debating what I should and shouldn't have done? I was used by the Norns. I could no more escape my destiny than I could stop the tide from turning. What was done was done. It was *wyrd*!

The End

If you enjoyed this story then there are 23 novels in the Dragonheart series. The first one is entitled **'Viking Slave'**.

The Bloody Hill at Senlac

I am a housecarl called Wolf, in the service of Harold Godwinson, King of the land known as Englaland, and I fought at the battle which finally broke the backs and the hearts of the Vikings in the north; the battle of Stamford Bridge. King Alfred, the one they called The Great, had not managed to end their stranglehold on Englaland but King Harold did. The mighty Harald Hadrada and the treacherous snake that was King Harold's brother, Tostig, had drawn us north to Jorvik where we had defeated them. They came in boats which numbered in the hundreds and they left in a handful. It should have been a great victory but it was ruined by the Normans! Taking advantage of our three hundred miles march to the north, Duke William with his Breton mercenaries had landed on the south coast. And, even though we were weary and hurt beyond words, as soon as we were ordered, we headed back south.

We had lost friends at the Battle of the Bridge close to Jorvik and, worse, we had left men too wounded to head south with us. Lord Aethelward was the most grievous loss. I am no general and I just wield an axe but Lord Aethelward was something more. He was able to advise the King and to choose strategies which helped us to win. It was his mind which had won the battle for us but he was wounded along with his kin, Aelfraed of Medelai. Aelfraed was young but he was, to my mind, the best of us. He had fought and defeated Norman horsemen long before the battle and he still had some growing. Along with his shield brother, Ridley, they had both been wounded too badly to head south. They were our shield brothers. When we next fought then their places would be taken by others. That they would be good warriors was not in doubt but they had not shared our fires nor our shields. They had fought in other parts of the line and there is something which is comforting about fighting alongside someone who is closer to you than any other man. When I swung my axe, I knew that Ridley and Aelfraed were protecting me and I had the confidence to strike when others might not.

There were just four of us left from our fire: myself, Osgar, Ulf and Sweyn. The rest were dead or wounded. If you fought us you might think that we were brothers who shared the same mother's milk but we could see the differences between us. Our mail byrnies looked, to enemies, to be the same but they were not. They each came down to our knees with a split at the bottom to enable us to move easily on the battlefield. They each had sleeves which were loose enough to let a warrior swing his war axe around his head. With a hole just large enough to allow a warrior to slip his head through the weight of the byrnie was spread across our shoulders. They all looked the same but if you examined the links then you would see a difference. Mine was the most expensive for each mail link was held to six others. It had cost me serious purses of silver to have it made but it was more than worth it. When we defeated the Normans then my shield brothers would use the coins we took from the dead to buy mail as good as mine.

  Our shields also looked the same but they were not. Each of us had painted a design on the metal-studded cover. They all had the red dragon of Wessex painted upon them but each was subtly different. Mine had a white-eye and I had given him a wicked smile with yellow painted teeth for I was Wolf and to be feared. We all still used the round shield. While some others used the kite-shaped shields favoured by the Normans we liked our big, heavy, but very effective round shields. Layered with oak and covered in leather and metal they were like a wooden wall when used by King Harold's housecarls. On our spears hung our helmets and they also looked the same. There was less of a difference in them. They were conical with a nasal bar to protect the nose. None of us affected the plume or tuft of hair which some thegns did. We were housecarls! Where we were identical was in the cloaks we used. They were oiled and they were thick, making them the same dull colour which could help to hide us if we needed to. One of the advantages of defeating the Norse was that we took from them great quantities of seal oil and that was a welcome bonus. On the march south, our cloaks would make a quickly erected tent or add extra warmth on a cold night.

  The road upon which we marched had been built by the Romans and went as straight as a spear shaft south, to Lundun. We would need to march there to pick up more men. We carried with us our weapons as we marched on the cobbled road built a thousand years ago! I had my ash shafted spear, of course from which hung my helmet. At my waist, I had the sword made for me by Aethelbert the Weaponsmith. I had used the gold we had been paid when we had fought the Welsh. The Welsh hills were poor grazing land but they had gold buried in them so that killing them was worthwhile. I had named the sword Dragon Slayer. When we had fought the Welsh, I had seen the dragon standard and it had made me fearful. Osgar had calmed my fears and after we had slaughtered them, I had decided to name the sword after the Welsh dragon on their banners as well as the Dragon of Wessex. The standard was a mighty beast and we had slain it. When Aethelbert had made the sword, we had tempered it in my own blood. The Norse and the traitors of Jorvik had much reason to curse my blade. The scabbard in which my sword rested also had as much love and attention as my blade and it was a richly adorned and well-made scabbard lined with sheepskin and had, woven into it, the hair of some of the men I had killed in battle. It would not please the priests but it pleased me. Along with the shield across my back I had my axe; the weapon of the housecarl. It was a single-handed axe but it had a long handle. Osgar favoured a two-handed axe with a larger head but I was happy with Widow Maker. Now as we tramped south, I was grateful for the fact that my axe was lighter than Osgar's for every piece of equipment had to be carried upon our backs. My last weapons were the same type as the others had in their belts. I had in my belt a seax which was as long as my arm from my elbow to my wrist. It was there in case the unthinkable happened and I lost my sword, spear and axe in battle. I kept it sharp but, thus far, I had never needed it. In a sheath behind my shield was a weapon I had used before. The seax which rested there was just the length of my hand. In the press of battle when a warrior could not wield a sword then Snake's Tongue could dart out and find the gaps between shields. Its bite was sharp and could find a warrior's manhood or eye more easily than Dragon Slayer.

Of course, only I used these names for my weapons and they were personal. Aelfraed of Medelai was the only of our small band who had a wife but we were, as yet, married to our weapons rather than to a woman. In the same way as a man with a woman might have personal, pet names so we had names for our weapons. Despite what the priests might say we believed that weapons were living things. Priests did not fight in battle. Oh, they were brave for they were in the thick of the fighting holding the banners and holy relics but they stood in the line knowing that if they died then they would go directly to heaven for they were priests. For a warrior that was always a doubt and we were never sure if our shriving before the battle had rid us of all of our sins.

The first day's march had been easy for we had just covered twenty miles stopping at the hamlet of Gulle where we crossed the river. When the rider came from the south to tell us that the Normans had begun to build a fort then the pace was increased and the second day, we almost ran down the road towards Lincylene. That was nearly the undoing of us for we travelled almost thirty-seven miles that day. The Romans built good roads and they were efficient. We passed their markers which told us how far we had travelled. That second day took us closer to Lundun but twenty men were no longer with us as we dropped our war gear inside the old Roman walls of the ancient fort. Some would catch us up but others, good men all, would still be marching south long after we had fought. Ulf shook his head as we lay on the ground, gasping for breath, "The King might be able to travel that far in one day for he is astride a horse and he has shield bearers to carry his weapons! I cannot do more!"

Osgar had his eyes closed and he chuckled, "You are like a woman, Ulf! Are you a warrior or a maiden? There are men lying on the battlefield north of us who would be more than happy to change places with you. If your feet hurt then be grateful for it means that you are alive!"

My stomach rumbled, "And I know I am alive for my belly thinks that my throat has been cut!"

Sweyn laughed, "And the world is as it should be! The Wolf is hungry!"

I stood and stretched, "I will find food if one of you will light a fire."

Ulf snorted, "Fetch me a horse with the skin on and I will eat it!"

I was the youngest, now, of the four of us and I was also the cleverest at finding food. King Harold would not condone simply taking even though we were fighting for those who lived in this town. That did not mean I would not steal, merely that I would be clever about it. I took my hessian sack and hurried towards the noise of the King and his party. We were the King's bodyguards but he had, with him, his brothers, eorls and his advisers. Aethelward was still in the north and the others would be vying with each other to become the new right-hand man of King Harold. They would all be crowding into the old Roman Praetorium building and that gave me the opportunity to find food. The Romans always had kitchens and I headed for them. I could smell food being cooked but that did not interest me. If there was food being cooked then there would be cooks. I saw a thrall hurrying from a building towards the light of the door of the kitchens. He had come from the granary. While the Romans had been quite organised, I knew that those who lived here now would not be. The granaries were good places to store all manner of food. They were better protected against rats. As I had expected the thrall had left the door unlocked and I slipped in. There was no light and that suited me. I had a nose and I would sniff out the food. The first food I found was apples. The early apples had been harvested. I took a dozen and dropped them in the sack. I had to feel my way along the sacks of grain. I detected a meaty smell and knew that there was some cured meat to be had. I found the leg of ham hanging from a hook. Even as I grabbed it, I realised that it had some slices already taken but that did not matter. As I slipped it in my sack, I heard the door and saw a flash of light. I ducked behind some sacks of oats. One was open and so I grabbed a few handfuls and dropped them into my sack.

I heard the thralls as they made their way towards me. I pressed myself into the shadows. I was not afraid of them but they would identify me and I did not relish being punished by the King.

"I am sure there was a leg of pig here!"

"Old Osbert will have finished it. They will have to make do with the fish stew that was prepared. Come, they are a bad-tempered lot!"

As they left, I breathed a sigh of relief. As the light moved, I caught a flash of muslin. I picked it up and sniffed it. It was a whole round of cheese! Slipping it into my sack I hurried to the door and, after checking that my path was clear, I scurried back to the others. No one noticed one warrior carrying a sack. We were amongst the fittest of the men following the King and we had followed his pile of horse dung so closely that it was still hot and steaming as we had passed it. It meant that the fort was filling up with those who were slower than I was. We housecarls were the biggest men in the army and the ones who I pushed aside were smaller, wearier warriors. I reached the camp and saw the welcoming flames of the fire and the water bubbling. We all carried certain essentials in our leather satchels, salt, an onion or two, wild garlic and herbs. Some would be in the water already. My three shield brothers looked up eagerly as I arrived. I took out the pig on the bone and, hiding it from the other campfires, slipped it to Osgar. He was now the leader and he grinned and nodded. I took out the cheese and hid that beneath my shield. We would share it later. Then I divided up the apples and gave them out; we would have something to eat the next day as we marched. We used our helmets as mixing bowls as well as emergency food and water bowls but I would not need to use my helmet. I had just enough oats to make them into a flatbread. I emptied the oats in my wooden bowl and, using the handle of my larger seax, began to grind them up into flour. We were a good team and all of us worked without words. Osgar was slicing strips from the pig. He worked his way down one bone and laid the meat inside his helmet. He was then able to break off the bone. Using his sword, he hacked into the bone to loosen the marrow and then threw it into the water. He added pieces of meat into the water to make a stew. Ulf was slicing onion and garlic into it while Sweyn put in pieces of bruised apple. Once I had the oats roughly ground, I went to the water fountain which the Romans had kindly installed close to the water trough and added enough to make a pliable paste. I shaped it into flat circles and slapped them on the outside of the pot we used to cook the stew. The upper part was curved and we had learned how to cook them without them falling into the fire. There would be pieces of soot on the bread but it mattered not. It helped to soak up the stew and fill a man up.

By the time the last of those who had managed to join us for the night had entered the fort the food was ready. I had turned the flatbreads and then piled them up to keep them warm. Osgar had secreted the remains of the pig meat in his bag and I still had the cheese ready to eat. We had had to use some precious coins to buy a jug of ale from an alewife who lived beyond the walls of the fort. The coins had come from a dead Viking! We ate with the dedication of men who are not sure if they will eat again. I ate the meat and tiny pieces of onion and apple I found in the thin stew. There would be more watery broth left in the cauldron for any who wished more. I then wiped my wooden bowl clean with my oat bread. As I had ground the oats in my bowl, I had more taste in my stew.

We were just finishing when there was a shout from outside the gate. We could not help it, each of us grabbed a weapon. The door opened and one of the priests who had followed the army shuffled in. He had upon him a brown habit and wore sandals. His shaven head suggested that he was a monk. He also looked young. I was the youngest of us and he was younger than I was. I was close enough to hear his conversation with the sentry.

"You are lucky I let you in priest! All the rest of the army arrived hours ago."

The monk did not seem put out by the aggressive tone of the sentry. We knew him. He was not a housecarl but wished he was one. He had been at the rear of those in the battle and I had yet to see him draw and use his sword. "I am sorry, friend, but there were some men on the road and one of their number was dying from his wounds. I gave him absolution and helped them to bury him."

The sentry, Wulfstun, narrowed his eyes, "And where are they?"

"Not with me. Is there food?"

"Find your own!"

I heard Osgar growl and I wondered if Wulfstun was in for a beating but, instead, he stood and said, "Come here, friend, we have a little and we will share it with a man of God."

He came over and I saw that he was shivering. October is not the time of year to be without a cloak. "Thank you, I am Brother Paul."

"I am Osgar, the ugly one is Ulf, the one who looks like he has eaten his own horse is Sweyn and the youth is Wolf!" I was a man grown with a full beard but I was the youngest! "Help yourself from the bowl although the meat has all gone."

I had not finished all of my oat bread and I gave him what was left. "Here, Brother Paul, there is some bread and when you have finished that there is," I lowered my voice, "cheese!"

He grinned, "Then I am in your debt and I shall say a prayer for you."

That was another reason for helping the monk. It did no harm to have prayers said for you. None of us had clear consciences and any help with the saints who guarded heaven's doors was always welcome. We moved so that he could sit and I took the cheese and cut it into two. I then divided one half into five and handed a piece to each of us. It was one of the local sheep cheeses from the uplands to the north and west, close to Jorvik. I had had some before because it was made close to where Ridley came from and he often shared one with us. It was a good end to the day.

When we had finished and given the last half beaker of ale to the monk, Osgar lay back on his war gear and said, "So, priest, as a story to send me off to sleep, tell me your tale."

"It is a simple one, Osgar the Housecarl, I was a monk who served in Jorvik and when Hardrada came some of his men decided to come to the small abbey in which I lived. They took the few things we had and decided to enjoy themselves with some of the younger monks. When we older ones objected then they turned their weapons on us. I would have died along with the others had not some men from the King's army come along. They managed to rescue me but were driven off. When the battle was fought, I joined them with a sword in my hand for the Vikings needed to be punished. I was not very good but I wielded my sword. All of the ones who had saved me were killed and so, after the battle, I determined to pay back King Harold by tending to his sick. "

All of us were impressed by his story. It took a brave man to fight a Viking if he had no skill with a sword. Osgar asked, "And where is the sword now?"

Brother Paul smiled, "Like me, it was not very good and it bent when I used it. I was lucky that another slew the man who was about to take my head and then the battle was over."

Osgar gave a glance to us all and then said, "Stay with us, Brother Paul, for a warrior needs someone to intercede with God for them and we will keep you fed and protected. Not all of King Harold's men are such as we."

He nodded and looked at Wulfstun who had been staring at us while we ate. "Aye, I know what you mean."

We were about to settle down to sleep when there was a commotion and we heard whispered, "The King comes!"

Sure enough, a few moments later we saw brands and King Harold and some of his men appeared. Men cheered. We did so too, albeit half-heartedly. A good king would have ensured that we were all well fed and he had not. He smiled, "Ah, some more of my loyal housecarls! We will show these Normans how real warriors fight, eh?"

We had all stood when he arrived and Osgar nodded, "Aye, King Harold. Where will we find these horsemen?"

"They show they are afraid by building a wooden fort on the beach where they landed. They wait for us."

There were some fragments of cheese lying by the fire and one of the King's servants whispered in his ear. The King frowned and said, "Ethelbert here tells me that some food was taken from the granary. A block of cheese and some pig meat. What do you know of this?"

Osgar smiled, "It was lucky that we brought some cheese from Jorvik, King Harold and had some wild onions or else we would have starved. I know not how a man can march three hundred miles without sustenance. Do you?"

One of his Thegns, Edgar of Hamwic, said, angrily, "This is not how a common man speaks with a King!"

Osgar turned on him, "Listen, little man, we are the King's bodyguards and I do not recall you on the battlefield at Stamford! Do not make me angry for I have eaten little today and it would not take much for me to remove your head. That might give some meat to the watery stew we ate." The words were spoken calmly but all knew of Osgar's skill and the Thegn took a step back for he did not wish to risk a fight, especially not with a housecarl.

King Harold snapped, "Osgar! Do not try my patience. Thegn Edgar, my housecarls are like highly trained greyhounds. When they have no enemies to fight, they seek battle with any. I apologise." He turned back to Osgar, "But I see your point, Osgar. There will be food and ale when we rest tomorrow. It will stop Wolf from pilfering from my stores!"

After they had gone Brother Paul nodded, "I can see that this will be a most interesting journey. I will try to entertain you with my words."

The long journey to Lincylene was the longest one we undertook. The rest were all in stages of about twenty-five or, sometimes, twenty-seven miles. It was to keep as much of the army together as we could rather than any thoughtful action on the King's part. Even so, the hard march in weather which deteriorated meant many men fell out. Some could not physically go on while others had had enough. None of the housecarls left the army and we all marched together. We bore the heaviest loads and kept up the fastest pace for we were the best. I think that there were many men who stayed with us because they wished to be like us. It was a dream for a man trained his whole life to be a housecarl. I had campaigned the least but Osgar had forgotten more than Thegn Edgar would ever learn. The further south we went the better welcome we received from the towns and villages through which we passed. Lundun was King Harold's centre of power and as we neared the cheers became deafening and would have turned other warriors' heads but not the housecarls. We let King Harold and his fawning thegns smile and wave. We marched grimly on knowing that, at the end of it, we faced a battle and all of us knew that it would not be an easy one. I was not alone in wishing that Aelfraed, Ridley and Aethelward were with us.

We had, with us, a couple of pairs of sealskin boots we had taken from the dead Vikings; we knew how to scavenge a battlefield. One pair was too small for any of us but they looked like they would fit Brother Paul and we forced them upon him. He was reluctant at first until we pointed out that we would be travelling faster and it would save his sandals for when he could wear them. If any of us thought that he would hold us up then we were proved wrong as the surprisingly fit priest not only kept up with our marching pace but was able to regale us with stories of his time in the priory. He was funny and knew how to tell a tale with excellent mimicry of men who were now dead. It made the next twenty-five miles pass quickly. The King was as good as his word and there was food awaiting us. Of course, when we collected our portion it would be augmented with slices of pig meat sliced from the bone and we still had the cheese.

Normally, when an army such as ours passed through a town then we were greeted with fear at best and aggression was more usual. The threat of an invasion by the Normans, however, meant we were greeted as heroes and feted well. We had heeded the threat to the North and while the North did not matter to the folk of Dunsby, the fact that Norman horsemen could sweep into their town filled them with terror and we were treated as heroes. Of course, each day we were bleeding men. The camp we made each night was marginally smaller. Five, ten, even fifteen men might disappear during a day of marching. Some might return but many would not and these men were irreplaceable for they had fought rebels and Norse and won!

When we reached Lundun we were a shadow of the army which had fought at Stamford Bridge. The King and his thegns had dug their heels in and left us on the road which led through the Bishop's Gate in the Roman Wall. Those who had travelled far, and there were a few, complained that Lundun was like an overgrown pigsty. They were the ones who had travelled with the King and had seen Lutetia and Rome! To us, Jorvik was a large place and Lundun seemed to us to have more people and better buildings within than every other town and burgh in the land! That is not to say that we liked it. The prices they would charge for everything would be double or treble of anywhere else. With the threat of a Norman attack, these prices were even higher. Worse, the overpriced beer we had to endure was little better than ditchwater. We thought that we would be there but a night or two but, in the end, we stayed five. None of us was privy to the machinations of the King, his brothers, bishops and thegns so I am not certain why we dallied. I do know that he sent emissaries to speak with the Normans.

Osgar had an opinion on that, "It buys time. Each day we waste here more men arrive from the battle. Every day that the Normans do not launch their horsemen means that more of the fyrd can be summoned to fight alongside us."

Ulf spat into the fire. The gob of phlegm sizzled. Ulf had been unwell since Stamford with the ailment most of us encountered during the autumn and the winter. It was a nose full of snot and a hawking cough. Weaker men went to bed; we carried on as though nothing was wrong. "The men of the fyrd are a waste of time and the Normans will sweep through them."

Sweyn was a cynic, "And if they slow the Normans down that will give us more time to hew them when they arrive. Besides, a large number of farmers with bill hooks and scythes will give this William the Bastard something to think about. These horsemen value their horses and a bill hook on a pole can enable even a farmer to slay a horse."

Brother Paul listened to it all with growing horror, "You speak of farmers as though they are unimportant!"

"And in a battle, they are." I shook my head, "Believe me, Brother Paul, I know the value of farmers. I come from farming stock and without them, this land could not grow but we are talking of a battle and a clash of steel between men who are the best at what they do. The Normans are the same. We use a shield wall and they use horses. We have yet to meet them in a major battle and the outcome will determine who rules this land."

Osgar laughed and clapped me on the back, "Our little Wolf has grown! That almost sounded like Aelfraed!" He turned to Brother Paul. "It is why Ulf says he wishes they were not there for they may get in the way and none of us can see a purpose for them. In the days of King Alfred, they might have had a role they could play but these Normans bring archers. We are safe enough for we wear mail byrnies with padded shirts beneath but they do not and the Norman arrows will decimate them. Then they will have to face the horsemen with their spears and lances. It matters not that the horses they ride are not large ones. When they charge the weapons they hold will come for faces and bodies with no protection. The fyrd's bowels will turn to water and those that can will run and then the Normans will come for us."

I stood and stretched, for I needed to make water, "And that is where we hope that the King chooses his battle site well. If we cannot be outflanked and there is a hill then we have a chance." I left the former Roman barracks and headed to the river. The building was no longer Roman for much of the stone had been robbed out but some Saxon King had used the foundations to plant large timbers and put a roof over the stone floor of the old barracks. It was dry and we had lit a fire in the centre. The stone walls which had once lined the river were no longer complete. Already, King Harold had men shoring up the gaps. It was getting on to dark and the workmen had gone. I headed for a gap and, after clambering through, dropped my breeks and added to the flow of water heading east. Close by me Beorhtric of Langhewis was using some dock leaves to wipe his backside, having emptied his bowels. He was a good warrior and usually fought to the right of us. He nodded at me.

Without looking at him I said, "There are fewer of us now than there were, Beorhtric of Langhewis."

"Aye, and after this battle, there will be one less."

"You will leave the King's service?"

He fastened his breeks and came to speak with me as I finished, "I cannot see the King holding on to this land." He lowered his voice. "It is said he is forsworn."

I had heard this rumour, "The shipwreck?"

"Aye, it is said that he swore an oath to Duke William that he would support the Duke's claim to the throne. He swore on holy relics and God does not smile upon such lies." I had heard this rumour and it did not sit well. We had not sworn such an oath but we followed a man who had. Where did that leave us? "We left many good men in the north. Had we met him, beard to beard without the treachery of Tostig, then it might have been different and we might have had a chance."

"And what will you do?"

"If we are not dead?" I nodded. "Then I will head east. It is said the Emperor of the Romans likes to employ barbarians such as we and he pays gold to do so. If I am to risk my life for a man then it might as well be for gold and if I cannot get there, I will take my son, Beorhtric, and hire my sword and axe to those who fight in Flanders and France."

I had heard others speak in this way. We were Harold's men but he had not treated us well. The days of gold after a victory had ceased once he became King. To many, Sweyn in particular, it seemed that he had used us to get where he was and we no longer mattered. We would fight for him for we had sworn an oath but that was all. We made our way back through the gap in the wall and we were both silent. He had planted a seed in my mind and it was growing.

The next morning, we marched south and west, heading through the Ardensweald. The few days of rest we had enjoyed enabled us to march seventy miles in two days. That was no mean feat and I do not think of any who could have done as we did. When we arrived at Caldbec Hill King Harold was so pleased that he gave us that rarest of rewards, praise. The place we stopped was the old muster point for the fyrd, The Hoar Apple Tree. We were so exhausted that we just collapsed at the highest point on the ridge. We were forgotten while the King sent out scouts and spoke with his brothers Gyrth and Leofwine as well as his other senior thegns. We chose a good camp. Brother Paul had proved himself to be useful in Lundun and had acquired some food for us. We ate better that night than we had on the march south. It looked a pathetically small army which was camped there. We just had six hundred or so housecarls, the thegns and servants. The rest of the army was strung out along the road to Lundun. While a pan of water was put on to boil to make a broth the four of us headed down the slope to spy out the land.

Sweyn knew the land and he pointed out, as we walked down the slope in the late afternoon, the salient features. "That is Telham Hill and the summit is called Hecheland. If I was Duke William then I would take that hill and use it."

I was the youngest and so I asked the most obvious question. "Then why do we not occupy it? It is obvious that it is higher than the other."

"Because it is a mile or so further away, Wolf, and the rest of the army would have to cross that stream. It is boggy and by the time the army had crossed then it would be a morass through which we could not fall back." Osgar spoke patiently, as to a child.

Sweyn said, "Besides there is a ridge here and a knoll. The stream, Santlache, will slow down the enemy as they climb here, to Santlache Ridge."

Ulf had good eyes and he pointed to the right, "See, there is a swamp. That will protect our flanks as will the woods. This is a good place to hold them."

"If we had the numbers."

Sweyn was right. We had barely six hundred housecarls and even if the rest of the army arrived in time, we would still have only eight thousand men. We did not know how many the Normans had brought from Normandy and Brittany but the odds were it would be a greater number. We made our way back up the hill and even I could see that the very top of the ridge, upon which the Red Dragon banner fluttered, would be the best place to defend. As we passed the other camps, I recognised Beorhtric and I waved at him and realised that he had not yet chosen to leave. When we reached our camp there was food ready for Brother Paul had not been idle. We even had a jug of ale and so we ate a good meal and then drank and sang songs about the warriors with whom we had fought. The others knew more than I did but I sang anyway for we were all brothers of the shield and the axe. Before I retired, I did two things. I sharpened all of my weapons and then I confessed to Brother Paul. My sins were insignificant, I suppose, greed, vanity and the like. I had never murdered and I had never been forsworn but if I was to die then I wished to meet my maker with the best chance of going to heaven.

We were all awake and preparing for battle before dawn for we had heard the scouts as they returned and they spoke of the approach of the Norman army. They were reported to be more than ten thousand in number. Tostig's name was cursed for we had lost many men when we had fought him. We made water and then ate. Osgar waved Brother Paul over. "We have enjoyed happy times since you joined us, Brother Paul, and for that we thank you." He took out his purse from his satchel. We all carried one. "I would have you watch this until after the battle." We all handed our purses over too. I felt embarrassed because mine was so small.

"Why?" The monk looked confused.

"If any die then you share out the remainder between the survivors and yourself."

"But I have done nothing!"

"You have shriven us and you have kept us amused with your tales and your songs. If we are to die then this is payment and we trust you. You will see that we are buried and as for the rest...?" He touched the cross around his neck. "A man will not need gold where we are going."

"And if you all live?"

He laughed, "Even now, you keep us amused, Brother Paul! On the off chance that all of us survive then we will give you a tithe of each purse for watching over it."

He took them but shook his head, "But I barely know you!"

Osgar was wise. I think he could have been a monk if he had not been so good with an axe. He smiled, "And how long does it take for a man to know he has made a friend. We did not choose you; God chose to send you to us and that is good. Now find somewhere safe from which you can watch this battle."

He made the sign of the cross, "May God be with you and watch over you!"

Ulf said, "Take the pot, food and our cloaks too. We shall not need them today!"

I almost laughed as the diminutive priest struggled to carry his goods to the trees. Whichever side lost they would take shelter in those woods. We picked up our spears and shields. Our helmets hung from our spears and our axes from our backs. We would wait until we discovered where we would be placed. I looked up at the sky. It was a waning moon and it was still bright. Far to the north Aelfraed and Ridley would be watching the same moon. I wondered if Aelfraed had recovered for his was a serious wound. When I had left, although his life was not in the balance, the odds on his being able to fight again were not in his favour.

It was the King's brother Leofwine who came to us. He was a little younger than Sweyn and we liked him for he had a sense of humour, something the King seemed to lack. "Are our blades sharp for we have Norman heads and horses to hew this day?"

Osgar spoke for us all, "Aye, my lord, and where does the King want us this fine morning?"

"You are all to fight with me and my housecarls. We have too few to waste men guarding his body. My brother and I will make the front rank and the fyrd will be behind us."

That was a relief. We all feared the fyrd. They had a tendency to run either forward or back when they could but they would be encircled by a belt of steel!

"We will be on the left side of the ridge. Fetch your war gear and follow me."

We headed, along with others who had been selected, to the left side of the ridge. It was almost a knoll and I saw that the slope fell away sharply to our left which made it safer so long as men stood there. As we were amongst the first, we were able to choose our position. We picked the flattest area we could and we picked out the features before us for a good warrior anticipated how he would fight based upon the ground before him. The slope was very steep and that would help. Leofwine left us to fetch others and we chatted with those to our right and left. I saw that Beorhtric was six men away and I waved at him. "Who is that?" Osgar asked me.

"I met him on the road south. He is thinking of serving the Eastern Emperor and says that he has had enough of fighting for the Red Dragon."

Osgar shrugged, "So long as he tells Harold Godwinson before he leaves then that is good." We had not sworn an oath to the King but Harold Godwinson. "As for me, I would rather fight in the land of my birth. I like this land."

There was a cheer and, looking behind us, I saw that the two banners, the Red Dragon of Wessex and the Fighting Man banner had been unfurled. It was significant for it would mark where King Harold would stand and so long as they flew then we would fight, even if the King was slain. I saw he was on the knoll which afforded a good view of the battlefield. We heard the sound of the bell in a nearby church sounding Prime and we had barely turned when we saw the arrival of the Normans. The Santlache meant that they had to cross in a column and it took them time.

Osgar shook his head, "If we had a few slingers and archers then we could make their crossing costly."

I turned and pointed to a small band of archers, "But we have some!"

"Not enough!" He took out a small bag. "And that reminds me, take out your stones. We might as well make it hard for them."

Ulf suddenly left us and raced down the slope. He came back with two fist-sized rocks. He looked happy, "See what I have found!"

The others also left the line and so I followed them. I had to go further down the slope before I found two which were the right size. I was confused but I would be told what to do. When we reached our line Ulf explained, "We tie cord to these and then throw them when the Normans advance. You can crack a skull with a well-thrown one."

It made sense and I took one of the spare bindings I had for my boots and, cutting it in two tied each length to a stone. All of this took time and the ridge had filled up so much that we were in danger of falling down the slope. Leofwine, who was in command of this side of the field shouted, "Form a second rank! Let the Normans struggle with the slope eh?"

As I looked back, I saw that we had ten ranks of men. It looked formidable but that was an illusion. Only the front rank and half were mailed men and the rest were the fyrd. We donned our helmets and stuck our spears, point first, into the soft earth. As the Normans, Bretons and French gathered less than eight hundred paces from us, men began to shout.

"Olicrosse!"

"Godemite!"

Osgar began to beat his shield with his spear and began to chant, "Ut! Ut! Ut!"

It was taken up by the ranks which had formed. It was almost hypnotic and then the Normans responded. A Norman knight rode up the hill to stop within a hundred paces of us. He lifted his helmet and then began to sing. I did not understand the words but the song itself sounded beautiful if sad. Leofwine said, "It is the song of a French hero, Roland!"

The knight then began to juggle with his sword. Ulf snarled, "Cocky bastard!"

I saw that half a dozen men, they were from the fyrd, had come around the edge of our line to stand before us and to view this spectacle. They were local men and each had a sword, shield and helmet. Suddenly the knight sheathed his sword and galloped at the six men. He was fast and his hand was even quicker. His spear darted out twice in rapid succession and two men died. He pulled back on his reins and another fell to the horse's hooves. That was too much for us. Osgar shouted, "Let's show the bastard what an axe can do!"

We were not the only ones and Beorhtric and his three shield brothers joined us as, leaving our spears in the ground, we took our axes and ran at the knight who was now chasing the three survivors up the slope. I was the youngest and the fastest. The knight pulled back his spear to skewer one of the fyrd and I swung my axe two-handed for my shield was still on my back. My axe hacked through his leg and the straps which held his saddle. They bit into the side of his horse. I am guessing that he was a dying man then but that did not stop us from hacking his body and his horse into pieces. It had been a piece of showmanship which had cost him his life. Our line all erupted in cheers and we returned to our place.

That was the end of the preliminaries. Both sides waited for the signal to attack. We would be awaiting the Norman charge and we knew that they would have to attack us. We had heard that a fleet had been sent from Lundun to attack the Duke's ships. If he did not attack then he would be trapped and already more men had been sent south. It was a nearby church which, unwittingly, signalled the attack. The bell sounded for Terce, the third hour of the day and the archers, followed a short while later by the heavily armoured men on foot, began the steady slog up the hill.

"Right men, shields and spears!" We all obeyed Leofwine's command as though we were all of one body. I locked my shield with Osgar and Sweyn. My axe was now hanging from my back and, at my feet, lay the two improvised throwing hammers I had made. There was little point in wasting them on the archers for they would outrange our throws. We would have to endure the arrow storm and then use our own missiles at the advancing foot soldiers. We did not lift our shields above our heads for that risked inviting an arrow beneath it. We angled them and then tucked our heads behind them. I peered over the top at the archers who scampered up the slope. They would find it easier than the ones who would follow. I saw that each archer had a sheath of, perhaps, twenty-four arrows. That was not a great number and I was relieved for holding a shield up sapped strength from arms. We were able to watch the arrows as they soared in the sky and, watching their flight, I knew that the majority would be wasted. I heard some thud into wood and spied others whose flight was so high that they would land behind King Harold. We had a few slingers and archers. They loosed from behind the shield wall and sent their own missiles at the enemy.

Both sets of archers moved when they had expended their missiles. Their archers pulled back and our archers picked up the ones sent by the Normans and which had fallen short. They would be reused. As they fell back, we each lowered our left arms. It would be foolish to take the shields off but the relief of a few moments without a raised arm might come to aid us at the end of what looked like being a very long day. As the archers retreated, no doubt to replenish their stock of arrows, the men on foot parted to let them through. Then they reformed and headed up towards us. This time we would get to hurl our missiles and when the spearmen closed with us we would have to battle with them.

Norman horsemen wore split byrnies to give their legs protection and some of those who advanced up the slope towards us also wore a longer byrnie but most had a short one which came to the waist. It was easier and cheaper to make and gave good protection against arrows. Their spears were longer and lighter than ours and could be used for throwing. Ours, too, could be thrown but they would not go far. The slope would increase the range. We picked up our improvised missiles and stones. Most of the housecarls had a sling from when they were boys and we could all use one. As there were no arrows being sent in our direction, we began to hurl our stock of stones. In many ways, it helped us to loosen arms ready for the wielding of an axe. The stones clattered down and the advancing Normans held up their shields. They had a variety of shields from round ones to kite-shaped ones. They would find it hard to lock them. When a stone hit, even if it did not wound the warrior, it would hurt, especially if it was an arm or a hand which it struck. If it hit a helmet the blow could render a warrior unconscious. Some of the stones made men stop and one or two fell. As my supply of small stones was expended, I picked up my first rope tied rock and, stepping forward, I began to whirl it about my head. I may have been a young warrior but I was as strong as any and when I hurled it the rock flew high to crash down on the advancing Normans. One fell. I did not see where the rock struck him. I would have been lucky to kill him but he could not advance while he was lying on the ground. Even as I whirled my second one, I saw other rocks flying through the air as well as throwing javelins and men fell. In the grand scheme of things, it was not a huge number but men fell and there were gaps. More importantly, it heartened us for it hurt the enemy

Eorl Leofwine shouted, "Lock shields!"

I picked up my spear. The embedded dirt which was on the spearhead would cause a worse wound than a clean blade. I locked my shield and, this time, kept it slightly lower so that I could see my enemy. The slope meant that they could not sprint the last few steps and would advance towards spears which were held at eye height. Our spearheads were bigger than the ones the Normans used and I knew that some men would empty their bowels in those last moments before they charged home. Every man in our front two ranks had fought recently while the Normans had been waiting since early summer to cross the Channel. We were sharp; they might be rusty.

As they closed you could see their eyes. Some burned fiercely with anger while others showed fear. We knew our reputation and the fact that they were keeping their best weapon back, the heavy cavalrymen, showed us great respect. They hoped to weaken us with this attack. I rested my spear on the top of my shield and Osgar's. There was a natural notch where the two shields met. I kept as relaxed and loose as I could for once we began to fight, we might have to go on for hours. I was not certain which of the two men who were closing with me that I would be actually fighting. They were not moving up the slope in a straight line as there were arrows and stones to negotiate. I turned to make certain that I could raise my spear and saw that the fyrdman behind me was short and the haft of my spear would be above his head; I could pull back my arm and punch. Despite the slope, the Norman line tried to run at us for the last few steps and it was a mistake. Some slipped and the line reached us haphazardly. It meant that I had a free strike at the Norman who was closest. His spear clattered into my shield and I rammed at him with my own weapon. His shield was smaller than was mine and the large head slid over the wooden top and struck his cheek. I pushed hard and it broke through his teeth and his jaw. Had he been able to then he would have screamed but I kept pushing and my spearhead ripped into the back of his skull. He slid to the ground and I pulled out my spear. All along the line, there were shouts and curses; there was the sound of metal on wood and metal on metal. It was a screaming cacophony of noise and death. I saw that Osgar, Ulf and Sweyn had ended the lives of another three warriors but that was the limit of my view. From behind me spears were thrust, blindly into gaps. Although they struck nothing, they made the advancing Normans have to keep their wits about them and any distraction helped us.

Pulling my arm back I thrust at the next Norman who had a kite shield and he blocked my blow before ramming his spear towards my eye. All that I needed to do was to duck beneath my shield and his spearhead slid across my helmet, rasping as it did so. I had quick hands and I pulled and thrust again as the fyrdman behind me used his own spear to jab down. Perhaps the Norman was distracted for my spear found his mail and my spearhead protested as I tried to force it between the links. I could feel my muscles burning and then the spear was through the mail, ripping and tearing a fist-sized hole in the byrnie. It carried on through the padded undershirt and into his shoulder. I twisted as I retracted and blood spurted and arched over my head as he crumbled to die before me.

In a battle such as this, you fought your own fight which was normally the length of a spear shaft all around you. For all that I knew we might be the only warriors who were winning but you just kept doing your job and the pressure from behind was reassuring. I saw a few arrows sailing from behind me and that told me that our archers were being employed. Of course, if the Normans rearmed their archers and returned then we might have to endure their attacks too. As Aethelward had once told Aelfraed and me, you fight one battle at a time and kill one man at a time.

My spearhead was no longer covered in mud. That had been replaced by blood, bits of bone and gore. I noticed as I raised it for a third time that there were small pieces of flesh attached to it. I stabbed down again and the warrior I struck had more skill than the other two for he deflected the head easily and then rammed his spear, not at my shield or my body but at my leg. I felt an excruciating pain as the small head tore into my flesh. The fyrdman behind me came to my aid, albeit unwittingly, his blindly struck spear hit the Norman's helmet. It pushed it down slightly over his eyes and in that instant, I pulled back and speared him close to where his mail ended at his neck. I found flesh and the Norman met his God. It was in that moment that some of those at the rear of the Norman line began to fall back down the slope. While they themselves had not suffered wounds, they had passed the bodies of those who were dead and saw the wall of spears still bloody. Some of the Normans and Bretons on our side of the battlefield began to head back down to the Santlache. It allowed us to see further down the line. Many of the Norman foot soldiers were still fighting but our stout defence of the line had hurt those facing us. I heard Osgar grunt and knew that he had been hit by a Norman spear. I had no opponent and so, ignoring my wound, I thrust my own spear at the side of his opponent's head. He wore a coif but it availed him nothing and my spear penetrated his ear, then his brain and then he died. A warrior with a sword suddenly rose from my right and sliced through my spear shaft. Before he could take advantage of my lack of an offensive weapon, Osgar had returned my compliment and skewered him. As he fell, he clutched at Osgar's spear. We both turned to grab our axes but the attack had broken down and the defeated foot soldiers streamed down the slope. Men left the line to despatch the wounded Normans and badly wounded housecarls moved to safety.

Turning to Osgar I said, "Where is the wound?"

He laid down his axe and pointed to his left side where the spear had broken the links of Osgar's byrnie and ripped into his side, "Here!" Bending down he tore some of the tunic from one of the dead Norman spearmen and, balling it, placed it beneath his mail to stem the bleeding. We both knew that he would be weaker for the rest of the battle. I also tore some material but I just made a tourniquet above the wound in my leg. I would have to keep releasing the pressure but so long as we did not have to move then I would be able to fight on. Looking down the line I saw that Ulf and Sweyn had survived as had Beorhtric but other housecarls lay dead.

Ulf was in a good mood, "Six Normans lie dead at my feet and I still have my spear!"

Osgar had finished tending to himself and he grunted, "Well it will be axe work now!"

I looked down the slope and saw the Norman and Breton knights preparing their charge. All of these had the kite-shaped shield. Some had lances but most had long spears. They were going to charge us. The slope, the bodies and the fact that over half his men on foot were still fighting meant that Duke William and his knights could not hit us in a solid mass. Their horses would not tower over us because of the slope. We had a chance and I tried a couple of twirls with my axe. Using an axe was all about timing. When I was satisfied that I was loose enough I kissed the head of Widow Maker. Ulf and Sweyn still had their spears but Osgar had slipped his shield around to his back for he had the Danish axe and it needed two hands. The deaths in the front line and the fact that some now used the two-handed axe meant that we were not as tight as we were before. Osgar needed room to swing his axe. The good news that it was horsemen approaching meant that we would not have as many men to fight but Osgar was at risk from a spear. All depended upon him maintaining his swinging rhythm.

    I saw their Duke leading his men. He had, behind him, the banner given to him, so some men said, by the Pope. He was heading for the part of the line defended by Leofwine. Beorhtric was now closer to the King's brother and there were some thegns now in the front rank. We had lost warriors. The horses were labouring as they came up the slope. They had to carry a mailed warrior up a slope slippery with early morning damp augmented with blood and gore. The foot soldiers had also churned up the ground as they had marched. The horsemen would not hit us at speed. I checked that I had room to swing my axe; the fyrdman had stepped back a pace and I would not have the protection of his spear. I held Widow Maker behind me and my shield before me. The knights who were riding at me would aim their spears and lances at my body. They would stand in their stiraps and ram their weapons at my body. I placed my right foot slightly behind me to help me brace. In a wedge, I would have the weight of other mailed men behind me but Stamford Bridge had cost us too many men for that luxury. I would have to use the Hill at Santlache to aid me. I saw, behind the line of horsemen, archers who were hurrying up the slope. Whatever happened when the horses charged, they would send arrows towards the Fighting Man Banner and King Harold. He might not be fighting yet but he would be a target.

    I wanted to loosen the bandage on my leg but the horsemen were coming closer and I did not want the distraction. I did, however, glance at Osgar and I saw blood dripping down his side. He was hurting, perhaps even dying.

    The line of knights did not hit us as one. Duke William and the oathsworn who protected him hit Leofwine and the men around him first. I heard the dying scream of a horse hit by a Danish axe. Splinters of wood from shattered lances and spears flew into the air and there was a collective scream as men used curses, oaths and anger to add strength to their strikes. I found it strange that both sets of warriors asked God to help them kill their enemies. He could not satisfy both! Osgar was not letting his wound impede him and he continued to swing rhythmically. I put all of that from my mind as I watched the knight who had chosen to try to kill me approach me. I could tell, from the way he rode his horse, that he was heading for me. It had been Aelfraed who had studied the Norman horsemen and it was he who had been the first to fight one. He had noticed how they had a longer rein than a Saxon thegn and that allowed them to use their kite-shaped shields to the greatest effect. The knight intended to present his shield to me and strike, with his wooden spear, over the top of his cantle. In that way, he would present his protected side to me. I had no intention of striking at his shield. I would kill his horse.

The irregular line of knights struck us. I heard cries around me but I fought my own battle, "Widow Maker strike true."

The spear was rammed at my shield even as I was bringing over my weapon in a horizontal arc. It was a good hit from the spear and if I had not had my shoulder pressing against the oak of my shield I might have been knocked back. As it was I held firm. Then Widow Maker hacked into the side of the knight's horse's head. It was the sort of blow a farmer might use to kill a sick animal and the horse died instantly. My hit meant that the horse went to my left as it fell, towards Ulf. I kept my eye on the knight and the horse. The forelegs folded beneath it as it crumpled to the ground. Its fall shifted the next knight to the right and I saw Ulf's spear strike the knight under the chin. Then I leapt from the line for the knight was on the ground. I lifted my axe and brought it down to strike him on the helmet. The helmet was a good one but Widow Maker was in no mood for prisoners. The helmet, head protector and skull were split in twain.

Ulf shouted, "Back, Wolf!"

I stepped back over the dead horse and took my place again. Ulf had slipped his shield over his back and he held his two-handed axe. His broken spear lay embedded in the knight's body. Osgar had also killed a knight but the horse remained alive. We now had a barrier before us but, as I rejoined Osgar I saw that he had been hit. A piece of broken lance was embedded in his left shoulder. With two wounds he was doomed.

"You are hurt! Go to Brother Paul and he will tend to you!"

He laughed, "And leave my shield brothers when victory is almost here? I think not!"

He was wrong. The battle was not almost won. While it was true that we had held our own I could see that Leofwine was down and that there were some thegns and their fyrdman fighting in the front rank. However, we still had men to fight for more horsemen came at us. These would have a much harder task for their horses would have to clamber over dead knights and two dead horses. The knights who came at us were angry for they had lost friends already and the three who came at my shield brothers and me urged their horses over the slippery bodies which lay before us. I punched at the spear which came down at me for the horse was rising as it struggled over the dead animal. The spear was not thrust as hard as the first one and I deflected it. I had intended to take the horse's head as I swung down but the horse slipped and dipped its head. The rider was thrown forward and Widow Maker hacked into the knight's shoulder. He screamed and, losing his grip on the reins, his body flew behind me. If he was not dead when he landed the fyrdman there would deal with him. If nothing else the man who watched my back would have a better sword.

As I turned to look for my next foe, I saw the spear slide into Osgar's chest. His two wounds and the two-handed axe had taken its toll. Even as the Norman knight was pulling back his arm, I swung my long axe and Widow Maker hacked into his arm and shoulder. The spear fell to the ground and I tore the axehead from the wound to swing sideways into his chest. He had good scale mail but it was not good enough and he tumbled from the back of his horse. We had broken this attack and I saw the knights and foot soldiers withdrawing down the hill to reform. I ran to Osgar who had fallen back. His helmet had fallen from his head and his eyes were still open.

I heard a cry from further along the line, "Duke William is dead! The Duke is dead and we have won!"

I dropped Widow Maker and cradled Osgar's head in my hands. He smiled and a tendril of blood oozed out, "See, I told you that we had won." Ulf and Sweyn had joined me. "I have done my duty and can go to God with a clear conscience. Tell Aelfraed…"

He managed no more for life left his eyes. He died happy thinking that we had won but that was a lie. The Duke was not dead. Even as Osgar's soul was rising to heaven, we heard a horn from the King and, standing, we saw that some of the fyrd had left the line and, thinking that the battle was won, had pursued the retreating knights and foot soldiers down to the swamp near to the Santlache. I watched in horror as the horsemen turned and butchered them.

We had lost heavily in the last attack. I saw Beorhtric's body lying close by Leofwine's. He had been slain defending the body of the brother of the King and he would not get to Miklagård after all. King Harold's other brother Gyrth shouted, "Shorten the line! Shorten the line! Housecarls to the fore!"

It pained us but we had to leave our shield brother and move closer to the King's standard. We had lost over half of the housecarls who had begun the battle. There were less than three hundred of us left. The three of us found ourselves close to Gyrth, the King's last brother, and just before the King's standards. Ulf and Sweyn shifted positions so that they flanked me.

"What…"

Sweyn growled, "You will be between us for that is what we all decided. You and Aelfraed are the youngest. Osgar always watched out for you. Just because he is dead does not mean that we shall forget our duty."

I saw a Norman rider halt before the knights who were falling back. He raised his helmet so that they could see his face and when men cheered then I knew that Duke William lived. Osgar had died thinking the Duke had died and we had won. The knights reformed as did the mailed warriors on foot. Norman and Breton archers, their arrow supply replenished, also gathered. We would have to endure another attack.

This time when they advanced it was at a walking pace and the men on foot were intermixed with the knights on horses. We were now fighting amongst less than half of the housecarls who had begun the battle. Behind us, we could see King Harold as he stood with the two standards. No matter what happened to us, we would fight for as long as the two banners flew. Our supply of stones and missiles had gone and as the enemy climbed the slope, we could do little about their approach. It was left to the steepness of the ridge to slow them down. In addition, they had to negotiate bodies both animal and human. Before us lay a pile of our own dead. Osgar was now to our left for our front had shrunk and now edged back to protect our fragile flanks. The attacks had weakened us more than the Normans. Some boys came around with ale and waterskins. The housecarls were given the ale for we were the last hope of the King. If we failed him then he was doomed. Even as I drank, I saw some of the fyrd slipping away. They had had enough of the slaughter. The ones who remained were the men of Kent and Sussex for they were defending their own land and, like us, they would give their lives to do so. The ale refreshed rather than inflaming my blood. Osgar was dead and I knew that I would follow him. The odds were against us as well as the numbers of the enemy. Tostig and Hadrada had given Englaland to the Normans and I hoped that they were rotting in hell.

Ulf wiped the froth from his beard with the back of his hand. "Just the three of us left eh? remember when we went into Wales to fight King Gruffyd? We were like a sea then and now our band is a pond!"

"Let us have a wager eh? Let us see who can kill the most knights before the end of the day."

Ulf was a gambler but he liked to win, "Starting afresh? For young Wolf here has slain more knights than we."

I laughed, "Aye, old man, I am just getting into my stride. I may only have Widow Maker, with just one blade but she is keen to add to her reputation."

Sweyn nodded, "Then whoever wins shares the money with Brother Paul."

In the grand scheme of things and God's plan, to which we were not a party, it was a small enough decision but it meant we turned to face the Normans with a smile and not a scowl.

Sweyn began beating his shield and chanting, "Ut! Ut! Ut!"

This time everyone took it up, even the fyrd and we all closed with one another as the mailed Normans headed towards us. As the men on foot and horse advanced arrows flew and, unlike the previous attack, men began to fall. Part of it was tiredness and some were slow to raise shields. For others, their wound or their death came because they had no mail or had lost their helmet. And then the Normans lurched at us. They, too, were weary and could not run but they urged their horses on. The Norman who came for me was on foot and had a sword. The Norman knights used the blade to strike and not the tip. He swung at my head and I raised my shield as I brought my axe from behind my head. His strike was nothing and I barely registered the blow. I struck for Osgar and I shattered his arm. His shield dropped and I punched him in the face with the boss of my shield. His nose, despite the nasal, erupted across his face and he stumbled. My axe bit into his neck and he fell. Ulf had used his axe to slay a horse and, as the knight fell one of the fyrd raced from behind us to leap upon him and slit his throat with a seax. He wanted the knight's sword but it was expensively bought as a second knight speared him with his lance. I used the body of the man I had killed to leap up and bring Widow Maker to hack through the helmet and the skull of the knight who had slain the fyrdman. As he fell, I was dragged back into the line by Sweyn.

"Do not get carried away and try to hit flesh. Your axe is becoming blunted!"

I looked and saw that he was right, Ulf and Sweyn had double-headed axes and when one side was blunt they had another which was razor-sharp. I turned Widow Maker so that I was using the flat side. I would use it like a war hammer.

As I stepped back, I saw Gyrth, the King's brother, fall as some mounted knights tried to get to the King and the two standards. Gyrth's oathsworn had been guarding both the King and his brother. Sweyn shouted, "The standards must not fall!" He turned to the men of the fyrd, "Take our place and may God be with you!" They nodded knowing that they were dead men walking. Some had picked up fallen weapons. I saw one with Osgar's axe. My friend would no longer need it and so long as it killed one Norman then it was worthwhile. The knights who were trying to get to the standards had to slay Gyrth's oathsworn first. They were good men but these were not the housecarls as we, we were the best. We were Harold Godwinson's men and we knew our business.

Ulf swung his axe sideways and chopped through the leg and the side of the nearest knight's horse. The blow did not kill them both immediately but it was a mortal strike and the horse pulled away. Sweyn's axe came from over his head and hacked into the arm and side of a knight. For my part, I swung the flat head of the axe at the knee of a knight. The kneecap was shattered and I swung again to break his thighbone. The knight wheeled away.

Sweyn had seen it and shouted, "He does not count for he lives!"

Men on foot had followed the three knights we had killed and they were easier both to fight and to kill. Widow Maker was a well-balanced weapon and when I struck a Norman it mattered not if it was his shield, mail or helmet. Something broke. I also knew how to punch with my heavy shield. Eventually, I would tire but I had to hope that I had more strength than the Normans. The three of us and survivors of Gyrth's hearth weru, his bodyguard, laid about us with our weapons until the last of the Normans had fallen. When the Normans fell back there were just five of us left.

King Harold shouted, "Well done! Now come and join my bodyguards."

As we made our way to the standards, I saw that Edgar of Hamwic had died defending the standards. He had been speared and then bled to death.

The King recognised us, "Where is Osgar?"

"He will wait for us in heaven, Your Majesty!"

Some of the fyrd, on the right, had seen the Normans retreating and tired of having to endure attack after attack many of them raced down the slope towards the stream. King Harold shouted, "No!" but his words were lost. More than a hundred of them chased the Normans and they were all cut down by Breton horsemen who had been waiting for just such a move. Not one thegn nor housecarl had moved but the fyrd were farmers and they died. Our line shrank even more. The last of the housecarls, less than two hundred of us were gathered around the King and the standards.

The Normans reformed and then attacked once more. It was then that the Norman archers showered us with arrows. We held up our shields and listened to the sound of arrows as they cracked into them. I was able to watch the fyrdmen die for they knew not the right technique. They held the shields too close to their heads and did not link them with others. We were all safe and then we saw the next attack begin. What surprised me was that Norman knights did not dismount. It cost them their lives for some of the younger fyrdmen were able to dive beneath the legs of the horses and use a seax to rip open the bellies of the horses. As the knights fell so the fyrdmen fell on them and slit their throats. Each time they did this a fyrdman died but a knight was slain also.

We were now a tight band of mailed men protecting the King and the standards. We were tight in the sense that we all had a common purpose but we were not shoulder to shoulder. Those behind us like King Harold could fill gaps and fight when it was necessary and then fall back. The three of us were at the forefront and had no such relief. There was no longer any order to the Norman attack but they were like animals which sense blood. We were haemorrhaging men and Duke William knew that unless he cleared us from this ridge and hill by dark then he had lost his gamble and his chance of gaining the throne. I looked at the sky. We had been fighting since Terce and it was after the sun had reached its zenith. If we fought until dark it would be a miracle. That the Normans were as weary as we were, gave me some comfort and the first horseman, a Breton, who pushed his weary mount towards our waiting weapons paid the price for that tiredness.

We were on the highest part of the ridge and for the horseman to struggle up and over the top, he had to lean forward. He jabbed his spear forward but I saw it and blocked it easily. Bringing Widow Maker over my head I smashed it into the back of his head and helmet. I knew that he was dead even as I pulled back the axe. His hand was on the reins and as he fell backwards, he jerked the head of his mount too and horse and rider tumbled down the slope cutting a swathe through the men who were still trying to get to us. I heard a Norman voice shout something, I knew not what but some knights dismounted. Perhaps they thought to save their horses or it might have been that they had seen the fate of the Breton. Our tight formation, especially in the centre, was helping us but I could see, as I sought another enemy, that our flanks were being pushed in. That our front line was holding became clear as both Ulf and Sweyn used their axes to take the heads of two advancing men on foot. I saw another warrior hurl a throwing axe at Duke William who was now just forty paces from our front line. The axe hit his helmet and dented it. He was not hurt but it brought a cheer from the beleaguered warriors on the front line.

Then they fell back and, as they did, arrows descended from the sky. The increasing weariness showed for we barely managed to react in time and to pull our shields over our heads. Some men were too slow. I saw one housecarl, Morcar of Wintan-Caestre with an arrow sticking from his shoulder. He would fight on for he was a housecarl but a man with such a wound could not last long. His wound, however, made me think of my own and I knelt beneath my shield to loosen the tunic tied around my leg. It was as I was rising that I heard a cry and turned around. I saw that King Harold had been struck in the cheek by an arrow. The archer had to have used a flat trajectory for the King's shield and that of his bodyguards were held above their heads. The King was alive but his bodyguards had to lay him down. The arrow had destroyed one eye and was lodged in his skull.

I turned to Ulf and Sweyn whose eyes were facing the foe. "The King has been hit in the head by an arrow!"

Ulf turned to look and nodded for he saw our fate in that moment. When he faced the enemy again, he said, "Some of the fyrd are fleeing for they know that we have lost. It is a pity that we swore an oath, eh? Still, we will have the chance for a glorious death and we will not be oath breakers."

The fall of the King, which was seen all the more easily by the Normans, Bretons and French encouraged them and they launched a ferocious attack upon us. They were trying to get to the standards. Even though the King was down, until the standards fell we would fight and Duke William knew that. The three of us fought as one. Sweyn's mighty axe swept from one side and Ulf's from the other. My blunted axe, Widow Maker, came from on high to use the flat head to crush and shatter bones. The first four men who advanced all fell but the next few fared better. Ulf and Sweyn were tiring and using a two-handed axe meant that there was no shield to offer protection. The Norman spears and lances had long been shattered and broken so that they used their swords. Although our next swings killed and wounded three men one managed to land a sword blow and hit Sweyn in the thigh. Blood spurted. I swung my axe sideways and the edge tore through the Norman mail exposing flesh and causing him to drop his sword. I punched him with my shield and he fell. I raised Widow Maker and crushed his face.

We had no time to tend to Sweyn for another wave of Normans raced up towards us and I could hear the fighting at the sides was growing closer. Our circle of steel around the standards was shrinking. One of the Normans had a mace and he swung it at my knee. I managed to block the blow with my shield but the weapon had a heavy head and my arm was numbed. Widow Maker was heavier and the blunt head hit his mailed shoulder. He lowered his shield and I punched with the axe at his face. The move knocked him to the ground but it also exposed my side. One Breton still had a spear and I felt it slide into my side.

Sweyn's axe took the Breton in the side of the face but that, too, exposed him and a sword hacked into his side. His only reaction was a grunt.

Ulf said, "We are exposed! A step back!"

I realised that we had a ring of dead before us while to the side were housecarls and fyrdmen who had died. As we moved back, we left a bloody track for Ulf had had his face laid open too. More arrows descended in the brief hiatus while we moved back. Sweyn's wounds meant that he was slow to raise his shield and an arrow plunged into his shoulder. He whirled his axe around his head and then threw it towards the advancing Normans. Even as he ripped the arrow from his shoulder, I saw the axe knock a horseman, lower down the slope, from the back of his mount. Sweyn drew his sword. His shield would have to hang from his left arm. He would not be able to raise it to defend himself. I would have to protect his left side.

When the arrows stopped, we knew they would come again. This time they were encouraged by our bloodied byrnies and obvious wounds. They targeted Sweyn whose movements were now much slower than they had been. His first two blows with his sword were rewarded for his weapon was lighter than the axe. As he hacked into the shoulder of one man, I blocked a thrust from a sword aimed at his head with Widow Maker and then I punched the Norman in the side of the head. As I brought down the axe to end his life, I realised that in blocking the blow the haft had been damaged and Widow Maker died on that bloody hill. I had no chance to mourn my axe's passing and I drew Dragon Slayer. Seeing my axe split a Breton had taken his opportunity to ram his sword at my good leg. My mail was good but he still broke the skin. Dragon Slayer tasted blood with its first strike and I thrust the sword into his screaming mouth. Tearing it out sideways split his face in two.

It was then that Sweyn fell. Some of our men had thrown axes at the Normans. They had been picked up and now one was thrown at Sweyn. I put Dragon Slayer up in a vain attempt to block the deadly flying missile but I failed and the throwing axe buried itself in Sweyn's forehead. I think he died instantly but I had no way of knowing for I had to defend myself against a ferocious attack from two Normans. Had this been the start of the battle then I would have had no trouble dealing with the two men but I was tired and my muscles burned. I was leaking lifeblood on the hill. I held my shield before me and brought Dragon Slayer in a high arc from right to left. The move exposed my right side and there was no Sweyn to protect me. His body lay to my right. As Dragon Slayer found first mail, then padded undergarment and finally flesh the Norman's sword broke my ribs and tore open the mail. I backhanded Dragon Slayer and it hit the Norman who had struck me in the side of the head.

I heard Ulf grunt and then he said, "Back!"

Pausing only to ram my sword into the neck of the stunned Norman I had just struck I looked at Ulf. He had lost his axe and shield. He now held his sword in two hands. We were both alone for the rest of the housecarls who had fought with us had fallen. I turned and saw the last stand of the housecarls around King Harold, who, miraculously, looked as though he still lived and the standards. The two of us walked backwards towards our comrades. A reckless Norman knight ran towards us. Ulf was more badly wounded than I was and I stepped forward to block the sword blow with my shield and then to swing my own sword at his kite-shaped shield. My left arm was no longer numbed but my body complained as the broken edges of my ribs grated against each other. I gritted my teeth for I was a housecarl and I would ignore pain. I turned my shield horizontally and brought the metal-rimmed edge to smash into the side of his head. He reeled and began to overbalance. I thrust my sword under his chin. Dragon Slayer emerged from the top of his skull, knocking his helmet down the slope. I stepped back as the Normans began to advance.

Behind me, I heard the men around the standard chant, "Wolf! Wolf! Wolf!" It was my moment of glory. I was one of the youngest housecarls yet here, at the end on the bloody ridge I was accorded such an honour.

I stood next to Ulf. King Harold was not yet dead and I heard him say, "Show these Normans how housecarls can die! Die hard and send them to hell!"

They came at us in a rush for we were few in numbers. Dragon Slayer was sharp still but most had blunted weapons. A housecarl who wields an iron bar can still break bones and maim men. That was what we would do. We would die but many of those who fought us would also die and we hoped that the survivors would never raise a weapon again. We might be dead but Englaland would live. Ulf was the first to die. I blocked as many of the blows aimed at him and it cost me another wound to my leg but wielding a sword two handed could only end one way and when he was sliced across the middle and I saw his guts pour forth I knew, even as I took the head of his killer, that he was dead.

Three men came at me when Ulf died for that side was now exposed. They rained blows on my shield and the inevitable happened, it shattered. Holding Snake's Tongue in my left hand I threw the shattered remains at them. I then darted at them to strike first with Dragon Slayer and hack across the leg of the nearest Norman and then thrust into the eye of a second with my dagger. The two fell dead but the third rammed his sword into my left side. It caught there and, as he tried to pull it out, I tore Snake's Tongue across his throat. I began to feel light-headed for my lifeblood was seeping away.

It was then that King Harold died. A knight slew Alfraed of Amsterley and then cut open King Harold's thigh. It was not the way to kill a king but it was effective. As the blood spurted and arced, I hurried to the two standards. They were surrounded by dead housecarls. I stood before them. The fyrd had fled and the housecarls lay butchered, I was the last of King Harold's housecarls and I shouted defiantly, "I am Wolf and I am the last housecarl! Who wishes to see God?" I doubted they understood my words but they rushed at me. I slashed my sword across their faces. I bit into the cheek of one knight with Dragon Slayer and rammed Snake's Tongue into the armpit of another but I felt a blade slide into my back and when I saw it emerge from my front, I knew I was a dead man. I stabbed with both of my weapons and headbutted the man before me. Then, suddenly I was alone and they all stepped back. I saw Duke William and he spoke but I did not understand his words and then I found that my legs would no longer support my weight and I sank to the ground. The last thing I saw before darkness overwhelmed me, was Duke William bowing his head and making the sign of the cross.

I am Brother Paul and I write this so that men, in the future, may know of the glory that was won by the Housecarls when they lost the battle of Senlac Hill. That we call the battle Senlac Hill is because the Normans won. We called it Santlache but they liked the irony of punning it and calling it Senlac, Bloody Stream. I daresay the housecarls would have liked that for they enjoyed words and wordplay. I was not with them for long but in the short time, less than a week, that I served with them I found them to be witty, clever, loyal, and, as they showed defending the standards, the bravest men I had ever met. They died to a man. I watched and saw Wolf as he placed his body before the standards and was cut down. I saw Duke William stop the slaughter and watched him weeping at the dead men. I went to collect the bodies of the four men who had taken me in. I was there when Duke William stripped the knight who had hacked into King Harold's leg with a sword of his knighthood for it was not honourable. I saw little of honour that day but when the Duke asked me what I was doing I told him for how could I fear him when I had watched my new friends die so well? And he nodded his agreement. He commanded six of his men to help me carry and bury the bodies. I collected the weapons from the battlefield. I could not find Sweyn's axe but the rest I did. We buried the bodies with their weapons and, after sending the Normans hence I said prayers and the four housecarls' souls ascended to God. I spent the night in vigil much of it weeping for I would miss the four of them. I had lost my fellow monks and now I had lost my newfound comrades. At the end of the vigil, I knew what I had to do. I must have committed some heinous sin to have brought such bad luck on those that I knew. I would make a pilgrimage to Rome and ask God's help. I needed to atone and I needed to make a life which would honour the dead housecarls. I took my purse of coins and the other things they had given to me and I headed east to take ship for I would leave Englaland and I doubted that I would return. I left the ghosts on Senlac Hill but I carried their memory with me; they would not be forgotten.

The End

If you enjoyed this story then read **Housecarl** by Griff Hosker which tells of the days leading to the Battle of Stamford Bridge. There are three books in the Housecarl trilogy.

Housecarl
Outlaw
Varangian

Wulfstan: the making of a Varangian

I am Wulfstan Oswaldson and I was born a Saxon but when the Normans came to claim England for their Duke that all ended. We became Norman or we would have done if we had accepted that the Norman Duke, William, had won. My father, Oswald Garthson, had been too young to fight in the shield wall at the battle of Hastings. He had been one of those who had used a bow and fought as part of the fyrd. He had slain a Norman; the tale was one I had heard every night as I was growing up for it was my father's proudest moment and made up for the humiliation of defeat and subjugation. The shield wall on the ridge was being assailed by the mounted Normans and my father had managed to send an arrow into a Norman horse and the knight had fallen from his mount which had trapped him. My father had taken his grandfather's seax and driven it through the knight's eye and into his brain.

That might have been the end of the story had not King Harold Godwinson been killed and the Normans fallen upon the housecarls in a bloodbath as the King's oathsworn died to a man. My father and the other Saxons had neither mail nor armour. They knew that they had lost and they fled but my father saw his chance and he took the knight's helmet, boots and sword. He was lucky and avoided capture and the inevitable death which would have followed but many of those with whom he fought died and died badly. My father had a weapon and he had hatred in his heart. He returned to his village, buried his helmet and sword and tilled his land for a short time. I was not yet born. Indeed, there would be two brothers and a sister born before me but I was the one who survived childhood and became a warrior trained by my father. I never knew my real mother for she died giving birth to me but I had a surrogate mother. My father's sister, Gertha, was my wet nurse and she raised me with her children. It was they who hardened me and made me the staff of iron I am now. The first step towards the change in our lives was made easier by my father's sister. I was big and I was handy for my cousins had used their fists freely with me and I learned that the only way to survive was to be stronger and tougher than they were. When I bit off the ear lobe of my cousin Edgar, who was a year older than me, they got the message and left me alone but my aunt took it hard and refused to feed me. We left the hut and his sister, taking with us the few belongings we would need to become outlaws, without a single look back. My father and I had to fend for ourselves.

I sit in the hall at the manor of Norton where I serve Baron Ridley. I look back on a life which has been interesting, to say the least. There were many events which shaped me and I did many things of which, now, I am not proud, but looking back they were necessary. Now I am well respected and live in a hall which seems like a palace compared with the hut in which I grew up. I do not know how much I have changed for a man cannot look at himself. He is judged by others and all those who were with me, in the beginning, are now dead and I am left with the shield brothers from Miklagård. I suppose that was where my life began properly.

It was when I had seen more than twelve or thirteen summers that my father decided to leave our hut. The decision was not taken lightly but neither of us was happy. His sister and her husband had more land and were more successful than we were. Farming suited neither of us for we had no animals and as soon as I could follow the plough my father was the horse and I tilled the land with him. We rarely grew enough to eat and so we poached from the Norman lord. We took his wood, illegally, to make our fires, we hunted his rabbits and deer and we dreaded the knock of the tax collector. When I was twelve and showed that I was almost a man he decided, we decided, that we had had enough of the life of a farmer. We had broken the law so many times that becoming outlaws seemed a natural step.

We headed for the many forests which littered the land. We found other Saxons who had either tired of a life behind a plough or preferred the easier life of taking from the Normans. There were only a handful of us and we avoided Norman knights and men at arms but there were merchants, churchmen, King William's clerks and tax collectors for us to rob. We became a band of friends and my father, for he was the oldest and had fought at Hastings, was the leader. He had kept the helmet and sword and he had used them to slay any Norman warrior that he could. Although it was only one or two he killed he was proud of ending their lives. They had taken his lord and his land and to my father that made every Norman an enemy. I acquired a long dagger, called a seax, and I already had a bow and a sling. Arrows were hard to come by and so I used my sling more often than not. The road that ran between London and the north passed within a mile of our forest home and we would go, sometimes together and sometimes with others to make the Normans who used that great highway fear for their lives. We took their purses and their food. We stole their animals and we lived better than when we had farmed. The forest was huge and we knew our way around it. We had trails and paths which only we knew. We were able to poach more deer for living in the forests showed us their trails as well as the Normans.

It could not last and the local lord, Gerlac of Bretuil who was the lord of Uppingham, tired of the banditry and hunted us down and, one by one, the men in our band were caught and hanged and their heads were displayed on his castle walls. Finally, only my father and I remained free. Those last weeks when our band was whittled down to just my father and I were the making of me. I learned to outrun horses and I learned just what I was capable of for the sight of the heads of our friends showed us that the price of capture would be death. Those months living in the forest made me stronger and my muscles filled out as I ate meat almost every day.

The final straw which drove us from the forest was one night when we came within a handspan of capture. The men at arms and crossbowmen of the Norman knight had begun to get closer and closer to us. I had woken to make water and it was I who smelled the Normans. They smelled of their own meat and it oozed from their pores. They drank wine and I could smell it on their tunics. These men who hunted us were piss poor at their job for they came downwind of us so that I knew where they were long before they knew where we were. It was dark and the sun had yet to rise. I heard them crunch twigs underfoot and worked out that they were still a good one hundred paces from us. I shook my father and put my hand across his mouth. With my head, I gestured towards the Normans. He nodded. We had little enough but we took it all. We both had cloaks. I had a bow, eight arrows, my sling and my short sword. There was still a hunk of cooked venison and I grabbed that and followed my father. He may not have had farming skills but he knew the paths and the trails. He also managed to run without stepping on dead wood. I heard the shouts when they discovered our abandoned camp and a horn was sounded. I knew that we had come almost half a mile but the horn was worrying. My father stopped. "They will have men waiting for us. The ones who came to our camp are driving us towards horsemen. I think we have taken one risk too many. Do you trust me?"

"Of course!"

"Then we wait here until they have passed us and head in the opposite direction. If they take one of us then the other should run."

I nodded and wondered if my death was just around the corner. I nocked an arrow and stood with my back to an oak. My father chose another oak just ten paces away. The sun would soon be up but we knew the forest and that it would take some time for its light to permeate down. He slipped his bow over his back and held his sword in two hands. We heard the Normans coming. We did not understand much of what they said for it was in Norman but the sound enabled me to estimate that there were just seven or eight of them. We kept still even when their voices appeared to be behind us. They were running and moving in a long line; I counted eight of them. One passed close to us and we could just make out the men at arms and crossbowmen who ran beyond us toward the waiting horsemen. In the distance, I could hear the sound of hooves. My father nodded and we stepped out. Fate intervened, there had been nine Normans and one wearing a mail byrnie stood just ten paces from me! He had a sword and a shield. I just reacted and I would not be alive to write this down if I had been slow. I drew and released even as I saw his mouth open to shout. The arrow struck his open mouth and drove through the back of his skull. Anywhere else and my arrow would not have hurt him for he wore mail and I used a hunting arrow. My father paused only long enough to grab the dead Norman's sword and we ran. That they would miss the dead man was obvious but they would have to return and to find him first. We ran until dawn, by which time we had crossed the great road. We did not stop until the sun was beginning to set again. Perhaps fate had intervened or it could have been that the Normans were incompetent but whatever the reason, we ran the twenty miles and reached Medeshamstede. The church ruled the burgh and we hid our weapons beneath our cloaks and sought alms at the abbey there. We were given some broth for our wooden bowls and a beaker of ale each. We augmented our broth with slices of venison. We used our cloaks to make a shelter against the abbey wall and, after we had eaten, my father told me his plans.

"Englaland holds nothing for us, my son. Sir Gerlac will hunt us down for we killed a man. We were lucky to reach here but we cannot count on luck. I have my sword and we have the Norman's sword. You are a fair bowman. I think we should head for Frisia and hire out as mercenaries."

I was dubious about the plan. My father had cunning but I thought that a mercenary would need skill. I could use a bow but I was not an archer. As for other weapons… I could skin an animal with my seax but I had never used a sword or an axe.

My father saw my doubt and smiled, "I killed a Norman when I was little older than you. You have heard the tale of Hastings, I know. You have killed a man with a bow. We can learn. There are bands of men who fight together for coins. We join one and take what we can get. If they are any good then we can improve both our skills and our weapons." He shrugged, "The coming of the Normans was a curse. This is the only way I can see to escape. If you know a better way then speak."

I shook my head, "I have no other plan and you are my father. I will trust you."

"Good, then tomorrow we head east and find a port and a ship."

We headed to Lothuwistoft to find a vessel to carry us to safety. Until we were aboard a ship, I would not be able to rest and each horseman and knight who passed us made me cringe with terror. It was there that my story truly began for before then my path had been set. I would have tilled the tiny piece of land and, perhaps, taken a woman and fathered a child and by the time I had seen forty summers, I would have been dead. As it was, I began a life which had both meaning and purpose; but not at first.

Hastings had changed my father. He had lost his brothers, his father and his friends on that October day more than twenty years earlier. When you lose so many who are close to you then part of you dies and you cease to see life as having a purpose. If life has no purpose then the taking of life becomes easy. My father was a killer. He had shown that when he had killed Norman merchants and clerks and he could always justify his murders but that is what they were. When we reached Lothuwistoft we had a purse filled with the coins he had taken back in the forest. He showed them to me when we neared Lothuwistoft and I was impressed that he had managed to collect so many. Once we reached the port, he set about finding us an employer. My job was to watch his back and I knew how to do that. I learned to look for the signs in men's eyes. I knew when one might be ready to threaten him and I could shout a warning or I could stick out a leg to trip them. His helmet and swords attracted attention but he was tough enough and hard enough to be able to handle any man, one to one. If there were more then I had to deal with them.

When we sat in the inn he spoke, after a jug of ale, about his father, "He was a warrior, a housecarl and feared no man. It took three Normans to kill him at Hastings. One day I would like to think that you could emulate him."

That day I saw a different future for myself.

We sought a boat to go to Flanders, Normandy or France. There were many wars and conflicts and my father knew how to wield a blade. He found us berths on a Frisian trader going to Dorestad. There would be no cabin for us. We were working our passage. The seas were filled with pirates: Norse, Danish, Frisian and whilst the rewards for trade were enormous the consequences could also be fatal. The Captain had seen that we were lean and hungry and took us on. The voyage could take anything from one to three days and so we went to an inn close by the quay which serviced sailors to fill up on food before we endured the cold sea between Lothuwistoft and Dorestad in the land of the Count of Flanders. The food was basic: it was a sort of fish stew with rye bread but it was hot and there was plenty of it. The beer was better than we were used to at home. As my father was fond of telling me my mother had brewed the finest of ale while Gertha would have been better serving up the piss pots the lords used!

The alehouse was filled for the food and the beer attracted customers. The land had been Danish for many years and despite the incomers, the Normans, it still felt more like Englaland than the rest of the land. For one thing, everyone here spoke English, albeit with an accent and so the atmosphere was cosy and almost companionable. There might still be fights but men with full stomachs were less inclined to fight and so I listened as my father sought the information which would indicate where we might find employment. We would be low down the order for there would be warriors with mail burnies and others who had fought in a shield wall but my father wanted me to be with a warband so that I could learn. Talking in inns with the other men such as us we learned that the men we sought as paymasters were not nobles; they were like us, little more than bandits with a mail hauberk at best.

As we mopped up the last of the stew with our bread, he nodded to a mailed Saxon warrior. "That is what I would have of you one day."

I looked up and saw a short stocky warrior. His mail and leather hauberk came to his knees and he had a good sword hanging from his belt. He had an open-face Norman helmet. I was bigger than he was. The man was speaking with two other warriors neither of whom wore mail but they had leather jackets studded with pieces of metal. "And who is he?"

"It is who he was that is more important. He used to be Beorhtric Thegn of Langhewis and his father, also Beorhtric of Langhewis, was a warrior who died at Hastings. His father had land in the next hundred to us. His son inherited the estate but was thrown off his own land. Men call him Thegn out of respect to his father and he is a warrior but he will never have land here in the land of the Normans."

"Then why do you want me to be like him?"

"For he is equipped for war and he can take land. With oathsworn around him, he can conquer some place and make it his. He can hold it and then, who knows, become a lord again. I want us to serve a warrior who can help us to become better equipped and then, who knows?"

"Why not serve him then, father? He seems as good a choice as any?"

My father shook his head and looked at the foam-covered barrel we used as a table. "I asked him and he laughed saying he wanted warriors and not the sweepings of Lothuwistoft."

Until that moment I was not particularly bothered by the thought of fighting as a mercenary but my father had been insulted. He had turned to banditry because of Hastings and yet he had fought for King Harold. My eyes narrowed. I would become a warrior just so that I could show the pompous son of a lord that he was wrong and that we were not worthless.

The inn became even more crowded and others joined us at the barrel. I saw that they were like us except that they had better weapons. My father's swords apart, we did not have much which was worth taking. Sigiberht and Tadgh were, however, good company. One was a Saxon and the other a Celt from Hibernia. Tadgh had a long, curved sword with a flat end rather than a tip. Sigiberht had a war axe. Both, however, had good helmets and shields. Tadgh had a small, round buckler type and Sigiberht the larger Saxon variety. I saw then that we should have each had one made. It would have marked us as warriors and that explained the attitude of the Saxon lord.

It turned out that they were on the same Frisian ship and so our conversation turned to the prospect of work in Flanders. Shaking his head, Sigiberht said, "Dorestad is merely the first step on a long journey. There are wagons which will head south to Paris, taking the wool that our ship will carry and those wagons and carts will need an escort. There are ships and river barges in Paris which will be travelling down the rivers to the Blue Sea and that is our goal. There the weather is warmer and there is more chance of finding a rich employer who needs good warriors. You should come with us. I can see that you do not have much but if you are any good then you will get the right weapons and war gear."

I asked, "And if not?"

He looked at the wooden crucifix I wore around my neck, "Then, if you have confessed before you fight you will go to heaven and there will be no more hardship for you."

"That sounds like cold comfort to me!" My voice was more belligerent than I intended it to be.

"You will learn, my young Saxon firebrand, that real warriors do not make their words and phrases flowery and full of glory. We are realists and know that death is just a seax away. Do not expect much from life and you will not be disappointed."

My father smiled for I think he was enjoying the company of these warriors. The men with whom he had robbed Norman travellers had been his friends but they were all dead and, sad though it was, I was his only friend until Sigiberht and Tadgh met us. We drank sparingly for none of us were well off and that was something else which annoyed me. Beorhtric Thegn of Langhewis appeared to have plenty of coins and was already staggering a little having consumed so much. It did not seem right that he was rich and we were poor. We left the inn and made our way to the quay.

The ship we had been hired to protect was a knarr. Faster than all but a longship they were wide and had a deep hull. We would be sleeping aboard and we were lucky, the bags of sheepskins had yet to be covered by the decking which lay on the quayside. I had the most comfortable bed of my whole life. With two new friends, a full stomach and a soft bed I thought I had died and gone to heaven.

The reality hit me the next morning as we were woken well before dawn to take advantage of a tide and a wind coming from the land. The Captain, a sour-faced Flemish seaman called Fótr, ignored the fact that our employment did not start until the sun had risen and he rousted us to haul on salt-covered and oiled ropes to hoist the sail to warp us away from the quayside. It was only as the coastline slipped to the west that he allowed us to make water, grab what food we could and prepare for the day. That the captain was tight-fisted became obvious when we saw that the only crew, apart from the ones hired in Lothuwistoft, were his two sons. Both were younger than I was and were as mean as their father. Apart from the four of us, there were two others. Unlike the four of us, they were sailors and not swords for hire.

Harald, the older of the two, told us that Captain Fótr was renowned for his mean character. "He will pay us off in Dorestad and then we will have to wait until he has a cargo or until we can get another berth back here."

"Then why do it?" Tadgh was a thoughtful warrior although, as I learned, in battle he could be as fierce and reckless as any Norse berserker!

"Simple, my friend, we have families to feed and sometimes ships which leave Dorestad require more sailors than they bring." He shook his head, ruefully, "The port has seen better days and is now full of pirates, cutthroats and killers. Often sailors are robbed and killed. If I had a choice, I would seek employment on a ship which paid me for the time we were in port!"

The two of them were honest men and they showed us what we had to do. It was hard work but I was nothing if not strong and I soon adapted to it. They helped us for the simple reason that in the event of a fight, the four of us would be their only protection.

The second day at sea saw the wind suddenly change direction and begin to blow from the south and east. At first, we tacked back and forth to try to make progress. It was hard work for little reward. Captain Fótr then decided to lower the sail and yard. He had us row. If I thought trimming the sail was hard then I knew nothing about being a seaman for within a short time of working the oars the muscles on my back burned as though I had been held before a fire. When darkness came, we stopped and I was so exhausted that I could not stand with the others to stack my oar. I ate because Tadgh and my father made me and my dreams were filled with screaming sea birds, which Harald told me were dead sailors' souls, and the sight of Harald's back!

We were roused at dawn and I dreaded the thought of another day of rowing. We were spared that but had to endure another, less natural danger; pirates! The captain's youngest son scrambled up the mast at dawn to spy the horizon and, as he looked east, he shouted, "Pirate ship! Ten lengths off the leeward bow!"

I did not know what a length was and ten did not sound much but I knew that one side of the ship was the lee and the other was the steerboard side. I ran and saw, alarmingly close, a ship which was roughly the same size as us but which appeared to be filled with men.

"Hoist the sail!"

This time we needed no urging and we hauled upon the sheets as though our lives depended upon it. As events turned out, it did! Once the sail was up the captain turned to take us south and west. We would use the wind! He shouted, "And now you four wastrels can earn your passage! Sell your lives dearly!"

This would be the first time I had fought for another. I did not want to fight for the captain. He was paying us a handful of coins; he had treated us badly and yet he expected us to die for him! I am not sure if Tadgh could read my mind for he said, "You do not fight for him, you fight for us. Today, we are your shield brothers!"

I was young and a little stupid in those days for I said, "I have no shield!"

He laughed, "No, but you and your father each have a bow and Sigiberht and I have shields. Let us see how good you are."

We ran to our gear and my father and I picked up our bows and strung them. They were better than hunting bows. We had made war bows for, when we ambushed, they were more accurate. That they were harder to pull was another matter but I was strong. We had but fifteen arrows between us and it did not seem enough.

My father said, "We cannot waste these arrows, Wulfstan. We wait until they are two lengths away and you must aim for flesh."

Tadgh said, "Wulfstan, come and stand with me at the stern. We will take the lee."

As we went, I saw that Harald and Edgar had both picked up two hatchets and the Captain and his sons each had a long seax tucked into their belts. It did not seem enough. I did not nock an arrow, I held it in my left hand. Tadgh hefted his shield and drew his sword. "They are Frisians. It could be worse, they could have been Norse." He smiled at me, "You need a helmet."

He was stating the obvious and I was keenly aware of my own shortcomings in terms of war gear. My father's plan was unravelling before my very eyes. "I need many things and we hoped that serving in a warband might get us what we needed." I wondered if I should have stuffed the spare Norman sword in my belt.

"You will get them but first you must kill and," he pointed to the pirate ship which was rapidly gaining upon us, "you must do so today. I am not certain if we will live to see another dawn but if we do then it will be because we fought better than they did and, perhaps, because we have a better captain!" He looked at him and shook his head, "So far I am inclined to think that it will be down to us!"

I took my carefully chosen arrow and nocked it but did not draw the bow. I knew my range and when the ship was two lengths away, which was what I had been told, it meant I could hit that at which I aimed. The wind was coming towards us but the sail of the pirate would help my arrow to fly true. I could now see the faces crowded around the prow of the pirate. Most appeared to wear helmets. I looked for one without a nasal. I had a strong arm and my arrow would fly so fast that it would beat a man trying to raise his shield.

The pirate was gaining. Tadgh said, "If they are foolish enough to come abeam of us then try to hit the steersman. They will be sending arrows at our captain soon enough. See how his sons guard his back with shields." I saw that the sons had huge Danish shields which would protect their father and themselves. Of course, once the knarr was boarded then it would make little difference to any of them. They would be dead.

Suddenly a flurry of arrows came from the pirate ship. It took me by surprise. Tadgh causally flicked up his shield and deflected one to rattle on the deck. He smiled, "You have another arrow now!"

I had been careless and now I watched the arrows. The pirates would be able to avoid our arrows too; the difference was that they were so tightly packed that if they moved out of the way then another would be hit. Sigiberht shouted, "Those who have not yet said their prayers then now is your time for soon they will be upon us."

I quietly said, "God, I am too young to die! Save me and I shall make something of my life!" It seemed a poor enough bargain but it was all that I had.

I heard the twang of my father's bow and knew that he had sent his arrow at the pirate. I pulled back on my own bowstring and saw six faces on the leeward side of their vessel. The first pull would be my most powerful and so, as I pulled, I intoned, "Fly true and flight straight!" I released and reached into my arrow bag for another. I kept my eyes on the arrow as it sped towards the faces. As I had expected they moved out of the way but, to my delight, the arrow smacked into the face of a pirate who had not seen me draw.

Tadgh shouted, "First blood to Wulfstan! Now it is your turn, Oswald!" He was a clever man and by making it a competition he made me forget my fears. I drew back and released aware that the pirate had drawn a little closer. I was drawing and releasing so rapidly that I barely saw my arrows hitting. The cheers from the other four crew members told me that my father and I were striking home. The pirate ship was almost upon us and I reached into my arrow bag and came up empty. I had used all of my arrows. I saw that my father was also empty. I laid my bow almost reverently on the ground next to me and drew my long seax. It seemed little enough but it was my own and I kept it razor-sharp and my sheath had been made by me. The spare Norman sword was wrapped in my father's cloak. I should have got it before the battle began.

Looking up, I saw that the pirate was so close that Tadgh could almost touch the bow. Suddenly six men launched themselves at our stern at the same time as arrows and spears flew from the pirate. I saw Edgar struck in the shoulder by an arrow while a spear skewered one of the captain's sons in the leg. Even as the men jumped the pirate changed course a little to come down our leeward side. I was inexperienced but even I could see that splitting our tiny number of defenders would guarantee victory. Even worse was the fact that the men who had jumped were all well-armed. Sigiberht, however, drew first blood for he swung his axe even as the first Frisian was in the air and his axe hacked all the way through the first pirate's leg to the bone. That the pirates were going for the captain was clear for three of them headed for the steering board while two came for Tadgh and me. The pirate ship had needed to move a little away from us so that the wind could slam her into our side.

Tadgh faced his man and said, "Wulfstan, strike hard and strike to kill. You have one chance and that is all!"

I knew that and I did not reply. I could hear my father and Sigiberht as they defended the captain and his son but I concentrated upon the Frisian. He had a good sword and a small round shield. His helmet had a nasal and he looked confident as he strode towards me. I had fought with a weapon although never against a man with a sword and a shield. I had stabbed a man before but not killed. I had merely sliced through his arm. I had to think and think quickly. Brute strength would not win the fight; I had to use cunning and the Frisian came, unwittingly, to my aid. I believe he thought to end it quickly and discounted my seax. He held his shield before him and, swinging his sword, took a step towards me. He intended to hack into my left side. Perhaps he thought I was terrified and would not be able to move but I was not. I dived between his legs and even before I had enough space to stand, I slashed with my seax at the back of the Frisian's knee. I cut into muscle and tendon and I slashed veins. He screamed like a pig and dropped to his good knee. I stood, aware that the pirate was swinging towards our leeward side. I heeded Tadgh's words and I grabbed the man's head, pulled it back and slashed his throat.

It was then I saw the arrow which Tadgh had deflected and, dropping my seax I picked up the bow and the arrow. The steersman was about to reverse his action so that his ship would nudge ours when my last arrow smacked into the side of his head. He had no helmet and must have died instantly. He fell away from us but he held on to the steering board. Instead of a gentle nudge, the pirate ship hit us hard and everyone on both ships was thrown to the deck. The pirate ship bounced away and the weight of the helmsman took it away from us.

I stood and saw that there were two pirates left and they were both fighting Sigiberht. Grabbing my seax I joined Tadgh as we ran to his shield brother's aid. I saw that although the captain stood and was steering us away from the pirate, he was wounded and his son and my father lay on the deck. Harald had been hit and was rising, groggily to his feet. I threw myself onto the back of one of the Frisians and held on tightly with my left hand. Tadgh hacked into the right arm of the other but Sigiberht had also been hurt. I pulled my seax toward the warrior's throat. I stabbed so hard that the tip of my seax came out of the back and pricked me. I jerked my head away and in doing so we both fell backwards and his dead body lay on top of me.

Laughing, Tadgh pulled him from me and said, "Today you became a warrior but this is not over. Get Harald and take him to the steering board!"

I saw that Harald had banged his head on the gunwale. "Can you steer? The Captain is hurt!"

He leaned on me, "You get me to the steering board and we shall see but if I cannot then the pirates will be upon us!"

Getting across a deck which was now slippery with blood as well as seawater was not easy. I saw that Sigiberht was seeing to the Captain while Tadgh was tending to my father and the boy. That meant my father was still alive. The Captain had been stabbed and when he saw Harald he nodded, "Use the wind! Take us back to the coast if you have to! Save my ship!"

Harald put his gnarled fingers around the smooth wood of the steering board and smiled. "I had my own ship once. She was not as big as this but I liked her." All the time he had been looking up at the sail and he made a slight adjustment to the board and said, "Wulfstan, go and tighten the fore sheet, eh? I spy hope!"

I did as he had told me but I failed to see how a tighter rope would help us. As I came back to the stern, I saw that he had been right. There was now a visible gap. We must have hurt them more than they hurt us. Harald was laughing, "Your arrow hit them hard, boy! Not only did it kill their helmsman, but the collision has also sprung their strakes. See, they have to bail!"

I saw then that was the reason we were leaving them behind. They had to save their ship. "But what of us? Are we hurt too?"

Harald shrugged, "I know not but we are still flying so perhaps not. You had best see to your father."

He was sitting with his back to the stern. I saw that his left arm had a bad cut. He smiled at me, "Tie some cord around my upper arm to stem the blood. The others are hurt worse than I." I did as I was told and he continued to speak while I did so. "I always knew that you were a warrior and today you showed it. You reminded me of my father, your grandfather. You are his double. We have done the right thing choosing this warriors' path."

Tadgh came over with some vinegar and honey, "You know what to do with these?" I nodded. "Take the cloth from the dead Frisians and use it for bandages."

I stood and went to the nearest Frisian. One side of his tunic was relatively free from blood. I then saw that one of the boys had died for he had a cloak over his body. Edgar had been tended to and his arm was in a sling. The captain and his other son were now the worst of the injured. I cleansed the wound and then smeared it with the honey. After I had bandaged it tightly, I loosened the leather cord a little. I must have done a good job for no blood emerged.

Harald shouted, "Captain, the pirates have given up. Do I keep heading for the coast or Dorestad?"

"Dorestad! When my leg is bandaged, I will join you for sailing at night can be dangerous."

Harald laughed, "I know I had a ship for twenty years but it seems to me that daylight can be as bad!"

"Aye, well there is a berth for you and Edgar when we have sold our cargo. I owe you." He looked over to us, "And you." He seemed to suddenly see that his sons were not there. "My boys?"

"The elder lives but your youngest is with God!"

"Then all this is for nothing!"

I did not understand the words although later when we were on land and speaking of it Tadgh thought that the younger might have been his favourite.

With the Captain steering once more we stripped the Frisians of all that was worth keeping before hurling their bodies overboard. We then swilled the deck. It was as night began to fall that Sigiberht divided the treasure. I wondered if I would get anything for I had been the youngest but Tadgh told me that fighting together made us brothers in arms. We would all share in the bounty.

I think that because of my actions, including hitting the steersman, I was given the better of the weapons. The helmet with the nasal was the best one and it had a head protector too. The sword I was given was as long as Tadgh's and I was given a leather jerkin which was studded with pieces of metal. The small shield from the first man I had killed was a good one too. It was well made and studded with metal. Carrying it made me feel like a warrior. We also shared in the coins that they carried. To the Thegn we had seen in the inn they would have been little enough but the coins I was given were more than all of us had between us! We were all a little richer. The coins meant we could be a little choosier about our employment. We would no longer need to take the first job that was offered to us. Of course, one problem we now had was that my father had a wound and we might have to wait for employment. As Tadgh told us that bridge had yet to be crossed. From their conversations, I gathered that Tadgh and Sigiberht were happy to carry on their association with us. I seemed to have impressed them. I knew not for I had done little save cut two men's throats from behind. I had not had to fight anyone! My father also gave me the other Norman sword which was better than the Frisian one. I fashioned two scabbards so that I could wear them across my back.

It took another day and half a night to get close to Dorestad and then we had to wait for a tide to take us in. We had buried Garth, the Captain's son, at sea when his brother had regained consciousness. I saw that the two of them were closer as a result. It also seemed that

Harald and Edgar now had a permanent berth for Fótr had realised the value of men he knew. When we had spoken, after the burial, Tadgh had pointed out that had we been members of the pirate crew then all three would have died. Often pirates joined the crew of a ship to help their comrades take it. Captain Fótr was changed after that single voyage. I rationalised that although I was changed, that was bound to happen regardless of the voyage. I had left the world I knew and entered a strange one!

Although we had only been on the knarr for three days it felt sad to be parting and yet when I had first met Captain Fótr I had not liked him. It was a lesson for me. Until you had journeyed with a man it was a mistake to judge him.

As we walked along the quay of the rapidly silting, dying port, I felt more like a warrior for I had a helmet hanging from one of my new swords but I was still glad that we had Tadgh and Sigiberht for company; not least because they knew their way around. They had never been to Dorestad but they had spoken with those who had and the inn they found for us, whilst not as clean as some, was run by an honest couple and we managed to get a tiny room in which we would sleep. Until we found work, we would be a warband, albeit a tiny one, and Tadgh would make the decisions.

Despite his wound, my father had never been happier. He had fought alongside other warriors and not been found lacking. He had not enjoyed being a bandit even though the ones we robbed were Normans but this future looked like it would be different. This was what he had sought since Hastings; men with whom he could stand and fight. Here, across the sea from our home, we had the opportunity to make something of ourselves.

The first two days were interesting for there was work to be had but Tadgh decided that escorting carts heading south did not pay enough to justify the potential danger. Ironically, it was a Norman who came to offer us work. Gerloc of the Haugr was an older sergeant at arms. None of us knew the title and we thought him a noble. He came to the inn and spoke with the landlord. His eyes took us in as he scanned the room. He paid for an ale, drank it and left. The innkeeper came over and told us the man's name and title.

Tadgh said, "I can see by his dress that he is a Norman. We saw enough of them after the Bastard took our country but what is a sergeant at arms?"

"He is a warrior who fights for a knight, a lord. He is here to recruit men for war."

"A war? Against whom?" Sigiberht was suspicious for the Normans back at home were always bringing fresh men from Normandy. We would not return home to fight our countrymen; that we had already decided.

The innkeeper smiled, "War is the wrong word. It seems his lord, Bohemond of Coutances, had his manor taken from him and given to a Breton, Alan Fergant, who served Duke William in the battle to gain his crown. This Bohemond intends to take his manor back." He looked meaningfully at us. "He pays well." Then, shrugging, he left with the words, "It is up to you but he waits in the town square and he leaves on the morrow."

My father shook his head, "I like not the idea of fighting for a Norman!"

Sigiberht smiled and shook his head, "In our line of work we cannot be too choosy. I think that we meet and speak with this Norman. The innkeeper seemed a little vague and I would know the details." He stood, "Tadgh and I will go and speak with this man. You can stay here if you wish. Each man makes his own decisions." He looked at me as he said it.

My father stood and took his arm from his sling, "I would hear his words myself and I confess that I am unwilling to break up this small band, Sigiberht."

His words obviously delighted our new companions and we took our new found weapons. I wore my shield across my back for that was what I had seen warriors do. I had yet to paint a design upon it and it still bore the Frisian markings. When we reached the square, we saw that Gerloc of the Haugr had three men who were squatting on the horse trough close by him. Dorestad had been a mighty port at one time and the Empire had guarded it well. Once it began to silt up then it became less important than Bruggas. That was reflected in the fact that the stone trough no longer contained water. It had become damaged and was not worth repairing. I later deduced this was why Gerloc had come to Dorestad, for he sought desperate men who could find no other master.

He stood and smiled at Tadgh who approached him. Tadgh would negotiate for us and also ask the relevant questions. I noticed that he spoke to us in our language. "I saw you four in the inn." He glanced at my father. "Has your arm been miraculously healed or do you try to deceive me?"

My father coloured. He did not like Normans and he did not like the fact that he had been caught out. "It is true I was wounded but my arm is healing. We come to speak of war and so I dress for war but if you dismiss me out of hand then my son and I will leave!"

Gerloc smiled, "Hold, friend, you have a temper and that can be useful. I am Gerloc of the Haugr and I fought with Duke William. I served for many years with Bishop Odo. I speak your language and I know your country." He waved at the three men who sat on the trough. "You three give us some space so that I may speak with these men." They left and Gerloc gestured for us to sit. There was not enough room for me and I stood.

Tadgh said, "We heard you sought warriors and we fight as a band of brothers."

Gerloc nodded, "I understand such arrangements but I have to say that only half of you look to be worth hiring. One has a wound and one looks as though he has barely begun to shave."

It was my turn to colour. Tadgh smiled, "Do not be taken in, Gerloc of the Haugr. The one you insult slit the throats of two Frisians who attacked our ship and it was his arrow which slew their helmsman." He waved at the three men who had just left us, "Have the others killed?"

He looked at me with fresh eyes, "You are right to berate me for appearances can be deceptive. I can see that he wears the spoils of war and that is good. Perhaps I have misjudged you. Let me begin again. My master fell out with Duke William. The matter need not concern you but you should know that my Lord Bohemond would take back his home. To that end, I am asked to find warriors for the purpose of retaking the Haugr. If you were taken on you would be paid each day until we have the Haugr and there would be a bonus once it was taken."

"And the pay?"

He rubbed his chin, "You say you fight as brothers then I would offer the pay to the four of you. That might suit for if one of you fell then the others would reap the benefit."

Tadgh nodded, "That sounds right. How much?"

He took out a purse and dropped five small silver coins into his hand. They looked to be the size of an English sixpence. They bore the head of the Emperor. "This for each day."

That was a good price. We had already been offered far less to escort wagons. "In advance?"

Gerloc laughed at Tadgh's words, "Do you think me a fool? Be here on the morrow to leave when they open the gates and the first day's payment will be here. I will find the food on the journey south for it will take us five days to get to Djupr where my lord is gathering his men. This is my last stop." He smiled, "And you will need horses."

Tadgh said, "At whose expense?"

"At your own but if they are lost then my lord will replace them." He smiled, again, "It is your decision but, trust me, you will not receive a better offer. Unless, of course, you wish to guard some fat merchant's wagons." Standing, he said, "I will be here on the morrow packed and ready to go with the other men I have secured."

Tadgh led us away and we headed silently back to the inn. We had almost had work and then it had been snatched from under our noses. We trudged back into the inn and the innkeeper, seeing our faces said, "You were not offered work?"

"We were but it necessitated having horses and we have none."

The innkeeper laughed, "And you cannot buy them?"

"Where would we buy animals? Do we look as though we can afford horses?"

"Will you be riding them to war?"

Tadgh laughed sardonically, "We fight on foot!"

"Then they do not have to be the best." He gestured with his thumb to the building behind his. "Theobald buys old horses and renders them down for glue. If you pay him what he would get for the bones and the glue then you would have four beasts." He shrugged, "It is just a suggestion and I am happy to serve you ale and food but we both know that there will come a day when you are without money and I will have to throw you out."

Our debate was brief and had only one outcome. We would try Theobald. If we had not taken the pirates' coins then we could not have done this but we had survived that trial. Surprisingly, after talking to Theobald we found that we could afford the animals although they were sorry looking and we had neither saddles nor harness for them but we had animals. I was terrified for I had never ridden before. Sigiberht had laughed, "These animals will be so slow that we could walk faster and your feet, Wulfstan, will almost touch the ground. The reason we need animals is to save our legs. When we reach Djupr then we can sell them for food. The Normans eat horsemeat!"

That night I spoke quietly to my father while Tadgh and Sigiberht played dice in the inn. "Are we really doing this, father?"

He smiled, "I know we fight for a Norman and I wish we were fighting for a Saxon lord but that day at Hastings changed all of that! We go to war and we learn." He chuckled, "You learn for I am an old dog as we saw on the knarr. I was wounded and slew no-one. You were unharmed and killed three. I will watch your back and you will become a sword for hire."

"What would life have been like for you had we not lost the battle?"

He shook his head, "I know not. Your mother and I and had a tiny piece of land but I did not enjoy farming. When my thegn died then all hope went. The Normans made me a thrall to my own land and we could barely find enough food to keep a body together. You are the only offspring of my loins who has survived and that says much about you. You fought for life just as you did on the knarr. That day showed me what you can become. I will do my part but the rest is up to you."

I was up early and I managed to find some pieces of leather traces and horse furniture in the stables where the doomed animals were kept. It was not stealing for they had been abandoned. I managed to contrive a harness for my horse so that it could carry my war gear. I would use my cloak as a saddle and carry my shield upon my back. I was ready to leave before the others. We did not risk riding the horses to the square in case they expired before we could set off.

Gerloc smiled but his nod showed that he approved. The other three men he had hired were better mounted and Gerloc's horse was a good one. "We have a long way to go, let us ride." I led my horse and Gerloc frowned, "I said, ride!"

I shook my head, "I will not slow you up, I promise!"

In the event there was little problem until we had left the town for the crowded streets meant we all went at my pace. There was a method to my apparent madness. I wanted my horse to last as long as possible. After I had made my harness, I had sneaked to the stable which was attached to the most expensive inn in Dorestad and put my old thievery to good use. I stole a small sack of grain. I doubted that it would be missed until we were long gone and I intended to fatten up my horse as much as I could. I had called her Mary after the mother of our lord. She was Flemish and would not understand English but I would teach her. I fed her handfuls of grain as we walked through the streets. Once we were on the highway, we were forced to go at the pace of the wagons ahead and I was able to walk and lead Mary. It was only when the wagons halted to adjust the harness that we were able to overtake them and then I had to run.

As I look back, I think that choosing to ride as little as possible was the best training I could have given myself. I ran and I kept up with Gerloc. He tried to lose me early on. I think it was a test but I passed for I did not stop. I learned to run at a steady pace and to run through the pain in my side which came every now and then. That was my first real pain and I endured it. That made me a stronger warrior.

Gerloc and my father kept glancing at me but I was always there and when we stopped to let the horses drink water from a stream we passed, I was not out of breath. I fed my horse some of the grain and put some of the oats in my mouth to chew too. My father said, "You can manage?"

"I can manage and I will ride but I will run more first. We have a long way to go and mine is the weakest of the horses!"

I heard Tadgh ask, "Are these the only men you bring, Captain Gerloc?"

Once on the road, Gerloc had told us that as we were now his men, we could call him captain. He shook his head, "Another of my men, Guillaume, has a further ten on the road ahead of us. Our lord will meet us in Djupr with other hired swords." He grinned, "You are the last sweepings and will do to stand behind a shield wall. We need numbers!"

If he thought to insult us, he failed. We knew that we were the lowest of the low but we also knew that we were being given a chance which we would not spurn.

I rode when it was the middle of the afternoon for I was tiring. Mary did not complain and seemed quite spritely. I had used a quarter of the grain and I would have to steal some more. Gerloc had said that he would feed us and he did but the food was not of the best quality and the farmer who sold us the food also served poor beer. Our accommodation turned out to be an outbuilding of a farm. It was sheltered and the old straw gave us a bed but it was not as comfortable as the inn we had used. Although I was tired, I took it upon myself to slip out and steal some grain from the farm's small granary. I had learned to sneak and move silently when my father and I, along with the others who had fought the Normans, had taken from our oppressors. The people here were not our oppressors but I did not know them and the quality of the food and the ale helped my decision to steal.

The farm had a dog but I liked dogs and they liked me. When we had come to collect the food, I had made friends with the animal. The result was that when I went, in the dark of night, it did not bark but licked my hand. After I had taken some oats, not enough for them to notice, I went to the place they hung their meat. It would have been tempting to take the pig but that would be missed. However, there were eight rabbits hung there and I took two. We would not be able to cook them until the next evening but I anticipated short rations all the way to Djupr. Finally, I took a dozen of the apples I found. It was one thing to steal but quite another to remain undiscovered. Stealing a sack, I put my booty in the sack and walked out of the farm, down the road until I came to an oak. I secured the sack to an upper branch.

Returning to the outbuilding I saw Gerloc cock an eye at me, "I needed to make water." He nodded but gave me a strange look.

As we were leaving the next day the farmer came and demanded the return of the two rabbits. I was surprised that he had noticed but pleased he had not seen what else I had taken. Gerloc looked annoyed and I was not sure who with. He invited the farmer to search us and I was given a cursory look for it was clear I had nothing with me. The farmer had to let us go with an apology. I ran and led Mary and, as with the previous day I ran at the back. It allowed me to collect my sack. Of course, Gerloc noticed it when we stopped but he was not angry.

"Resourceful! I can see a warrior in you, boy. You just need more meat on you. Those rabbits will be a start!"

The journey to Djupr was a journey to becoming a warrior for me. I learned the best way to carry my shield. I developed a better harness for my horse and I listened as the others spoke of wars and battles. My father and I were silent.

When we reached Djupr we found Lord Bohemond and around sixty men. Two or three were mailed and I recognised the Thegn from the inn, Beorhtric. He was a hired sword too and that surprised me. I had thought that if one was a lord then he needed not fight.

Once we reached the port it was as though we did not exist. Gerloc took us to the camp and then abandoned us with the message that we would be told what to do, eventually. We gravitated, quite naturally, to the Saxons, the English. They were gathered around a fire and we heard their voices and knew that they were friends, even before we had met them. The Thegn we had seen was with them but he was not the most powerful of the men. There were two who stood head and shoulders above him. While he had a short byrnie, they each wore one which went to their knees. They were housecarls and we went as close to them as we could for they were the greatest of all Saxon warriors and just being close to them would be an honour. We knew our place and we stood with others like ourselves, meanly dressed and poorly prepared for war. As I would later learn we were axe fodder. Leaders would use us ruthlessly to blunt enemy weapons and to weaken shield walls.

This time there was food and the pot which bubbled on the fire smelled so good that my stomach actually hurt. In anticipation, I took out my wooden bowl and a wooden spoon. I hoped for an ale but food was a priority. A one-armed man stirred the pot. I learned later that Edward had fought at Hastings too but his wounded left arm had become poisoned and he had lost it above the elbow. He had learned to be a cook and was able to hold food in place with his stump while he cut it. He was a good cook. I let my father and the others listen to the conversations around the fire and I drifted towards the pot.

The cook looked up at me, "It isn't ready yet, young 'un!"

I nodded, "My stomach will enjoy the smells and that will ease my hunger."

He laughed, "Aye, you look to be at the age when you can never be filled. Here, make yourself useful and I will make sure you are the first served after the housecarls." He handed me some root vegetables. "Wash those and then chop them up as small as you can. I had not expected Gerloc back so soon!"

I took the vegetables and washed them in a nearby pail. "You have served with Gerloc for long?"

"A year or so. Lord Bohemond pays well."

"But he is a Norman and you are a Saxon."

He nodded, "Aye, and I lost my arm to a Norman but in war, such things happen. You cannot bear grudges all of your life. We lost Englaland when King Harold died. The man was a foolish lord, brave but foolish. The Fates conspired against him and his brother too. Had not Tostig joined Hadrada and the Danish scum then he would still be sitting on his throne. The world is wide, boy, especially for a hired sword." I had chopped some vegetables on the tree stump and I dropped them in the pot and went back for more. "There is war in Italy and in the Empire. Then, if you are good enough, there is always the Eastern Empire where they pay good money and you fight with the sun on your back. You are young but you have chosen well. Do not fight for a country, fight for coin!"

I put the last of the vegetables in the stew, "You sound bitter. Surely a man should fight for his country."

He pointed his ladle at the two warriors who were talking with Thegn Beorhtric, "You see those two, Ralph and Garth?" I nodded, "They are housecarls and fought at Hastings. They slew many Normans but their lord, Thegn Osbert, changed sides during the battle and ordered them to leave with him. Men fight for lords, lords fight for kings and kings fight for power. When the Bastard took the crown, he rewarded Thegn Osbert who tried to rid himself of all vestiges of his Saxon past and that included his men."

I looked at the two men. They looked to be younger than my father and yet that could not be for they had fought at Hastings. "And that is why they hire out their swords and axes?"

He laughed, "Aye, they slew their lord and taking his gold, they fled. There were ten of them then and now there are two but if you do fight then stay by those two. They are survivors. It is they who will lead our contingent. The Thegn is young and it is just a title he clings on to. He knows who are the better warriors and that shows that there is hope for him." He gave the pot a stir and after tasting it, said, "It is ready, go and get your bowl. You are a good worker and you have knife skills. If you survive a year then who knows?"

The stew which was made up of ham, dried venison and offal as well as huge amounts of green and root vegetables was, indeed, tasty. The oat bread was filling and I was seated with a brimming bowl and my own small loaf even while my father and my brothers in arms queued.

When they sat down Tadgh laughed, "You have the look of an old campaigner, Wulfstan!"

I smiled as I began to use the bread to mop up the last of the stew, "What can I say, I was hungry!"

We met the Norman lord the next day. He was a powerful-looking knight and had a long scar running down his cheek. He did not speak to us, we learned he could only speak French and Norman, instead, Beorhtric spoke his words. "You are all here to serve Lord Bohemond. Today I will take those warriors who come from the land that was Englaland and we march towards Lord Bohemond's home. We are to await his arrival with the Breton and Norman men who fight for him and we will fix the enemy's attention. There will be a bonus of one gold piece for each man when the castle at the Haugr falls!"

That brought a cheer although I wondered where this lord had acquired such a large amount of coins. It was much later that I discovered he did not have that much gold but he assumed many of us would die. The majority of the hired swords worked for themselves. We were expendable.

Mary had improved since I had bought her. I do not think she had deserved to die in Dorestad and, thanks to the oats, apples and my running, I was able to ride her. Our war gear was carried in a wagon driven by Edward who had his pot in the back. This time Gerloc would stay with his lord and the thirty of us rode beneath no banner. As we gathered and mounted our horses it was not the Thegn who spoke to us but Ralph, one of the housecarls.

"We are travelling through land which fears men like us and we can expect no welcome in any of the places through which we pass. We will avoid castles and any towns with a wall. Where we can we will pay for what we need to eat." His eyes fixed on me, "I have heard that some of you have scavenging skills and that will be useful. When I say it is permissible! We ride with weapons ready to be drawn. Garth and I will speak with each of you as we ride for we must decide who fights in the shield wall and who does not!"

We set off and, as the least experienced, we were relegated to the rear of the column, I did not mind for Edward was there with the wagon and I rode next to him and chatted to him. My father was of an age with Sigiberht and Tadgh and they talked easily to one another. When we camped, I helped Edward unload his gear. With one arm he needed help. Once the pot was suspended upon its tripod he pointed to some nearby woods. "Gerloc said that you were resourceful. See if you can hunt something to augment the stew. The salted meat has to last another five days!"

I did not mind although I had only six arrows left to me. They were the ones I had recovered from the deck of the knarr. I would need to find either an ash tree or a poplar and make some more. The metal for the heads would need a blacksmith and I had already collected goose feathers when we had stopped at farms. The wood would be vital. Taking my arrows, I hurried off to the woods. I had learned to hunt in Englaland but I knew that Norman law meant only the lord of the manor could sanction hunting. If I was caught then I could be blinded or lose my fingers. I did not intend to be caught. I was patient and I was silent. At dusk, the animals came from their burrows. I had used two snares and I caught one that way but the second I hit with an arrow. Leaving two snares in place I gutted the rabbits and left the offal well away from the snares and then headed back to the camp. I had the two bunnies in my sack.

When I reached the fire, I saw that Ralph was speaking with Edward. Ralph was not wearing his byrnie. Instead, he had a hide jerkin. I learned that it could stop an arrow and provide protection against swords. I wished that I had one. The leather I wore needed metal and that made it heavier and less effective than a hide one.

"So, this is the resourceful Wulfstan, eh? I have heard much about you."

I was stunned that I had been noticed. Taking out the rabbits I began to skin them, "I caught two. I will check my snares before we leave in the morning."

"Here, I will help you." Ralph took out his own seax and began to skin one of the animals. "I am told that you and your father would be warriors?" I nodded. "Yet you have no experience of fighting in a shield wall?"

"I have killed three men!" Even as I said the words, I regretted them for they sounded petulant.

"And that speaks well of you but to stand in a shield wall means you lock shields with another two men and endure the enemy striking at you. You cannot flee. You cannot step back. You either win or you die. It is a battle between men to see who wishes to live more. Are you prepared for that?"

I shook my head, "I do not know for I am still young but I would hope that when I have taken weapons, mail and gold from an enemy, when I am bigger and stronger and after I have learned to use the weapons I have taken, then I might be able to answer you. I am young and I have much to learn."

He laughed, "A good answer which shows that you have a brain."

We had both finished skinning the animals and we handed them to Edward who just threw them in the pot whole. They would cook slowly and fall off the bone. When we ate the stew, knowing that it was rabbit we would eat carefully and any bones we found would be kept. They could be fashioned into needles, brooches and even tiny crosses.

Ralph nodded over to my father and said, quietly, "You know that your father can never stand in a shield wall."

"He is brave and fought at Hastings!" I was tempted to say '*and did not run away*' but I knew that would be wrong.

"And he killed a man but he is older and has not the time left to him to learn the new tricks. You will have to leave him behind if you are to become a warrior."

My shoulders slumped, "Then I will not become a warrior for I will not desert my father."

Surprisingly Ralph smiled, "And that is also the right answer, for a man who would leave his father so quickly would not be one I would have in a shield wall. I will watch you, young Wulfstan, for I see something in you."

By the time we reached the land to the south of the Haugr, I felt one of the company. Edward used me as his assistant and Ralph spoke to me each day. In addition, I had managed to get a branch from a poplar tree and could begin to make my own arrows. We camped by the sea. Ralph had spoken to me often and he took the time to explain Lord Bohemond's plan. When his ships arrived, they would sail along the coast and we would march parallel to them. Both the ships and our small warband would arrive at the same time. The Norman knew his own land well and he held the secrets of the small castle in his head.

"The men who follow this Breton, Fergant, will not dare to stay behind the walls. They will have to come forth to fight us. Lord Bohemond hopes that they will see our small warband and attack us before his lordship can land his Normans and horses."

I had grown up since leaving my home, "He expects us to die and then he will not have to pay us." It was not a question, it was a plain and simple statement,

Ralph smiled, "Now you see what it is to be a warrior for hire. Do you still wish to learn the skills?"

"I do not want to die before I have planted my seed and made a mark in this world!"

"You have made a mark already but fear not, you will not die." He pointed to the warriors who were gathered around Garth and the Thegn. There were twenty of them. "We will make a shield wall. Those like Sigiberht and Tadgh who have fought before will be the second rank. There are ten of you who are left and you will be the ones who use your bows to harass the enemy when they try to get around our flanks."

That seemed a daunting prospect and I only had a few arrows. I set about making new ones while we waited for the ship. We knew that our presence would be reported to the men of the Haugr but we were far enough away for them to merely wonder. As Ralph told me, if they came prematurely then that would help Lord Bohemond. The easiest part of the arrow making process was splitting the poplar. I managed to make eighteen blanks. We did not have all of the tools necessary; we did not have a shooting board nor a finishing plane. My father managed to make a gauge which would ensure the arrows were all the same thickness and the nearby seashore yielded sandstone so that we could smooth and shape the arrows. We had saved eight arrowheads from the pirate attack and we managed to make and fletch eight arrows in one day. That meant I now had more arrows. We fletched another eight arrows but they had no heads.

When the four ships hove to off the shore, we were ready to go to war. We left our horses tethered at our camp and one-armed Edward would watch them. I did not envy him his lonely vigil but he seemed happy enough. My shield still bore Frisian markings but that did not appear to make a difference. I saw that Ralph, Garth, the Thegn and six others all had a long axe along with their ash shafted spears. They were the ones with the byrnies and I knew they would be in the centre. From my talks with Ralph, I learned that the main disappointment would be that they would not be fighting beneath their own banner. Men, he told me, fought much better with their own banner above them. The fact the Lord Bohemond had not provided one said much about the Norman's view of us.

As we marched up the road which ran next to the sea, I saw that the mailed men were at the fore. They wore their helmets but carried their shields across their backs. We marched at the rear and we, too, had our shields across our backs. I was next to my father and I realised that since the pirate ship we had been together but rarely spoken. He seemed to enjoy the company of Tadgh and Sigiberht. Now we were forced to speak as we were almost the last two in the column of men.

"You and this Ralph appear to get on, my son." I felt suddenly guilty as though I was being disloyal to my father. He smiled, "It is good. He is the warrior I might have become had we not lost at Hastings. Watch him and learn. I think that Tadgh and Sigiberht will follow him when this is over and I would like us to accompany them too. If they will have us."

"I have spoken with him and know that he intends to head for Italy where the two Empires battle for land with the Normans who are there."

"Good." We walked in silence then he suddenly said, "If I should fall know that I am proud of you. I did not give you all that I could and for that I am sorry. I wonder if I was cursed by a witch when I was young. We should have done this years ago."

I shook my head, "No father, for if we had then I would lie dead like Garth on Captain Fótr's ship. This was meant to be. We were meant to travel on the knarr and to pass the test which God set us. Before then I would have been too young."

"Aye you are right and you are grown wise! I expect you get that from your mother for she always made better decisions than did I." His words made me think that I wished I had known my mother.

The Haugr stood out above the surrounding landscape as it had a stone tower. I also saw a stone breakwater which led to an island which looked as though it was defensible. Our Norman leader had taken his ships north and passed the breakwater. He knew of a beach where he could land his men and horses. Ralph halted us four hundred paces from the wooden walls of the castle and I wondered why he had not gone closer. The answer became clear as we climbed the slope to the top of the small knoll. Sigiberht told me, as we arrayed in our ranks, that the word haugr was Norse for mounds and I saw many of them dotted around. The castle was built upon the largest of them.

That we had set a problem for the Bretons in the castle became obvious when they did not suddenly rush out to attack us. They had seen the ships and would wonder at their purpose. The castle gates remained closed. Tadgh was just in front of me and I asked him how we would take such a castle.

"The walls are not high. We would use our shields to boost men to the top of the walls and do so at a number of places. The tower would be the hardest part to take for they have put the door higher up the wall and we could not batter it down. If they have enough men within the walls then they will try to sweep us from this knoll."

I did not like being bait and I did not like the waiting. I spent the time choosing my best arrow. Ralph had told us, once we were arrayed, that he would allow each archer and slinger to choose his own range. With so few arrows I would wait until they were close for I wanted to hit and hurt with each one. Once they were spent then it would be down to my Norman sword which I had never used in anger. I had swung it and practised but that was not the same. I had not risked hitting my blade against anything solid. I knew now that was a mistake. I had taken the boots from one of the Frisian pirates and I had a dagger in the top. With my Frisian sword, I seemed to have enough weapons but I had only used my seax to slice into flesh. This day would either see me dead or with some lessons learned.

The defenders left their castle. Twenty horsemen emerged followed by another twenty men on foot. Only ten of the horsemen looked to have mail of any sort and it only covered their upper bodies. I adjusted my helmet and nocked an arrow. I need to empty my bowels but I did not have enough time. When we had fought on the ship, I had not had enough time to be afraid. The horsemen formed up in two lines while the men on foot lined up behind. The horsemen all had lances and long spears. I noticed that there were still some men on the walls. The Bretons were taking no chances.

Unconsciously I found myself stepping closer to my father who said, quietly, "We need space for our bows!" I nodded and moved away again.

We were on the extreme right of the line and were the closest to the sea although it was still a good four hundred paces from us. I saw that Tadgh had a spear but Sigiberht, next to him, still swung his axe one-handed. I saw a horseman raise his lance and shout something which was in a language I did not understand but it must have meant, charge, for they began to gallop at us. That day was the first time I faced charging horsemen and I have done so many times since. It never gets easier although, with time, I have gained in confidence and trust in the shield wall. I heard my father draw and I emulated him. I saw that the riders on the flanks wore no mail but I was not sure that my arrow would pierce the leather that they wore. The horses seemed a better target and I aimed at the closest one to me. Two of our men had slings and I heard them whirling.

"Steady! Steady!" Ralph's voice was, somehow, reassuring.

The horsemen were just one hundred and fifty paces from us when the ground began to rise slightly. The riders leaned forward. An arrow flew from the left side of our line. I caught its flight from the corner of my eye. When my father sent his arrow, I released my own at the horse on the right. I actually saw both arrows hit and that was a mistake for I should have been nocking my next arrow. My father's arrow hit one rider in the leg while mine hit the horse in the eye and it must have killed it instantly for the horse's head came down catapulting the rider through the air. His head smashed into the ground and he lay still. My father sent another arrow and I nocked and released a heartbeat later. I should have aimed for my arrow merely struck a second horse in the rump. By now they were just forty paces from us and I knew, even though this was my first battle, that I would only have one more arrow and I determined to make it a good one. They were so close now that I was confident of my aim and I sent an arrow into the screaming face of a young warrior, I later learned he was a Breton. The range was so close that I hit him in the mouth and the arrow drove his head back.

Dropping my bow, I swung around my shield and drew my Norman sword. I knew, as the horsemen struck our line, that I should have sent my arrows sooner and then I would have hurt them more. If I died then it would be my own fault for failing to have faith in myself. It was not just the sound of the lances and spears cracking and shattering on the shields which alarmed me but the fact that Tadgh and the others took a step back. How could those in the front rank endure it? Then there was the noise of horses struck by spears and the death cries as men were killed. The men on foot had raced after the horses and they had spread out. Harlan, a Saxon from Lundun shouted, "Ware right!"

I turned just as a spear came towards me. I realised then that the ones on the left of our line had the protection of their shields but I did not. I flicked up my sword and, by some miracle, deflected the spear. The Breton had a pot helmet and no armour and his head was, invitingly, at my waist height. I punched at him with my shield. There was no boss on the shield but I am strong and I connected well. He reeled and blood burst from his nose. When I had fought my cousins, I had endured many a bloody nose and I knew that it made eyes water. I swung my sword from behind me and hit his helmet. It jarred and numbed my arm but he sank to the ground. I had no time for self-congratulation for another man with a javelin and a small shield ran at me. This time I was prepared and I angled my body to the right so that I could use my shield for protection. In doing so I unwittingly left a gap to my father.

The javelin was lighter than the spear which I had deflected but the Breton had quick hands and he almost took my eye. The nasal on my helmet was not very large but the javelin hit it and it so shocked me that I forgot I had a sword and brought up my knee. I drove up between his legs and, as he sank to his own knees, I swung an awkward blow to the side of his head and when my hilt connected with his head, he tumbled down the slope. As he fell, he knocked two others to the ground and I had a moment to look around. Looking towards the Haugr I saw the banner of Lord Bohemond as he rode towards his home. The gates were still open and I did not think that the defenders had seen the threat for we were now surrounded and men assailed us from all sides. There were bodies both before us and behind us for men had died.

I saw Sigiberht step forward and swing his axe into the side of a horse's head. Tadgh had impaled a Breton with his spear and now wielded his sword. I faced a warrior with a thick hide jerkin and a sword. The man looked as though he knew how to use his weapon and he swung it at my unprotected legs. I had to step back to avoid it and that allowed him onto the flatter ground I had just occupied. Worse it made a hole in our line so that my father was no longer protected by my shield. The Breton saw that I was a novice and he swung his sword hard at me and I barely blocked it and when I did so my arm was numbed by the force of the blow. I had to take another step backwards and that helped me for my enemy stumbled and I blindly swung backhand; I was lucky and my blow connected. I was on my feet and he was reeling to the side when I stabbed at some flesh I glimpsed close to his neck. There was a point to my sword and I penetrated the skin and my sword slid down to his wrist. I was unlucky not to strike a vein but I must have damaged a muscle or tendon for his sword fell from his fingers. I swung my shield to hit him hard and he rolled away from me.

I heard my father shout, "Wulfstan!"

I looked around and saw a spear coming towards me. I had used my shield as a weapon and my left side was exposed. I would have died had not my father thrown himself with his sword held before him, at the man. His sword went in to the depth of a hand. I saw another Breton seize his opportunity and he began a swing which would have taken my father's head. I leapt across the gap and held my shield over my prostrate father. The sword blow was so hard that it almost shattered the shield but I had enough of my wits to hack into the side of the man's leg. Blood gushed and the Breton began to back down the slope. I saw as I raised my father to his feet, that the Haugr had fallen but that would not help us. There was a sea of bodies both Breton and Saxon all around us. I had no idea who survived for the only ones of importance, at that moment, were my father and me.

I said, "Back to back and let us see if we can survive!"

He nodded and laughed, "Who is the father now?"

It felt reassuring to have my back protected and I held my shield tighter to my body. I saw that my Norman sword had a couple of nicks and I would need a whetstone if I survived this combat. I suppose I could have drawn the Frisian one which was sharp but I did not wish to risk sheathing a weapon. I was facing the sea while my father faced the Haugr. We were both on a flat patch of the mound. I could hear the clash of steel and the cries of men who were hurting but I seemed to have calm within me and I knew not why for I was about to die. I watched the mailed Breton dismount his weary horse and walk purposefully towards us. My father and I were the last two who were left to guard the right flank of the housecarls. It must have seemed an easy task to shift the two poorly armed men and then attack the mailed men in the rear. I saw just mail and thought my end had come. I would have to slow down the man as much as I could and hope that Ralph and the others would defeat their enemies. This was my initiation into the world of warriors and it might also be the end of my life as a warrior.

I was aware, as he swung his sword to intimidate me, that the blows I had taken on my shield had weakened both my shield and my arm. I would not be able to endure many blows. Behind me, I heard the grunt as my father blocked a blow. He was also being attacked and I had to fight as long as I could. The Breton was more experienced than I was and I would lose if I traded blows with him. As on the ship I had to use cunning. The man's byrnie came to his waist and that gave me hope. As he took two strides towards me, he began his swing and I simply dropped to my knees and raising my shield above me as I did so, I rammed my sword blindly upwards. His sword struck the air and my weapon ripped through the cloth and up into flesh. Blood flooded over my hand and arm as he screamed. I pushed harder until the hilt of my sword touched bone. The man's body began to fall over me and I had no choice but to let go of my sword or risk my arm being broken. He landed on me and I knew he was dead. I wriggled and pulled myself free and stood. I turned to find where my father was and I saw him. He was dead but he had a smile upon his face. I was also aware that there was no longer the sound of metal on metal. All was quiet except for the moans and groans of the dying. Ralph, Garth, Thegn Beorhtric and five others remained on their feet. All else were dead. I saw that Sigiberht and Tadgh had both fallen.

That did not matter to me and I dropped to my knees, throwing my almost shattered shield away. "Father!" I saw that he had been cut many times. He had not died of one wound but many. It showed me how lucky I had been. He must have kept fighting even though he knew he was dying. Even his last words to me, *'Who is the father now?'* may have been uttered when he knew his life was ebbing away. I could not help the tears which coursed down my face and I cared not who saw me. I was now alone in the world and while I could live with that, I was not certain I could live without my father. We had lost all of our friends in Englaland and that had, somehow, made us closer. The fight on the knarr and the journey here had made us brothers in arms and I had been anticipating, had we both survived, a future where we both earned a living with our weapons. While I wept, I was reflecting that I was now a warrior. I had lost count of how many men I had killed and my last victory, whilst won with a trick, had been against a mailed horseman.

"Wulfstan!" I felt a hand on my shoulder and looked up at Ralph whose byrnie was besmeared and bespattered with blood and gore. "It is over and your father is dead. You are now a warrior. Have you any hurts?"

I stood and looked down at my clothes. It looked as though I had been working in an abattoir. The last man had bled out over me. I shook my head, "I know not how, Ralph, but I am whole and yet my father lies dead."

"It is because you are a warrior."

Garth came over, "And if you would we would have you join us when we leave this place." He pointed at the Breton I had slain. "His helmet and byrnie are yours. We won this battle and all that is here is now ours!"

Thegn Beorhtric nodded. "Aye, for we were abandoned by that Norman! We were sacrificed!"

Ralph shook his head, "We are hired swords and we chose the wrong master. We take our pay and we take this booty. I know not about the rest of you but Garth and I will head for Italy."

Beorhtric shook his head, "I will take my men," he laughed wryly, "both of them and return to Englaland with the money we have earned and with my share of this booty. I will seek some land there. I am English and I will fight the Normans any way that I can!"

Although our dead needed to be buried and the mound seemed a good place to do so we knew that we first needed to collect all that we could from the Breton dead. Already Lord Bohemond and his men had raised his standard above the Haugr and would soon be heading to the mound. Thegn Beorhtric sent his men back to Edward for the wagon and the horses. I first went to recover my weapons. The bow of my father and mine were both broken. I would use a bow no longer. I took my sword from the dead Breton and then stripped his byrnie and the aketon which lay beneath it from his body. I took his sword and his shield as well as his helmet which was better made than the Frisian one. I was going to leave his body when Ralph said, "The rings on his fingers, Wulfstan, are valuable."

I nodded and began to prise them from his fingers. He also had a purse and I found, within it, one gold mark and twelve silver coins. I learned that many warriors carried a gold coin if they died in battle then their comrades would give them a decent burial. The Breton's body was rolled down the mound to lie with the other dead Bretons.

The wagon and our horses had arrived by the time that Lord Bohemond, Gerloc and five of his oathsworn rode towards us. They had their helmets on their saddles and their coifs hung around their necks. He did not dismount but said, "You have done well. We will take this treasure into the Haugr."

Ralph had just picked up a good spear and, throwing it to me he shook his head and said, "Here Wulfstan, for you! No, my lord, you will not take what we have earned. You will pay us what you owe and we will leave. We have done all that we were asked and more. Our dead are a testament to that!"

The knight coloured, "You dare to speak to me who is lord and master here in such an insolent manner!"

Thegn Beorhtric said, "You are a Norman and we should have learned, after Hastings, that you are not to be trusted. There are few of us left but by all that is holy if we are not paid that which we are owed then we will join our brothers in arms as will you, Lord Bohemund!"

I thought that the Norman would draw his sword and I would have to use the spear which I now held. It was Gerloc who spoke, "My lord, I was the one hired these men and they are right to ask for what is due them. We made a contract. Would you break it for I know we shall need to hire more men to replace those who are lost? We will have to defend what we hold. We will be able to hire few men if we are seen to break contracts."

I saw then that Gerloc was more than just a sergeant. His name, Gerloc of the Haugr told me that this was his home too and he appeared to have an influence. Lord Bohemond nodded, "Then pay them, uncle, but I want them off my land by dawn!" Wheeling his horse, he led his squire back to his castle.

Ralph said, "Uncle?"

Gerloc dismounted, "Aye, his father was my brother and when he died, I watched over his son. He is a good man, really."

Garth snorted, "He has a strange way of showing it!"

Ralph asked, "Why did he not come sooner? Some of those who died might have lived had he done so."

Gerloc looked almost embarrassed, "Lord Fergant fought hard and it took us time. I am sorry for your losses. Truly I have never seen such a fight." He looked at me, "I am sorry that you have lost your father and the other two. Know that I will honour the contract you made. You will have the five coins for each day."

"I would rather be poor as a church mouse and have the three of them alive."

Gerloc nodded, "Then you have taken steps towards becoming a warrior. May fortune favour you, Wulfstan the Saxon."

Ten days later we were approaching the Rhone valley. There were just five of us, Ralph, Garth, Edward, Harlan and myself. I now looked like a warrior. Ralph had told me to take Sigiberht's axe as we buried our dead with their swords. I had my long ash spear, two helmets and three swords. The dead Breton's horse was better than Mary but I had kept Mary as a packhorse and because she was a reminder of Dorestad and the start of this journey. As we rode down the road towards the coast to Nissa I asked Ralph what was our plan.

"Winter will come soon enough and we have money enough to keep us comfortable. You have the makings of a warrior but you need to be trained. We have the winter to hone you like a good sword. When the spring is here, we take the road to Italy and seek a paymaster but this time we will fight for either one of the Empires or the Normans of Sicily."

I shook my head, "Normans are all untrustworthy."

He laughed, "I agree and the Hautevilles are more ruthless than any but let us not rule out any paymaster. Who knows what a year will bring?"

I liked Nissa which was an independent city supporting the Papal States. In fact, I could have stayed there if there had been work but it was now a peaceful little port. We found an abandoned hut in the hills and lived there. The local lord was happy for us to do so as the Saracens had raided and pillaged the land many times. He asked only that should the bell be rung from the tower in the port we would go to their aid. The Saracens had not attacked for almost a generation but the people there had long memories. The climate was clement and the food to my taste. I ate well and became bigger. I thought I had stopped growing but I had not and soon I was the size of Ralph. My beard came and I filled the byrnie which had been a little loose when first I had owned it. I also became stronger. Ralph made a pel; this was a post driven into the ground and he made me a heavy wooden sword. Each day I worked at the pel and learned how to make better strokes. Then Garth showed me how to use my axe. Used two handed it meant a warrior had no shield to face an enemy but a line of such swinging weapons was daunting. Over the winter and, as spring approached, I became a warrior. When we left, in March, I was no longer a callow and untried youth. I was almost a man and no longer discernible as the weak one from the warband. Ralph put my growth spurt down to the good food, climate and the work I had done. He was convinced that I would grow more.

While we had been in Nissa we had not been idle. Ralph and Garth had regularly been to the port to speak with the captains as they brought their boats to land. In this way, they learned of the world beyond our doorstep and could plan both where we could go and how we might earn coin. Sea captains knew where there was conflict for they could both profit and suffer from such wars. We had not been profligate and we had not wasted the money we had earned but it would not last another year. It was from these sea captains that we learned of a war which was brewing in the east of Italy at a place called Benevento. There, it seemed, Count Lando of Capua was recruiting men to take back his family's lands from the Norman Duke of Sicily. There were also rumoured to be Papal soldiers as well as Imperial ones. The fact that we would be fighting Normans appealed and all of us agreed that we would travel across Italy and offer our services. Despite the clement climate wars were still fought in the summer and so we left Nissa in early spring. We had spare horses, which we could sell and we had plenty of food. I would not have to scavenge and we headed south and east.

During the winter I had learned a little of the local language and I was able to ask for things when we stopped on our journey south. The others normally used me to do the speaking as I looked less fierce than they did and, added to the fact that I was younger, was less intimidating. We were viewed with suspicion but my halting and imperfect words seemed to endear me to them and I was able to prove an asset to the company. I was desperate to win their approval for I felt I had not yet earned my place amongst them.

The more we spoke with the locals the better became our ability to ask questions and we learned that the two belligerent sides were busy seeking allies for the war for this part of Italy. The Empire was suffering further south and the Normans had also suffered a defeat when they lost Capua to Count Lando. This would not be a clear-cut war and the posturing and diplomacy meant that we might earn more than we would elsewhere. The two sides sought the best men. The land was rich and we were told that the wages to be had were high. One old soldier, wounded and heading home with a full purse told us that axemen such as we would be most useful as their opponents were Norman knights. He also told us about the Varangian Guard who were regiments of soldiers in the employ of the Emperor. He explained how they were feted by the Emperor for when the Norse, Angles, Saxons and Rus gave their word they kept it. The fact that they were paid higher wages also appealed. The more he spoke the better it sounded. When we continued our journey, I spoke with Ralph.

"I feel a cheat, Ralph, for I have used a sword but not a spear nor an axe. I may jeopardise your chances of employment."

"Wulfstan, we often spoke with your father on the road to the Haugr. I think he knew that he would not live long. Some men have that curse, that they see their own death. Whatever the cause we promised him that we would care for you if he fell. A promise made to a dead man is a sacred thing and besides, you do not know yet what skills you will have. You are much younger than I am and when I was your age, I had not yet developed skills with an axe. You practise each day and you are strong. You will get better."

His words gave me comfort and set me to thinking about my father. Had he felt a failure because of Hastings and was his death on the mound at the Haugr atonement? I would never know for I had had no last words with him. Our banter as we had stood back to back was the last exchange we had had. I kept those words in my head for they were the last link to the man who had raised me.

When we reached the city of Benevento, we found a city prepared for war. It was surrounded by armed camps made up of different nationalities and types of warriors. Ostensibly a Papal city we saw the banners of Count Lando all around the camps. We also spied Imperial troops; they were a mixed bandon of spearmen and archers. I confess that none of us knew the words we were about to learn but, as we ended up camped close to the Byzantine troops, we learned their words and their structure. We discovered that they were commanded by a pentekontarchai who had sixteen subordinates called locaghos. I confess that at the time it seemed confusing but, now, as I sit in Norton and recall my youth it is like revisiting old friends. The pentekontarchai was an officer called Basil. He had many other names which followed Basil but we could say that word and he seemed amused by us and humoured us when we used it. It was only later we realised how senior he was. We learned all this, not directly, for we could not speak his language but through a priest who was with them. He had been an English monk who had gone on pilgrimage and was now attached to the Imperial troops. Brother Paul was a real character for he carried a sword with him and hated the Normans as much as he hated the Muslims. He was the embodiment of a warrior priest. At that time there were none and I fear that Brother Paul was born before his time although when we met him, he had grey hair. He had a story which he kept hidden from us but the fact that he became so attached to us made me think that he had known warriors like Ralph and Garth. He helped me much and almost took the place of my father, briefly.

It was he advised Ralph on the best way to approach the Count's man, Robert of Benevento. The two of them left our camp and went to the castle to seek terms. We explored the town. That our lives are not our own became apparent that day. I was just enjoying being in the city for I had never been as far south nor east in my life and it seemed an exotic place. The smells and sights were unlike anything I had seen, even in the Italy through which we had travelled. Those who ran the businesses in the city were pleased to see us or at least they feigned pleasure at our presence. I suspect they were just glad for our money although some may have been pleased that we were there to stop the avaricious Normans from taking their land.

Edward was looking for ingredients for his food. He had been a warrior and could still fight, after a fashion, one-handed, but he loved cooking and was keen to be a better cook. We had heard that, as this was a port which faced the east, there would be exotic spices for sale. As such he was desperate to get to the market. Garth and Harlan were equally keen to find somewhere to drink. We found a small tavern. We had learned that the beer which was drunk in this land was not to our taste and the others had developed a taste for wine. I found the beer acceptable: I was still young and knew no better in those days. As we sat at a table, outside, for that was the custom in this part of Campania, the others looked to me to order for I had taken to Italian far better than they had. I think it was my age and the fact that I absorbed knowledge quicker than they did. A young blond girl came over and I tried my Italian, "A jug of wine and a beer, please!"

She cocked her head to one side and said, "You are from the north?" She spoke English and we could all understand her.

Edward was the one who was the poorest of us when it came to speaking other languages and he beamed, "Aye, we are! And how is it that a young beauty such as you can speak our language?"

She smiled, "I am named Margaret and I was taken with my mother as a slave when we travelled with her master on pilgrimage to Jerusalem from the port of York. Our ship was taken by pirates and the Arabs who took us separated us and I ended up serving an old Arab and his wife for I had just seen eight summers and they trained me." She shrugged, "I was lucky and I served them for six years and was treated better than most slaves. They came to Rome to trade and they both died for they were old and little ailments can hurt the old. I knew that my fate would be to service men and I ran before the bodies were discovered. I kept heading south and begging until I reached here and the owner, Mistress Sophia took me on." The place was filling up and she shook her head, "and now I had better fetch your order or she will flay my back!"

That meeting changed Edward's life. We did not know it then although we saw that he was much taken with the girl. I confess that I felt my loins stirring when she had been close to me for she was comely. I was young and my thoughts, at that time, were turning to girls. Edward was much older but, it seemed, his thoughts were too. We did not get to the market, that first day, for we spent the time in the tavern and when we left, in the middle of the afternoon, the market had closed. The other three had consumed four jugs of wine between them and we had eaten well. As we headed back to the camp Edward was slightly drunk and loose-tongued.

"Margaret was a beauty was she not? And she has steel in her. She has survived as a slave! I am not sure I could endure the whip and not react."

Harlan shook his head, "A man can never know how he will take such an indignity. Perhaps life becomes so precious that a man would do anything to hold on to it."

Garth snorted, "I would die with my axe in my hand rather than suffer slavery but I can see that, for a girl, it is different."

I was young and naïve, "Why?"

Garth looked at me, sadly, "What do you think happened to the mother? If the daughter is anything to go by then the mother would have been a beauty. The Arabs like pale women and use them for their pleasure."

"Oh."

Garth laughed, "Oh indeed! It is time that you had a woman. We will find a brothel for you!"

Harlan pointed, for we neared the camp, "You need to look no further than here. There are women who follow the warriors and they will show you how to be a man for a silver coin."

I flushed and shook my head, "Thank you but I will wait!"

Ralph was waiting for us and he looked less than pleased when we arrived, especially as we were empty handed. Garth was the subject of most of his vitriol for they were shield brothers. "I leave you one task and that is to procure food and we have none! What will we eat this night?"

I could see that Edward felt guilty for he had been the one who kept us there. "Do not worry, Ralph, I can come up with something and we will get to the market early on the morrow. Had we managed to buy anything then all the best would have gone."

I did not like discord and I had become the peacemaker for there had been arguments and disputes on the way south and I tried to ease the tension, "Have we employment?"

"We have but the Count is not a man to trust. He thinks we are like the Normans we fight for we come from the same part of the world. We are paid now and when we fight then the pay doubles on the day that we do battle. However, we have to feed ourselves." He glared at Edward and Garth. "Make sure we spend our coins wisely." He handed over a small purse to Edward. "Here is the pay for this week. I want you to make it last two. We may need young Wulfstan to scavenge once more."

The fact was that we spent longer waiting for battle than we expected. Brother Paul was the one with his ear to the ground as was the pentekontarchai, Basil. Edward was a good cook and each morning he went early to the market and returned with a wide variety of provender. He found spices which made the food taste most interesting. The consequence was that Brother Paul and Basil often joined us. The Normans, it seemed, were not enjoying the same success they had when first they had come. Allied to that they were also fighting the Saracens for Sicily. The Count was still building up his forces. We no longer needed Brother Paul to translate as we all spoke enough Italian to get by. Occasionally the priest would have to translate a Byzantine word but by and large, we got by.

When he gave us advice, we felt that it was sincere and well-meant. I noticed that, when Basil spoke, Brother Paul's eyes seemed to stare at me. I know not why. "You four should go to join the Varangian Guard. They are well paid and earn half a pound of gold a year. That is all profit for they are clothed and housed at the Emperor's expense."

"That is a great deal of gold and what does he expect for that?"

He turned and smiled at our leader, "Simple, Ralph, he expects you to be axe-bearing barbarians who fight to the death as your armies did when the Normans came."

I saw the others taking that in and weighing it up. Housecarls believed that they were the best warriors in the whole world. I was young and did not yet consider myself a housecarl so I wondered at the truth of this but Ralph and the others did not believe that they would be defeated. They regarded Hastings as an accident that would never be repeated.

Edward looked at the pentekontarchai and said, "You said four and I am guessing that I am not included."

Basil was an honest man and he nodded, "There would be no need for you but why leave here? You are a good cook and your food is better than in any of the taverns in the city. When this is over and paid off you could buy somewhere and make more money that way."

I saw that he had not considered that but he had been with Ralph and Garth for a long time, "These are my brothers in arms. I do not want to leave them."

Brother Paul shook his head, "Sometimes the good lord shows us a new path and a man is a fool if he does not take it. I was on one path but thanks to wild Vikings I now tread this one! I would still be a priest in an abbey but for that accident. I have seen much of this world and I have changed myself from that which I was. Look at yourself, Edward One Arm, and ask what it is that you really want." Brother Paul was the wisest man I ever met. I wish that he had told us his story but he never did.

The time we waited was not wasted for we worked on my skills with an axe. Each day I grew stronger and I learned to wield the one-handed axe I had been given, better and better. The others used a two handed one but they saw the advantage of fighting with someone who could hold a shield and guard the left side. So, when the war came, we had a way of fighting with which we were all comfortable.

And then the Normans chose to bring us to battle. Benevento was too hard a place to try to assault the walls and so the Normans used their horsemen to begin to raid the land around the city. The Count did not have the horsemen to thwart their attacks and so he gathered his army to force the Normans to battle. We marched south to their camp leaving the walls of Benevento well-defended. We left Edward there to watch our horses and spare war gear and we marched with the Byzantines and the other mercenaries. There were Swabians with their two-handed swords and Pisan crossbows. There were even some Cretan slingers and archers from the Balearics. Then there were the Lombards who were, basically, the warriors whose home was Italy. We were amongst the few who were mailed. The skutatos, the Byzantine spearmen, wore a short mail corselet and the Swabians wore hauberks which made us the foot soldiers who would face the Norman horses. That also made sense for we were all foreigners and, largely mercenaries. If we died then the Count would not have to pay us.

The army marched south towards the Norman camp. They had Breton light horsemen and they knew we were coming for these men who had fought at Hastings were like a swarm of flies which buzzed ahead of us as we marched towards the Normans. The enemy had chosen a camp which was on a higher piece of ground and between us would be a small stream and a shallow valley.

Garth was convinced that once the battle began that would become a quagmire and he warned me of the consequences. "Those without mail will cross easily but once the horses have ridden over it then it will become churned up. If we have to cross then beware for if you are stuck there then the lightly armed men can dance around you and you will die."

I nodded and thought back to the battle of the Haugr. There I had not been mailed and I had had the advantage over the mailed men.

We did not fight that first day. Instead, the two armies sent out scouts to assess the numbers of their opposition. The second day there was a truce and the leaders met to discuss surrender. Ralph told me that it was all a formality for we would fight. The Normans had not come all this way just to talk and any negotiated deal would be detrimental to the Count. We would have to go to battle. The next morning, we were up before dawn. The winter in Nissa had been important for I had watched the rituals of my shield brothers and now, as we went to battle, I used my own. I had long hair and a beard. The first thing I did was to comb my hair and beard and tie up the ends of both. Then I donned my aketon, the padded tunic which went below the mail. The hauberk was lifted over the aketon. When I had first donned it, I had struggled to get it over my head but now I did it easily. It had a hood, called a coif and that was a comfort for it protected my face. I put on my boots and slipped a dagger into the top of each one. The Norman sword my father had taken from the dead Norman was the one I favoured and I strapped on the baldric and scabbard. I placed my arming cap on my head and then my helmet. This was not the cold north and I did not need my cloak. I slung my shield over my back and hung my one-handed axe from my belt. With my spear, I was almost ready but the last part of my ritual was to kneel, alone and to pray to God.

That day before the battle, as I stood, I saw Brother Paul behind me. He looked at me with sad eyes, "Wulfstan, Ralph has told me that this will be but your second battle. A word of advice from one who has seen many battles and many men die. You will not run for you are amongst housecarls but the Count is not your master. He pays you. Live!" He made the sign of the cross and I think I saw the hint of a tear in his eye. I could not understand why but I felt better for having been given his blessing.

As Basil had predicted we made up the centre of the line. We anchored the left of the line while the Swabians manned the right. The archers were arrayed before the Skutatoi and it would be us who endured the attacks of the Norman crossbows and horsemen. Our own horsemen were on the left and right flanks. Our reserve was made up of the familia of Count Lando.

We did not fight that day but it was not through a lack of courage. It was the weather. A storm of Biblical proportions meant that neither bows nor crossbows would be effective and the horses would struggle on the muddy ground. When it became obvious that the day was wasted, we retired to our camp where we ate cold fare for the rain had doused the fires. I wondered if we would ever fight!

The next day God sent us sunshine and heat. Once again I went through my ritual but there was no Brother Paul to bless me for he and Basil had been ordered into position early. Basil's archers were a key part of the Count's strategy. A thin fog filled the valley bottom and once it had been dissipated by the sun, we saw that the battle would commence. As usual bishops and priests blessed their men. Brother Paul did so for us as well as his Byzantine men. The priest had a two-handed sword and stood with us; he smiled and nodded at me as he took his position. I was the one closest to the horsemen and I felt a little isolated. Behind me, I had Lombard spearmen. They did not fill me with confidence and I wondered if I would still be standing when the day ended. I knew that I would not desert the others. I had stepped back at the Haugr and my father had died. I would not do so again.

Once the priests had gone, we tightened our helmets, hefted our shields and had a practice swing or two with our weapon of choice. We had left our spears at the camp. I glanced at my three brothers in arms. Their shields were across their backs and their only defence would be their swinging axes. A lance could spear them or a horse could trample them. At least I had my red painted shield with the white horse upon it for protection. That the Normans would attack us was never in doubt. They had far more horsemen than we did and they had conquered half of Italy as well as the whole of England and half of Scotland with their knights. It would be as my father had said about Hastings. They would advance with crossbows to weaken us and then charge. The difference would be the Imperial archers who fought in a much more disciplined way than the fyrd had done at Hastings. They would send volleys of arrows which could penetrate mail and when they withdrew there would be a wall of spears with veterans behind them. If I had not already fought against horsemen at the Haugr I suspect that my bowels would be emptying themselves of their own volition but I had faced greater odds with less protection. Even though it had cost me my father I had needed the battle of the Haugr to temper me.

The crossbowmen began their steady walk towards us. They were closely followed by their mailed horsemen as they did not want to risk the vulnerable crossbowmen being attacked by our horsemen. I saw that although the ground had dried out a little on the upper slopes, the lower ones were still sticky and claggy. Once they had passed the valley bottom and the horsemen waited at the stream where their horses took advantage of the water, as yet unpolluted by blood, the crossbowmen halted just two hundred paces from us. As the crossbowmen loaded their weapons the lochagoi in command of the Imperial archers ordered their men to nock and draw. I did not understand the Greek they used but I recognised the action. The crossbows were pulled back but not loaded. You did not march with a quarrel in your crossbow. The arrows fell amongst them and their ranks were decimated. Even as bolts were loaded and crossbows raised another flight hurtled towards the crossbows and more men died. As the crossbows sent their first volley the third flight of arrows thinned their ranks by a further third. They had done their work and the lochagoi ordered their archers to retreat behind the Skutatoi.

The crossbows belatedly loosed their missiles and they rattled against shields which were not penetrated. Barely a handful of Imperial troops were struck. The demoralised crossbowmen marched back across the stream leaving large numbers of their men dead and wounded; the horsemen prepared their charge. I could see that the horses would not be approaching us at quite the speed they would have wished. There were bodies to negotiate on an already slippery and boggy ground. The horsemen formed an arrowhead. I learned from Basil that the Byzantines had recently been defeated in Greece by a Norman army of horsemen. It might have explained the confidence of the Norman knights as they came directly for the Imperial troops. Of course, it may have been because there were horsemen on our flanks. The Norman foot soldiers, their spearmen advanced towards the Count's horsemen. It was a clever strategy as it prevented our horsemen from engaging the Normans; they did not want to risk a flank attack.

Next to me, I heard Harlan singing a song. It sounded sad and mournful. My father had told me that he had heard the housecarls of Harold singing before the battle of Hastings. Perhaps that was what housecarls did. The formation used by the Normans meant that the arrows of the archers behind the skutatoi were more spread out but, even so, some horses were hit and threw their riders from their backs. The kite-shaped shields looked awkward to use but they afforded protection to the more experienced Normans who held them over their heads and their horse's too. The formation also meant that the Normans did not hit as one. There was a ripple of cracks as the Norman spears shattered on Byzantine shields.

My own shield suddenly felt too small and inadequate. I braced myself as Ralph had taught me with my left foot forward so that I could lean my left shoulder into the shield and keep my axe behind me. In the time since the Haugr I had grown and the horse which came at me did not seem as big as those first horses in Normandy. Its head would be level with my arm. I saw the horseman, he wore a long byrnie with a split to allow him to ride, as he stood in his stirrups to punch at me with his spear. I had used the axe many times but we had not been able to practise using it against horsemen and I knew I had to time my strike well. As the spearhead raced towards me, I began my swing. I had long arms and the haft of the axe was as long as my arm. Even as the spear hit and shattered on my shield my axe head was biting into the side of his horse's head. I had seen men despatch horses with a hammer and my axe did the same. The horse was mortally wounded and its legs buckled. I knew enough to move away from the dying horse which was hurling its rider from the saddle and the knight sailed through the air to land amongst the Lombards behind me. I heard their steel as they butchered him and I stepped back into the line.

I saw, as I did so, my three brothers in arms and Brother Paul swinging their two-handed weapons almost as one. Nothing could get close to them and I saw why my father had said that at Hastings the housecarls had stood on the ridge for so long. The Imperial arrows had thinned out the horsemen while the Norman spears had formed a hedgehog to stop the Lombard horses from flanking their own. This battle would be decided by the battle in the centre, my battle. The Norman spearmen to my left had some archers with them and they boldly stepped before their spears and began loosing hopeful arrows at the Lombard horsemen. It was nothing but when one of the lords there had his horse struck then they began a wild charge towards the annoying archers. It had not been planned but I had no opportunity to see if it succeeded or failed for the next line of Norman knights approached and this looked to be a familia for they all had the same design upon their shields. They were more disciplined and came as a line of eight. They were heading directly for the five of us. Now that the Lombards had deserted us we were a weak point in the line and if we could be broken then the horses could flood through and roll up our line. They would begin with me and then work their way along. My shield was Harlan's protection.

I risked taking a step to my right to bring me tighter to Harlan. I had to leave enough space to swing my arm but I found a flat piece of ground upon which to plant my feet. Two spears came for me and I suppose I should have been honoured that they thought me worthy of two spears. They could not see my face for my coif covered all but my eyes and they would not know that I was not quite a man. When the spears came at me, I would only be able to block one. I watched the two knights pull back their arms to strike at me and saw that one would come for my shield and one for my face. The slope and their control meant that they were not riding as fast or as recklessly as the first knight I had faced. The odds were that they would strike accurately and I dared not risk a swing yet. I heard a horse scream as Harlan's axe took a chunk from its shoulder. Even as the dying beast fell between Harlan and me the lances were coming at me. The lance which struck my shield shattered but it was the dying horse which saved me. It struck my right side and shifted me to the left so that the lance which had been coming for my eye scraped and scratched along my helmet. More crucially, the knight riding the doomed horse fell to his right and clattered into the knight who had just missed my eye. It was then that I brought over my axe from behind my head. The knight who had tried to take my eye was trying to pull back his arm to finish me off when my axe connected with his shoulder. His horse had lowered its head and I was level with the knight. The razor-sharp axe had only struck the horse and now it hacked through the mail and the gambeson beneath. The weight of my axe head and the strength of my arm drove it hard and it tore through muscle and then fractured the bones which were there. The knight screamed as I pulled back my arm for his horse had taken him beyond me and I did not wish the axe torn from my hand.

 The horse spun me around and I saw the two knights who had attacked me, one mortally wounded and the other with a shattered spear, surrounded by Lombards who hacked and chopped at them, As I swung around I saw that Harlan was exposed and a knight's spear drove into his unprotected left side. I was not there to protect him. The mortal wound did not stop him. He continued to swing and I ran at the knight who threw away his broken lance and began to draw his sword. I felt I had failed Harlan and I determined to make up for it. My axe came from on high to smash and hack into the Norman knight's right side. His mail split as though it was parchment and his scream was not only one of pain but of anger. I pulled back and swung sideways. He and his horse were stopped and I hacked through his leg below his byrnie. I took the leg in one blow and he fell to the other side of his horse, blood pumping from the wound. I charged the horse with my shield and the beast, now relieved of the knight turned and tried to run away from me. It was stopped by the other Normans who were trying to get at Ralph, Brother Paul and Garth. The Norman horse became our ally. As the horsemen tried to control their horses the axes of my brothers in arms took a terrible toll. The familia all died on that hillside.

I reached the side of Harlan who was barely standing. He nodded, "Thank you, Wulfstan!" Those were his last words to me for, summoning all the strength he had left to him he suddenly barged through the Norman knights swinging his axe like some kind of demon. He hit two knights and a horse before he was hacked and chopped by Normans whose spears had shattered but who had swords. Harlan died but he died like a man. I stepped close to Ralph. I saw that his mail was covered in blood and his axe was notched yet he appeared to be unhurt. The horse I had shoved and Harlan's actions had broken up the attack and I saw the Normans reorganising.

Ralph said, "That was a good death but let us hope that it is the last!"

I had heard that the Normans could fight on foot and I wondered if their long kite shields would hamper them. As they came towards me, I swung my axe a couple of times. My arm would begin to burn soon but all the practice in Nissa had paid off. The kite shield gives protection but it is difficult to lock with others and so the knights who approached us came as individuals and I looked at the knight who came at me. I could see just his eyes. His shield and surcoat showed horizontal stripes of yellow and red. Unlike my axe head which was notched his sword was sharp and keen. He swung his sword at my head and I saw then that I was a head taller than he was. I took the blow on my shield. When we had been in Nissa I had strengthened it with metal and the edge scraped along metal. His sword was no longer razor-sharp. Ralph had taught me to make blows with the flat of a sword to break arms and keep the edge. I brought my axe from behind me once he had made his strike and I brought all the force I could muster. He brought up his shield and I saw how narrow it was. The axe might be notched but it had a heavy head and was still sharp enough to cut into the wood. I saw his eyes widen as my blade bit. He reeled for I had hurt him and I stepped forward, swinging again. This time he could not raise his shield for his arm was either broken or so numbed that he could not. My axe split open his helmet and skull but his dying body dragged the axe from my hand.

I drew my sword and this time knew that I had a weapon with an edge. My last attack had taken me towards the Normans and two came at me. They had to negotiate bodies to do so and therein lay hope for me. Turning my sword so that I presented the flat side I swung towards the heads of the two Normans while holding my shield before me. They, too, stabbed and thrust at me but the flat of my blade connected with the shield of one of them and my swing was so hard that he lurched into the other. Their blows, in comparison to mine, were weak;

I was stronger and I twisted my sword and swung again at the nearest reeling Norman. He almost managed to block the blow with his shield but the hilt of my sword hit his shield and the blade hit him on the crown of his helmet. His eyes glazed as he fell backwards and I punched my shield into the face of the other. It was then I received my first wound. My attack had taken me towards the Normans and a knight to my right slashed at my leg. Although the byrnie took most of the force the edge laid open my calf. I had committed to my attack and so I ignored the pain and brought my sword up to strike under the arm of the knight with whom I was fighting. A second blow to my back knocked me and the knight to the ground, driving my sword up and through his body. He was dead but my sword was trapped. I turned to see the knight who had stabbed me and struck my back standing over me with his sword raised. I was young and I was quick. I had my dagger drawn and driven up under his byrnie to slash into his thigh before he even began his swing. I did not know it then but there is a mighty artery there and the Norman was transfixed above me for a heartbeat before, as blood cascaded over me, he collapsed across me. Had the battle not ended at that moment I might have died for I could not move. As it was, I heard horns and the Normans withdrew.

A grinning Ralph held his hand out for me as Brother Paul and Garth shifted the dead Norman from me. Shaking his head Ralph said, "One berserker is enough, Wulfstan! You did well but let us get your hurts attended to and your weapons recovered. This battle may not yet be over!"

Brother Paul tore a piece of the yellow and red surcoat into strips. "You were lucky, young warrior. I will stem the bleeding and after the next attack I will cleanse the wound properly!" He shook his head, "I see that you did not heed my advice but I am just pleased that Wulfstan lives!

I could see, just twenty paces from us, the body of Harlan, "Why did he rush to his death, Ralph?"

"Because he knew he was dying and better to take enemies with you than wait to be butchered."

I shook my head, "I did not mean to leave a gap. Have I killed Harlan as I killed my father?"

Ralph grabbed me by the shoulders, "You are a good warrior and did nothing wrong in either fight. If you had been in a shield wall like the skutatoi then perhaps there would be justification but you had the hardest task of all. You guarded the end of the line and when those Lombards forgot their own orders then our whole battle plan was in jeopardy." He pointed to the remnants of the cavalry who had charged the spearmen. "They have paid the price!"

Garth wandered over with my sword and my axe. "And you handled yourself not like a young warrior but a veteran. You did not get those skills from your father. God must have favoured you."

"Do not blaspheme, Garth. God does not make warriors!" Brother Paul shook his head.

"Believe what you will, priest, I know what I know and I have seen some men who should not be warriors and yet they seem to have ability born into them. Wulfstan is such a one."

Basil came over. He had bloody mail and I saw that his sword was badly notched. His helmet had dents, dints and scratches all over but he looked happy, "It looks like the battle is over. See, the Normans withdraw."

"They are defeated?"

"No, Wulfstan, but they have not won either. There must have been a plan and we know not what it is."

Brother Paul cleansed and bandaged my wound properly and we collected what was our due from the field. That evening we headed back to our camp and we heard that the Normans had, indeed, withdrawn back to the Dukedom. It was months later we learned the reason. The attack had been to fix the Byzantine attention to the north. They captured major towns to the south of us from the Byzantines. For them, this was a victory. When we reached our camp, with Harlan's body on the back of a captured horse and with our booty on other horses, Edward had food ready for us. He smiled when I asked him how he knew that we would be back.

"Riders brought news that our line had not been breached and that many Norman knights had died. I knew then."

Ralph said, "Before we eat let us bury our friend. Brother Paul will say the words." There was a small church close to the camp and men prayed there. There was a tiny cemetery and we buried Harlan. Ralph told the mound of earth that we would remember him with tales and stories. That was all that was left of warriors once they died. The memories of what they did and how their brothers in arms remembered them.

Reaching the camp, Edward waved at the pot, "And now I will head into the city."

I was surprised but the other two were not. We had been five and now, as Edward left us, we were three. I must have looked depressed for, as I picked at the food, Garth asked, "What troubles you, Wulfstan?"

"Harlan is dead and I thought that Edward would want to hear of the battle."

"And you wanted to tell him how well you fought?"

I coloured, "No, I, that is…"

"He will be back and then we will tell him how bravely you fought."

I looked at Garth for any hint of sarcasm or irony. There was none. "But why has he gone?"

Ralph laughed, "He has an itch and it needs scratching." I must have looked confused. "Margaret, in the city. They like each other and I think that it will just be the three of us from now on."

I was young and did not understand such things. I had lived with my father for so long alone and without the presence of a woman that I found women a mystery. When Edward did return, he was keen to know all that had happened. After we had told him he gave us news from the city… "The Count will come tomorrow to pay off the mercenaries. Our work here is done."

I shook my head, "And poor Harlan died and will have no reward."

"Not so, Wulfstan. The papers I signed were for the company. The money due to Harlan we will receive and he would be glad for us to have it. The money will be split four ways."

"But I am the youngest!"

"That makes no difference. We all took the same chances."

Edward put his good arm around me, "And even a one-armed man can be rewarded if he has loyal friends but I have to tell you, Ralph, that when we are paid off, I will stay here."

"Margaret?"

He smiled, "Old Sophia now has grandchildren and her daughter's husband has land. She is willing to sell the tavern."

Ralph said, "And with your share of the payment and the share from the sale of the booty you should have enough."

He shook his head, "I cannot take your booty for I did nothing to earn it!"

Garth snorted, "You are of our company! And you have fed us well, none of us, even the boy here, would deny you a quarter share."

"I thank you."

"And besides when we are tired of warring we can come and drink in your tavern."

"Where you will be more than welcome."

Knights had been captured and ransoms demanded. That, allied to the fact that we had not been defeated, meant that we received all that we were due. I did not understand it until Edward pointed his good arm at the harbour, "This port receives trade from the Empire and that is the lifeblood of the city. Had the Count lost it then he would have lost all of his money and his power. It is money well spent but he will be glad when you all leave. Already the Imperial ships have been summoned."

One of the conditions demanded by Old Sophia was that Edward marry Margaret and so we attended the wedding with Brother Paul and Basil. As we headed back to camp, all of us having enjoyed Sophia's hospitality, Basil announced that he and his bandon would be gone by the end of the week.

"We will miss you. For Greeks, you were quite pleasant company!"

Basil laughed, "And my men appreciated your efforts when you fought alongside us but you should come with us."

"We are no skutatoi!"

"No, but the Emperor needs Varangians and after the battle of Dyrrhachium, he needs to fill the ranks again. I would speak on your behalf. The money is better than you received from the Count."

We had been paid, I thought, a fortune and if we were paid more then I thought it worth doing but I was the youngest and knew that I had little say in the matter.

Ralph said, "When my head is clear we will speak again."

The next morning, I was given the task of cooking. I had watched and helped Edward so often that I could emulate him. As I did so we spoke of the offer. Garth said, "We have little to lose. If we do not like it then we leave and find work elsewhere."

Ralph was not convinced, "But we do not know what the world will be like. These are Easterners! They have different customs!"

Garth laughed, "Since we left England every people we have met have different customs! We hew heads and it matters not the colour of the skin or the religion of the man we kill. We work for pay and we are men without a land but let us ask Wulfstan. He has stirred the pot but not ventured a view."

"Me? I will go along with whatever you two decide."

"No, Wulfstan, you are an equal and you have an equal say. What is your opinion?"

"I agree with Garth. We have no land and we cannot return home. If we did then we would be regarded as an enemy and while I do not mind fighting and killing Normans they are like fleas on a dog. It seems to me that we can still fight Normans and be well paid for doing so."

Garth beamed, I had given him the answer he wanted, "Good, then I will speak with Basil and we will sail for Miklagård."

As we headed south-east in the imperial transports guarded by Imperial vessels, I could not know how much my life would change. I could not know that I would never see Edward again nor that I would return to England for those parts of my life had not been written but from that moment on I never regretted for one instant the fact that I had joined Ralph and Garth on an adventure into the unknown. I had lost one father at the Haugr but gained two and I was all the richer for it. I would no longer be Wulfstan the English warrior I would become, along with Garth and Ralph, a Varangian Guard of the Byzantine Emperor!

The End

If you enjoyed this book then try reading **'The English Knight'**, the first book in the Anarchy series by Griff Hosker

The Hostile Land

I am Sir Robert of Jericho and I live with my wife and stepson in the land where Christ was born. I did not choose this life; fate chose it for me. I began life as a humble man at arms, Robert of Mont St. Michel and I was a Norman. I was not born of a noble family; my father had been a man at arms and when he had been wounded, he returned to the farm where his parents had lived and he eked out a living making salt and raising sheep. He ensured that I was trained as a warrior from the first moment that I was able to run. He did not enjoy the life he led but knew that he could no longer fight as a man at arms. When I was big enough then he gave me his mail and his sword.

My life might have been spent in Normandy if the Warlord, the Earl of Cleveland, had not hired me as a man at arms. The Warlord was fighting in France for the Empress Matilda and her son, Henry. Battling the French and King Stephen was expensive for men died. He saw in me a good warrior and I was hired. I followed his son, William of Ouistreham, to the Holy Land and there I was knighted. King Baldwin gave me the manor of Jericho. Some thought it was a poisoned chalice but I was given it when I married the widow of the knight who had died defending it, Lady Sarah. Taking her and her son Henry into my life was the best thing that I ever did. True, when Sir William left for England, I chose to stay in the land of the Turk and the Frank. It was a hard decision to make and I felt the loss severely for only Edward, my squire, remained. However, life was good and for a few years, we were happy. The manor was a poor one but I tried all that I could to make it worthy of my wife. I hired half a dozen men at arms and I began to train the Christians who farmed in the manor. They were not the men I had fought alongside with Sir William, but they would do. Edward was a good squire and learned quickly. More, he helped to train Sarah's son and he would, in turn, become a good warrior. Life was good and I envisaged a peaceful end to my life of war. That dream was shattered by two things, the rise of Nur al-Din and the infighting between the Frankish rulers of the lands of Outremer. Even King Baldwin and his brother Amalric became involved in what was, effectively, a land grab.

At first, I was unaware of these changes. I had much to do ensuring that my lands were safe from bandits and that my farmers prospered. In ancient times Jericho had been a large and important city. Now it was little more than an overgrown village. I was a warrior and not a farmer and I had to rely upon the Franks who lived in my manor.

The first moment I knew that something was amiss was when I received a summons to join King Baldwin who, it was rumoured, intended to head towards Egypt to deal with an attack on the southern lands by the Egyptians. Since the battle of Ascalon, that border had been safe. The Knights Templars, Hospitallers and Teutonic knights all maintained garrisons in the castles they had built. In a perfect world these warrior monks would all have had the same purpose; to make the Holy Land Christian, but, like Count Raymond of Tripoli and Humphrey of Toron, they were more concerned with strengthening their own lands. I had no choice for King Baldwin was my liege lord and I had to take men to follow him. We were to muster at Ascalon which was where I had fought for the last time with Sir William.

I was unhappy to be called forth to fight for it meant leaving my manor unprotected and I took just four of my men at arms with me. Wilfred, Jack of Tilbury, Karl the Swede and Ralph of Tewksbury were all good men and I was happier knowing I had left my wife and family protected by the rest. Henry, of course, wished to come but I denied him the opportunity. Part of it was a concern for his safety but more important was the fact that I did not know if he had the required skill! The Holy Land was not the place to learn to fight!

I was not a young man when I married and I enjoyed my married life. So it was that leaving my wife was harder than I had expected it to be. I wondered if the years of peace had softened me. I had put that life from me as I prepared the animals and war gear that we would need to fight in the inhospitable lands south of Gaza. One resource I had accumulated was good horseflesh. The Holy Land seemed to eat horses. Both Edward and I rode coursers and the palfreys my men at arms used were solid horses. The spare horses carried the war gear we would need. I used spears instead of lances and that was because the Warlord had used them. They were easier to transport and, in my view, a better weapon. Only I wore a full mail hauberk. My men at arms and Edward wore the short one which left their legs exposed. We needed more money to buy better hauberks and I needed all the coin I could manage just for the upkeep of the manor. Until we had sustained peace then we would be living from hand to mouth. If we could defeat the Egyptians then that might bring peace but I was not confident about that outcome.

The road from Jericho to Ascalon was not an easy one for there were many brigands and bandits on the road. They preyed on Christian and Muslim alike. Women might be safe but only in as much as they would be ransomed. Men would be slain. I had not fought since Ascalon and I had not fought with my new men at arms. I was confident in their ability but there was something about fighting with a man that you knew which increased your chances of success. This campaign would show me the mettle of my men. Edward had improved since Ascalon and, as we rode south and west, I saw him scanning the hillsides for signs of danger. The other four were too and showed that they had fought in this land long enough to be wary and vigilant. Each time we approached travellers our hands went to the weapons hidden beneath the robes we wore. We had learned to wear clothes such as those worn by Muslims. Plain and white, they kept us cooler than wearing a surcoat and mail. You could always tell those who were new to the Holy Land. It was not just their red faces, it was that they wore their livery for all to see. Even the military orders wore the garments but they had their order's marks upon them.

Once we reached Jerusalem then we could breathe a sigh of relief. It was only fourteen miles from my manor and we arrived in daylight and were able to find accommodation. King Baldwin was still in his palace but, as we spoke with the other knights who had heeded the summons, we discovered that many had already left for the muster. The King's steward explained to me where we would muster and my commitments. He handed me the warrant which would grant me refreshments and shelter, should I need them, on the road to Ascalon. As so many knights had left already for Ascalon I was invited to dine at the King's table. He would not be eating with the knights who attended for he was a solitary man. It gave me the opportunity to meet some of the other knights alongside whom I would be fighting.

Most of them were like me, knights who had been rewarded with parcels of land as a thanks for service to the King of Jerusalem. As such, I got on well with them. One I did not get on with was Hugh de Lusignan for he was a newcomer who had done nothing for King Baldwin and yet appeared to be feted and honoured just for being in Jerusalem. His family were powerful in Poitou and thought that they should rule. I had met many like him when I served Sir William for there were Normans and English knights just like him; self-serving. Hugh de Lusignan sought a kingdom and if I had been King Baldwin then I would have had him sent from my land for it was obvious to me that he sought Jerusalem. The evidence was clear to see. Although the King was not in attendance there were important counts who owed fealty to King Baldwin and they occupied the high table. Hugh de Lusignan had managed to inveigle himself in their company. I had been born a common soldier and Sir William had elevated me and I recognised someone who had not an ounce of nobility in their body in an instant. Hugh de Lusignan was such a one. He smiled and fawned at the counts and lords but sneered at the knights who were on lower tables. I was just glad that I was not in his eye line. Had he sneered at me then I would have spoken to him. I was not one to suffer insults for I was born a warrior and knew my own worth. There were few men who could last long in a bout against me.

I turned, instead, to speak with the knight next to me, Amaury of Senonche. He had come with King Louis as a crusader and had met and married the daughter of a knight of Anjou, Guy of Tours. He was younger than I was and reminded me of Sir William. He had yet to fight in the Holy Land but he was keen to do so. His manor was a rich one and it showed in his garments.

"I was lucky, Sir Robert, when Eloise's father died without a son, I inherited his manor. It has terraces and grows good wine I cannot imagine how you survive in Jericho. The Turks raid there do they not?"

I washed the food down with wine and nodded, "But not since I have been there. We keep a good watch and the battle of Ascalon ended that threat, albeit briefly."

"What do you mean?"

I lowered my voice, "I know that this Nur al-Din is a threat but, thus far, he has not made an attempt to attack the fortresses which lie to the south of us. They were built for a purpose. Now that he has Edessa, he seems content to stay there. I believe we go to take land from the Egyptians and that that the King has been badly advised. This campaign can only stir up a hornet's nest."

"But the King must know best!"

I nodded towards the high table where their strident voices showed the effects of wine, "The King listens, I fear, to the voices of others."

"Yet you will ride behind his banner."

I nodded, "For I owe him fealty and I am a man of my word but that does not mean I am happy about this."

"I would ride with you and your men on the morrow, if you are happy to do so."

"Of course. The journey is better undertaken with pleasant company."

After we had dined, I headed back to the inn where my squire and men at arms awaited me. Wilfred was the closest in age to me and he watched me approach, "Did all go well, my lord? We still ride to Ascalon?"

"Aye, we do, Wilfred." He simply nodded. Nothing seemed to upset Wilfred who was something of an enigma. When he had come to me, I had asked him his name and he had replied, simply, '*Wilfred*'!"

When I had pushed him, for most men had some association with the place they were born, he had simply said, 'I am Wilfred and I was born in a camp in Aquitaine. *Wilfred of some long-forgotten road in Aquitaine who never knew his father and whose mother died when he was still a babe*, seems a bit of a mouthful, lord, and so I am Wilfred. It suits me and men know me. I am content.'

And that was his way yet he was one of the most skilled soldiers I had ever known. I had been born the son of a wounded warrior forced to become a farmer fisherman and had not relished the prospect of making salt, raising sheep and gathering shellfish. Wilfred had been born to a band of hired swords. I suspected that they had been brigands at times but I did not press him. The fact is he had learned skills which I could only dream of. I could use a sword, axe and spear but Wilfred could also use a warbow and he handled pole weapons with such dexterity that men soon learned to fear him when we trained.

"We will have to keep our wits about us on the road tomorrow, my lord. If knights have been travelling south then the bandits will be watching for a small contingent. We would seem to fit the bill."

"We do not ride alone. Sir Amaury of Senonche and his men will ride with us."

He looked relieved, "Where do we meet them?"

"David's Gate."

"I will tell the others. Goodnight, my lord."

It was strange, Wilfred was doing the same job I had done for Sir William and yet I still did not feel like a knight. Sir William had dubbed me and I wore spurs but I felt a fraud. I knew that had I not been a lord then I could never have married Lady Sarah and saw, in that single act, the hand of a higher being for Sarah and I were meant to be together. Henry needed a father and although I doubted that I would ever sire a son of my own, Henry was everything I would have hoped for in a son. When I returned from this campaign I would begin, in earnest, his training.

Sir Amaury was obviously wealthier than I was for he had ten men at arms and eight crossbowmen with him. I would have preferred archers. I had seen how effective they could be but they were as rare as hen's teeth here in the Holy Land and the Seljuq Turk was as good an archer as I had ever seen. Despite the fact that Sir Amaury's men outnumbered mine it was Wilfred who took charge and gave commands. It says much about him that none took offence. His voice was commanding and demanded respect. He and Jack of Tilbury rode ahead as scouts. Edward and Robert, Sir Amaury's squire, rode behind.

Sir Amaury had been accommodated in the palace and he said, confidentially, as we headed south and west, "De Lusignan is a powerful man."

I nodded, "How do you know? Did he tell you?"

He laughed, "Are you a fortune teller that you can know such things? Aye, he did."

"Then he has no power at all for those with power do not boast of it. A word of advice, Sir Amaury, watch how men fight on a battlefield before you judge them." He nodded. "You have fought over here, have you not?"

"Aye, but not in the major battles. However, I know what you mean. I will heed your advice for I can see by the scars you bear that you have been a warrior and your men have the look of stout men who know their business."

We reached Ascalon without any attacks materialising and we made our camp amongst the small army the King was sending south. As with all such camps, there was a hierarchy and the higher one's standing, then the closer to the King one was placed. Sir Amaury had more standing than I but I had so few men with me that we were able to fit into the space we were allocated. I saw that de Lusignan had a very high standing indeed for his tents were placed within twenty paces of the King. His time in the palace of Jerusalem had not been wasted!

The King followed two days later. I wondered at this delay for we were on the main road to Egypt and the Muslims would know that we were coming. Sir Amaury did not seem concerned. "We have a mighty army, Sir Robert, and the military orders will almost double our numbers."

That worried me for, thus far we had only seen one company of Hospitallers. In my experience, they were the most reliable of the orders but one company would not save King Baldwin. We did, however, meet other knights in whom I did have faith. Like me, they had few retainers and were the remnants of other expeditions to save the Holy Land. While we awaited the King's arrival, we spent time together. Such meetings were never wasted for you learned much about a man from the way he spoke of his experiences in battle. Sir Amaury was the youngest of us and it showed in his naïve observations and conclusions.

When the King did arrive, he met with his leaders and they held a council of war. Of course, none of the nights who had been rewarded with manors for their fighting ability was invited despite the fact that we had much collective experience of fighting the Seljuq Turks. We all gravitated towards the King's tents where his bodyguards kept us a respectful distance. The council did not last above an hour and it became clear that Raymond of Tripoli was the most important leader other than the King when, at the end of the council, he and the King retired to the King's tent. De Lusignan was with them!

The King's Lieutenant and standard-bearer, Geoffrey of Nablus, waved us all closer and the guards let us approach, "The King's Council has made its decision. We will head south, towards Gaza, on the morrow. We depart at Lauds."

That made sense. The church service, Lauds, which was held in the hours of darkness was the coolest time to travel. I began to become more hopeful. It was only as we took the road, while it was still chilly, that I realised the only military order which rode with us were the Knights Hospitallers and that we were woefully short of archers. Geoffrey of Nablus knew me for when King Baldwin had agreed to allow me to marry Lady Sarah, he had been a young knight in the King's retinue and had been charged with dealing with me. As he passed us, I hailed him, "Sir Geoffrey."

He recognised my voice and rode next to me, "Sir Robert, I hope that Lady Sarah and her son are well?"

"They are."

"Good."

I lowered my voice, "Sir Geoffrey, where are the Templars and the Teutonic Knights?"

He leaned towards me, "There has been a falling out between the Masters of the orders. It is a dispute concerning a castle which lies close to the County of Tripoli."

My heart sank, "And the Hospitallers?"

"The Grand Master, Hugues de Revel, is away on some mission to Cyprus. There is also in-fighting going on there which is why we have but one company." He smiled at the obvious dismay upon my face, "Fear not for we have Count Raymond and he is a wise head and brings almost half of our army. It is good that the other leaders support King Baldwin."

"But the Holy Orders?"

"We can manage with what we already have. And now I must organise the baggage."

I was less sure that we could manage and, as we headed south, I began to fear for this expedition. The Muslims had to know that we were headed for Egypt. Why else would a Christian Army under the King of Jerusalem gather at Ascalon? I did not think, for one moment, that they would wait for us to arrive at their borders and then muster an army to meet us. They would fight as far north from their borders as they could and make us bleed on our land. Gaza and Darum were the border fortresses but Darum, although a royal castle, had a small garrison. It was there we made our last halt before heading towards the border. The lord of Darum was an old Crusader knight. Sir Hugh of

Darum had been part of the Second Crusade. He hailed from England and I knew that Sir William had respected the old knight for he understood what drove him. He was a knight to whom honour and duty were more important than land and power. Sir Hugh was more like Sir William's father. The King, Count and their entourage were accommodated in the keep with Sir Hugh. I met with him in our camp, and I was greeted like an old friend for he respected warriors above all else.

"Good to see you thus elevated, Robert. You deserved it. And how is Sir William?"

"He has gone back to England to fight for his father in the war against the Usurper."

Sir Hugh nodded, "I was torn between following the cross and following the Empress." He looked sadly south, "I wonder if I made the right decision. This host is not big enough to defeat the Muslims, Robert, you know that." I nodded. "This is like taking a stick to poke into a snake's hole. All that it will do is to annoy it for we cannot hurt it but one bite and …this cannot end well. The King, I fear, is ill-advised."

I wondered then about the hidden motives of the Kings advisers. You cannot see into a man's mind and that had been another reason which had driven Sir William back to England. There were other knights like de Waller, the knight who had tried to kill Sir William and the family of his wife, Rebekah, and they sought a different outcome to this Holy War than did King Baldwin. The King wished peace in Jerusalem while for others it was in their interest to maintain the conflict as they gained land and power when there was war.

"And have you any intelligence about the enemy?"

"I fear my garrison is four knights, ten archers and twenty men at arms." He waved a hand around the camp, "I see as far as this and no further." He looked old and sad, "I will die here in this last outpost of the Christian world. I pray that it guarantees my place in heaven for if not then I have deserted my own country for nothing."

I fell into a pit of despair for I had hoped that I had been wrong and, perhaps, there was a good reason for this ill-advised expedition. I saw now that I was right. Had I doomed Lady Sarah to becoming a widow for a second time? I could not do as my heart wished and leave to return to her side; I had to see this out to the end. I had learned, from Sir William and his father, that it was always better to keep your own men informed and so I took a walk to the horse lines with my squire and four men.

"I fear that this expedition is doomed." They merely nodded and, Edward apart, showed no emotion for they were all professional soldiers.

Edward chewed his bottom lip and asked, "Then should we not leave?"

Wilfred snorted, "Master Edward, you have a long journey before you can become a knight. Our duty is to fight for Sir Robert and his to fight for the King of Jerusalem. You do not cut and run because you think you might die! We all die and it is just a case of how we face that death that marks us as men. Sir Robert, what do we do?"

"When we fight then, regardless of the orders, you five will ride behind me. We will fight as the men of Jericho. I want you all close enough to hear my commands and to obey them regardless of any horns. I do not intend to throw our lives away here in this wasteland but neither will I desert my King, while he lives." I am not sure that Edward understood the importance of my words but my four men at arms did and they nodded. It meant we would leave the battlefield when the King died and not wait for the banners to fall. I began to see why Sir William had headed home; this was not a place where men fought for God. This was a place where men fought for what they could grab and hold.

We seemed a small number as we headed south from Darum. Sir Hugh and his small garrison remained behind the walls of Darum, or, as the Egyptians called it, al-Darum. They were like a monastic community. There were no women and their existence was a bleak one. When we left they would have to await our return either as victors or, as I suspected, the vanquished. Worryingly we did not ride with scouts ahead of us and we moved at a snail's pace, not that I had ever seen a snail in this hot land. Once again, we had left at Lauds to travel in the cool of the night and when we stopped shelters were erected for the King, Count Raymond and the other leaders. The Hospitallers prayed. I had ensured that we had plenty of water as Darum had a good well. I had advised Sir Amaury to do the same. He seemed to be willing to take suggestions from me and, indeed, appeared to regard me as some sort of mentor. He was unique in that. The other knights did not regard me as a knight but a lucky sergeant who had had one promotion too many! I did not mind as I knew my own worth. The Warlord and Sir William had been good teachers and, more importantly, the best judges of men that I had met. We drank and we made certain our horses did too.

We left when the heat of the day had passed and it was a mere ten miles later that we found the Egyptian army. They appeared as a dusty mirage on the southern horizon. If we had had scouts then we might have spotted them. In light of subsequent events I am not certain that would have helped us for it was a huge army and more than half was mounted. We immediately halted and I turned to Sir Amaury and the men I led, "Prepare for war!"

My men obeyed instantly and, like me, they rolled up their cloaks and fastened them to their saddles. Sir Amaury asked, "Why? It is clear that there will be talks first!"

"Sir Amaury, if you wish to see another sunrise then do as my men do. We do not fight a Christian army we fight Muslims. When they come, they will come as swiftly as a leopard hunting a gazelle and we will be that gazelle."

He did as I said. Even as I watched the Fatimid Egyptians formed their battle lines. They had a large number of mercenary mounted horse archers and they formed up before their askari who were the Muslim equivalent of knights and men at arms. The half which was on foot, the Sudanese, formed a solid third block. I saw, whirling around the edges of their army the Bedouin who were wild warriors wearing no mail whatsoever and riding both camels and horses. They were the most unpredictable element of the Fatimid army for each followed their own clan leader and could be as braves as any or they could run if the mood of the leader changed. As I mounted my horse, I saw that the King had finished his discussion and Count Raymond took his contingent, more than a third of our army, to the right. We were given no orders but I led our handful of men to join those who were arrayed to the King's left. The Hospitallers were sent to the far left where they could protect that flank so that the King had the knights of Jerusalem around him. We had some archers and crossbowmen and they dismounted and formed a frighteningly thin line before us. Sir Amaury's crossbowmen had left their horses and gone to join the other crossbowmen. They were all good men but I wondered if they were marching to their deaths. At least we had a line to face the Egyptians. Even as our priests were walking down the line to bless us and as men prayed, the Egyptians charged.

The ground over which they charged was flat and covered in scrubby plants and rocks; I could only hope that their horses might trip in some hole or stumble across a rock. I lowered my face mask and pulled up my shield while I rested my spearhead across my cantle. My world narrowed to the slits in my helmet. There were ten other knights between the King and I. Sir Amaury and I were the only ones with our men at arms lined up with us. Edward rode at my right and Wilfred at my left.

I heard King Baldwin shout, "For God and Jerusalem!" It made me turn to look at him and, as I did so I saw Count Raymond lead the knights of Tripoli north, towards Darum! The treacherous snake had abandoned us and we now had our right flank exposed and barely half the men who had arrayed before the Egyptians! I would reflect on the desertion later but, at that moment, I just began to work out how we could escape this death trap. We were already outnumbered and now had no chance of victory. If we turned and fled then the archers and crossbowmen who had dismounted would be slaughtered while the horse archers would pursue us and rain arrows on unprotected backs and I knew enough of King Baldwin to know that he would never abandon Christians. Fortunately, the men who had the bows and crossbows had not seen the men of Tripoli flee. They assumed that all was well. In ignorance lay bliss for if they fled then the whole army would be destroyed.

Horse archers are good but they have some weaknesses. Firstly, their bows do not have the range of a warbow and their quality is varied. When they are good, they are deadly accurate but as with all such conscripted armies, there are weak areas. They would only release their arrows when they were less than eighty paces from us. They would rely on the large number of arrows they sent hitting enough of us to weaken us. The crossbows and war bows which faced them had a much longer range. The arrows would be sent into the air while the crossbows would send their bolts on a flat trajectory. The captain who commanded them knew his business and the arrows and bolts flew when the horse archers were one hundred and fifty paces from us. They punched a wide hole across the front of the line of charging horsemen. While the crossbowmen laboured to reload the archers had sent a second and third flight at the horse archers. Some of the crossbows managed a second flight before the Egyptian arrows flew. The men on foot had done enough to diminish the Egyptian arrow storm but men still fell and they were the archers and crossbows. Their captain hurriedly pulled them back behind our line of knights. Sir Amaury had lost three of his crossbowmen and the rest ran back to their horses. A crossbow cannot send a bolt on any other trajectory than flat. The Egyptian arrows had been aimed at the King and the men closest to him. Two of the knights to my right fell and the standard-bearer lurched.

"Edward, move your horse to the right, closer to the King!" We had all trained well and our horses crabbed sideways. It would put us at risk but we had to protect the King. I could not understand how the men of Tripoli could have abandoned their post.

Behind the horse archers, I saw the askari galloping towards us. The horse archers sent one more shower at us before wheeling away. While all of my men had the technique of using a kite shield to protect horse and rider from the arrows one of Sir Amaury's did not and I saw him fall. Two of those assigned to protect the King had also sacrificed themselves by using their shields to stop the arrows hitting the King. The arrows did not pierce their mail but the knights were wounded. One man who had stayed with the King was a former Templar, Henri of Chartres and it was he who gave the only order which might save us, "Sound the charge!" It was the right order to give, although it sounded suicidal. If we allowed the askari to strike us while we did not move then we would lose. Our only chance was to use our greater weight of mail and horseflesh and smash into them. The horn sounded and I spurred Remus. He was a good warhorse and he leapt forward. I lowered my spear and looked for an enemy.

Our line was not as straight as one might have wished. Some men were fearful and did not ride as hard while others did not have horses which had been watered at the rest and were tired. We were, however, all moving forward and together. Edward was slightly behind me and I did not mind that but Wilfred's right boot touched my left and I felt confident. The askari warriors who faced us wore the bayda, or egg-shaped helmet and some had a full-face mail ventail. I knew that below their tunics they had a lamellar cuirass. My men, Edward included, knew the best place to spear these askari but I had not had the opportunity to tell Sir Amaury or his men. They would learn that the best place was just above the cantle of the saddle and that a downward struck blow would drive the spear under the cuirass into soft flesh. As Remus was larger than any of the askari horses I saw then I would not need to stand in my saddle. The amirs who led the askari were encased in mail. I was just grateful that we faced none. They were riding for the King and I did not envy Henri of Chartres and those who were protecting him and the standards!

All of that went from my head as I closed with the askari. I saw that two of them were edging towards Edward. He had an open-faced helmet and wore no spurs. The Egyptians would go for an easy kill if they could. I began to turn Remus and spurred him to prevent two men from skewering my squire. The result was a good one. I managed to strike the nearest askari in the side. I had no cantle to surmount and my spearhead slid, unobstructed into the Egyptian's side. Even as the man tumbled from his saddle to hit the other warrior, I felt an askari lance hit my shield. All the years of training paid off and I barely moved. Edward made his first kill as he speared the askari my dead enemy had struck and I saw the horse of the askari who had struck me, riderless. Wilfred had done his job. We had punched a hole in the Egyptian line.

The second line of Egyptians had left enough space before them for men to fall and so I had the chance to rein in Remus and allow Edward and my men to catch up with me. Sir Amaury was also there but he had lost men. The furious and fierce battle was around the King and the standard. To my left, the ever efficient Hospitallers had won their battle and we were, in effect, swinging our front around. Had the Count of Tripoli still been on the field we might have held them but the King was being assailed on two sides. I shouted, "Begin to wheel right!" By doing so we would be exposing the men on my left to the full force of the Egyptian attack but we would relieve some of the pressure from the King.

It was only a subtle change for we were moving quickly and we had to stay as close together as we could. I knew that I was putting at risk Sir Amaury's men but we had no choice; if the King or the standard fell then the army would flee and more of us would die. It also meant that we were striking the askari from their spear side while our shields would protect us from their attacks. Remus was a warhorse though and the askari horses were weaker; he began to snap and bite at their animals. My horse was as good a weapon for me as my sword. Some of the Egyptians saw what was happening and tried to wheel to face us. It merely accelerated their fate. One jerked his horse around too much and the animal could not keep its legs. It fell in a tumble and would have brought down Edward had he not had the wit to stand in his stirrups and pull up the head of his horse to leap over the Egyptian and his horse.

And then I had to focus on the men before me. I rammed my spear not just into the side of the amir I faced but through him. His mail hauberk tore the spear from my hands but he was dead for I saw the spearhead protruding from the other side of his body. I drew my sword as our wheeling line began to turn. I saw that the King and his retinue were completely surrounded. "To the King!" Edward's leap had helped him to spear another askari and Wilfred and my other men had hacked their way through the amir's bodyguard so that we were behind the askari trying to get at the King. It meant our backs were exposed and we would be reliant on the men of Sir Amaury; this would their test for they could protect us or run!

The askaris and their amirs were trying to get at King Baldwin. He was a brave king but he was no warrior king. I watched as two Egyptians surrounded Henri of Chartres. He fought one but was lanced by a second. Still, he did not cease fighting. With a spear sticking from him he laid about with his sword. He was buying the King time and I spurred Remus towards them. I was too late to save Henri but he wounded both of his opponents. One askari lasted a heartbeat longer than Henri. I brought my sword across the back of the askari and cut through to the bone. The amir who had killed the King's lieutenant turned and swung his sword at me. Standing in my stirrups I blocked the blow with my shield and then hacked down towards his shoulder. The Muslims wore good mail but my sword was expensive and one of the best that money could buy. Razor-sharp, it hacked into the silk outer tunic, through the mail and into the shoulder. I heard the crack as his collar bone broke and I was able to push him from his saddle.

Wilfred and Karl the Swede were ferocious. If they lacked some of the skill of the Egyptian amirs they faced, they more than made up for it with sheer power and strength. They slew the three askari trying to get at the standards. We had been lucky for we had attacked the rear of the Egyptian but both standard-bearers were wounded.

I raised my face mask and shouted, "King Baldwin, we must fall back to Darum! With the men of Tripoli fled we will be butchered." He hesitated and I could not see his face. I pleaded with him. "So long as the standards remain then men will die!

He nodded and turned to his squire, "Sound the retreat!"

As he turned so I shouted, "Protect the King! To me!" and then lowered my face mask.

I had Edward and four men with me. I looked and saw that Sir Amaury had four men and his crossbowmen left. Most of the King's bodyguard had perished at the hands of the Egyptians. As the two standards turned and the others heard the horns so men fled. This would not be pretty and many men would die but fewer would die than if we stayed to be butchered. The ones with the better horses and mail would be the ones who would survive. I saw that the archers and crossbowmen had seen the end was nigh and they were already half a mile up the road. Many would be caught but some might escape.

Without being told my men spread out behind me and Sir Amaury and his surviving men were behind us. The King and his two wounded standard-bearers, as well as his squire and the other wounded knights, had some protection but we had many miles to go to reach Darum. My hope was that the wretched Count of Tripoli and de Lusignan would have warned the garrison there and they would give any who pursued us a hard time. The Egyptians had to deal with those who were slower than we were and, sad though it was, the deaths of those men bought us time. We also passed men on foot who had fled first and begged for us to ride double. It was a hard decision to make but we had to refuse. Had we done so then we would have all been captured and killed and nothing would have been achieved. When the Egyptians caught up with them their only hope was to fight and to try to capture a horse or two. The men we passed were, in the main, archers and crossbowmen. They had a chance, slim though it was.

Our horses were tiring. We had been riding since before dawn and although we were not galloping hard, we were still sapping energy from them. The Egyptians, in contrast, had fresher horses and being without mail were catching us. We would have to fight them before we reached safety. I glanced over my shoulder to work out when we would need to do so. The flight of our army had actually aided us for men did not keep to the road and used the land on either side. The fact that it was rough did not appear to bother them as they hunted the isolated groups of men who had fled there. The pursuit was equally spread out. I also saw that we had, miraculously, managed to save more of the army than we might have had we stood and fought. The better knights were using their horses to try to get away from the Egyptians.

It was their archers who caught us. The first we knew was when one of Sir Amaury's men shouted and clutched his shoulder. He was a man at arms and his mail was not of the quality of mine or his master's. He was a tough man and he stayed in the saddle with the arrow sticking from his back. Wounds to us and our men we could cope with but not wounds to our horses. We had passed the place where we had stopped to rest and I knew that we had just eight miles to go to reach the sanctuary that was Darum but it would be a long eight miles. I had allowed the King to get further ahead of us but when one of his standard-bearers fell from his horse the King stopped.

I cursed under my breath, "Noble fool!" The standard-bearer was expendable; the King was not. I shouted, "Ride, Your Majesty, we will see to him!" If I had to, I would leave him for this was a ruthless and unforgiving world. Edward and King Baldwin's squire picked up the man and his standard. They dumped him unceremoniously on to his horse and tied the standard and the man to the saddle. The squire took the reins and we set off. The delay could not have been shorter but arrows flew toward us. Edward, for his trouble, took one in the shoulder and I felt three hit my back. I was a big target. Wilfred was struck in the left arm.

Shouting, "Ride, King Baldwin!" I turned my horse and growled, "Let us bloody a few noses."

I knew from the punch of the arrow that they were close and the last thing they expected was for us to turn. We rode, filled with anger at our wounds, and clattered into the nearest band of Egyptians. A horse archer wears no mail and rides a light horse. They rely on speed and being able to gallop away from trouble. Our sudden attack took them completely by surprise. My sword's slash almost severed the body of one archer in two. I saw Wilfred's sword actually take the head of another and it sailed through the air! The effect of our attack was instantaneous. We slew nine before they realised we had turned and then they wheeled around and ran. I had done that which I had hoped and I said, "Back to the King! Well done!" An empty saddle showed that another of Sir Amaury's men had paid the price of the Count of Tripoli's treachery.

The gates of Darum were closed as the King and the knights and men who had gravitated to him approached the fortress. My men and I had dropped back a little in case there was another incident. The doors only swung open as the King closed to within two hundred paces of them. Just before we passed beneath, I saw a bareheaded Sir Hugh on the gatehouse's fighting platform. He had a face as black as thunder. Once in the outer bailey, we dismounted. It was only after I had stepped down from an exhausted Remus and asked Sir Amaury to see to our men, and raced up the steps to join him, that I realised that darkness had almost fallen. The last few miles had been ridden through the twilight. It was no wonder that the gates had remained barred. They could not discern who we were.

As I reached him, he shook his head, "A grim business Sir Robert! When the Count and his men headed north without stopping, we feared the worst. Thanks be to God that King Baldwin survived."

"It is worse than that, Sir Hugh. The Count and those who fled never even drew sword. They ran when the Egyptians arrayed."

He looked shocked and then nodded, "Just so! This was treachery!" I cocked an eye. "When you stayed here on your way south one of my servants reported to me that he overheard a knight, he thought it was de Lusignan, asking what would be the signal. The Count became angry and told him to be silent. Had the Count not done so then Peter would not have suspected anything but he thought it strange that there was a signal which was a secret one. Peter had been a Crusader until he was hamstrung. He knows how to fight a battle." I said nothing but stared at the stream of men who fled to the castle. The Egyptians had slowed their advance and those who were still alive had a chance. "Sir Robert, you are silent. Speak, I pray you for we are now the King's hope."

I nodded, "I had thought my mind was too convoluted and full of snakes. I believed I saw plots where there were none but now, I can see that I was wrong. I wondered at this campaign which seemed to me a pointless and dangerous exercise. De Lusignan was at the King's side until the Count of Tripoli arrived. We must speak with the King."

"Aye, for if the Egyptians have routed the army of Jerusalem then that will encourage them to finish us off. It is many miles twixt here and Jerusalem. The King is not safe!"

The King was with his wounded men in the hospital in the fort. He looked up when we approached. King Baldwin had a skin complaint, perhaps it had been a severe attack of smallpox; I heard only rumours and knew not the truth of it. He always wore gloves and, we had been told, when he was in the palace, he kept his face covered but, as he spoke with the wounded, I saw the marks of the disease. This was the first time I had seen him without his helmet and the disease had ravaged him since I had first met him all those years ago. It was all I could do to hold his gaze and not to touch my cross for protection.

I knelt, as did Sir Hugh, "King Baldwin, we must speak for we are all in great danger and there is much to debate!"

He nodded, "Raoul is dead!" Raoul had been the standard-bearer who had almost cost us dear.

We stood and Sir Hugh said, "And more will join him unless we can devise some plan to extricate the remains of the army from this disaster."

He smiled and nodded, "You are right. We will do what is necessary for the dead when we have seen to the living."

We went to Sir Hugh's solar. Two other senior knights close to the King had survived: Sir Raymond and Sir John. They were with us. Sir Hugh knew the Egyptians better than any and he spoke first, "King Baldwin, we shall wake on the morrow and there will be a ring of archers around this castle; within the day they will add their camps and begin a siege. We have supplies for a month but that is for my garrison. I can feed this army on the barest of rations for less than six days."

"How many have survived?"

I shook my head, "We cannot know yet. The gates are now closed and none more will be admitted until dawn but there must be many who are still heading north. In the castle?" I shrugged, "There are, perhaps two or three hundred."

Sir Raymond and Sir John were in as big a state of shock as we were. They were still stunned and they just took in my words and those of Sir Hugh.

King Baldwin said, "And the Hospitallers?"

I had been the closest to the warrior monks and I shook my head, "When I brought my retinue and Sir Amaury to your aid I lost sight of them. My move left their right flank exposed."

King Baldwin nodded, "Then they might well be lost but you did the right thing for you saved my person and the standards. While we are free then there is hope. But what do we do?"

I was the most practical soldier there. I had fought with the Warlord and Sir William enough times to be able to think quickly and find a solution to what appeared to be an insoluble problem. I had learned to look for any hope and cling to it rather than to fall into the pit of despair which was the mistake others made. "We cannot leave this night for we would be caught on the road to Gaza. I have no doubt that there will be archers there watching now. We have to make the Egyptians believe that we intend to hold out here." The King nodded. He knew we could not leave. "I suggest that we take those with the better horses and break out tomorrow as soon as it is dark. We ride when the Muslims are at prayer and head for Gaza."

The King asked, "And the rest?"

Sir Hugh's grim face told me that he already knew the answer but I had to say it aloud so that the King would know the ramifications of such an action. "Hopefully, when the Egyptians know we have left then they will follow but I believe that they will reduce Darum."

Sir Hugh nodded, "Aye, Sir Robert, but we will hold them up long enough for you to escape."

Sir John said, "But if we reach Gaza then…"

Sir Hugh said, "Then you will find a castle with as few men as we. Gaza will be a brief stop to get better horses and then race for Ascalon. If you reach Ascalon then you have a chance to be safe."

"Aye, King Baldwin, but that will be all. You will be safe but the flower of Jerusalem lies on the desert south of here. You will have to regroup and build up your forces. Ascalon will become the new frontier." Sir Hugh's words sounded like the death knell of Jerusalem.

Sir John and Sir Raymond stared at Sir Hugh and the King nodded, "Then that is what we shall do. Sir John and Sir Raymond, go and have the men rest. We will not eat. Any food which is in the castle must be left for the garrison. Have the helmets and mail burnished. When dawn comes, we will stand on the walls and make the Egyptians think we intend to stay and fight." Once they had left us, he shook his head, "I have been betrayed and, except for you two, I know not whom I can trust. My mother, the Queen, warned me of the Count of Tripoli but I saw a way to form a new alliance and keep the Holy Land Christian. De Lusignan…!" For the first time I heard the anger in his voice as he shook his head, "He was the one whom I had close to me and I had promised him good lands and estates! He was the one who whispered in my ear. He was like the snake in the garden of Eden and I believed his honeyed words. I can now see that he was planted by the Count of Tripoli."

I pieced together the puzzle, "One of Sir Hugh's servants overheard something which suggests that the Count planned to leave your side all along. King Baldwin, whose idea was this campaign?"

He gave me a wry smile, "You know the answer already, Sir Robert, it was the Count's suggestion! He and de Lusignan persuaded me that the time was ripe to make the south safe and we could make up for the loss of Edessa by striking at the Egyptians while they were weak."

It all made sense now. "And that would leave Jerusalem undefended and ripe for him to take over."

King Baldwin smiled and I noticed the pain it caused him to do so, "Then they have reckoned without my mother and my sister. Before I left, they told me that they would guard my kingdom. Jerusalem will be held safely for me but for the rest I am uncertain. Will Gaza and Ascalon side with the Count?

"We try Gaza and see how we are received. If we have to then we ride across country. It will not be an easy journey and not one a king should have to undertake but needs must, Your Majesty."

"Do not worry about me, Sir Robert. My father, King Fulk, trained me to endure all kinds of hardships. My affliction will not affect me; flaking skin merely looks unsightly." He stood, "And now we should go and speak with our people; I beg you all to have a positive face. They do not deserve this fate."

King Baldwin was a good king. As we headed down to the shocked and shattered men, I knew that he was in an impossible position. Jerusalem would always be the target for others. The Muslims wanted what they regarded as their Holy city returned to them while Christians saw it as the ultimate power. I found Sir Amaury with our diminished number of men. In one day, he had grown up immeasurably. He had lost more than a third of his men and had to fight for his life. "The men have all eaten, Sir Robert, and the horses attended to. I fear that another day such as today will see the end of them."

"They will have a whole day of rest and the next time that they are ridden will be in the cool of the evening." I saw the question in his eyes. "Do not ask yet, Sir Amaury. I will tell all when I can. The King is still in command."

"Was the Count afraid and that was why he ran or …?"

"What do you think?"

He shook his head, "This was my first real battle but I think that spear to spear we could have held them. I am not sure we could have driven them from the field but having fought them I can see that we had a chance. The Count is an experienced warrior and has fought them before. Why did he come all the way south with us just to abandon us when battle threatened?"

I lowered my voice, "To ensure that the King had to fight and then lose. I do not think the Count thought that any of us would escape. He wanted the flower of Jerusalem crushed. We have a chance, one with barely a glimmer of hope, but a chance nonetheless." I spread my arm. There were many knights and nobles in the bailey. They had with them some of their men at arms and squires. "More have survived than should have. That was down, quite simply, to Henri of Chartres who bought us all time to get to the side of the King. Now make sure that all the men rest and then when day comes, we will sharpen weapons, groom and tend our horses and pray that God aids us when we implement our plan."

After we had removed the pieces of arrow and fletch which were caught in our mail, I went with Edward to the chapel to pray. Our good mail had saved us and I was glad that we had invested our tiny amount of treasure wisely. The castle chapel was, perforce, a small one and lit by candles but that intimacy made it easier to kneel on the cool stone floor and speak with God. Since I had come to the Holy Land with Sir William, I had discovered that prayer in this land always seemed to bring a warrior closer to God. I felt his presence in the chapel and so, when I spoke aloud my prayers, I truly believed that he was there in this Christian outpost and heard every word. Priests had told me that was true in every one of God's churches but I had never felt his presence as much as I did in the Holy Land.

"Lord, I pray you to aid the King when we ride forth. He is a good man and he was betrayed. I beg you to punish those who deceived him for they do not do your work. If I am to die in this venture, I pray that you will watch over my wife and stepson for they do not deserve to be abandoned a second time. In return, I swear that I will try to be a better man. Amen!"

As we left the chapel Edward said, "You think that we will not get home, lord?"

I smiled. Edward, too, had grown but he was still young and he had lost his father already in this land. He feared he would end his days here. "I know not but if we do escape and return to Jericho, then it will be because God wishes us to live and I take that as a hopeful sign. Do tomorrow night what you did today and all will be well!"

He yawned, "I confess that although I never lost my fear today my training took over and I used my spear and shield as though they belonged to another and that gives me hope."

"While a man lives there is always hope!"

As much as I wanted to stay awake and watch from the walls, I knew that a tired man makes mistakes and so I found a corner amongst my men and, curling up in a ball, slept. They say that mail is uncomfortable but, that night, I slept as though wrapped in a blanket.

My cloak was my bedding and my arming cap my pillow. I woke as the first rays of the sun struck the walls of the keep. I went to the gatehouse and used the garderobe there. I joined Sir Hugh who peered south.

"Did you sleep, Sir Hugh?"

He smiled, "Soon, Sir Robert, I shall enjoy the eternal sleep," He pointed to the south where I could see the advance guard of the Egyptians. They had taken advantage of the cool night to march towards us. "Some rode north during the night. My men say that they have made a camp just eight hundred paces from our north wall." He saw me calculating how that would affect our plans. "It is rocky there. I am not saying that they cannot dig ditches merely that they cannot dig them in one day." He smiled, "They are Bedouin and do not dig in any case. I know the Arab and he is looking for what he can get out of this battle with the least effort. The Sudanese foot, spearmen and archers, are more disciplined. They will be coming from the south and they are the ones we watch."

"Your castle just has one gate?"

"That is what the Egyptians think but there is a sally port on the western side of the castle. This is not a large castle but it is a cunningly constructed one." He pointed to the one tower which was bigger than the other three corner towers. "That is one example for it is the same height as the keep. The sally port is hidden by an abutment so that, from the north wall, men can move out without being seen. It was built that way for this castle was first built to defend against Ascalon when it was in Egyptian hands. You can all walk your horses through the gate and then mount where there is a piece of dead ground to the west of the castle. By walking your horses, you can approach to within two hundred paces of their camp. You are the warrior and not the King. You will need to judge the most judicious moment to mount and ride through their lines. I would make it a count of forty after you hear the call to prayers. By then even those on sentry duty will be on their knees and abasing themselves. A man cannot hold a weapon while he does so. They are Bedouin and they may or may not pursue you. If they know the King is with you then they will do so; I would have the banners hidden and the King disguised. They may think you are deserters."

Other men were rising and one of his men at arms approached, "Lord, we slaughtered a lamed horse last night and we have cooked it."

"Then we will descend. Make sure that those who fight on foot eat first." The man at arms was no fool and knew what that implied. He nodded.

"And how long can you hold out?"

"The Egyptians will need to fetch wood to build siege engines. I think our food will run out before they are built. I think a month at the most but, let us be hopeful. Once they realise that the King has fled, they may leave."

"But you do not think so?"

He shook his head as we descended the stair, "No. Thanks to the Count of Tripoli we have awoken the beast and he will rid himself of these annoyances like al-Darum and Gaza. He may even retake Ascalon, who knows? We are in God's hands now."

By the time the Fatimid army had begun to build their camps, we had eaten and the King had the walls lined with every knight wearing burnished mail and helmets. It was a splendid sight. The men at arms lined the towers and the top of the keep so that the sun, which God sent to shine, flashed from their spear points. It told the Fatimid leader that we were going to defend al-Darum! When the sun reached its zenith then the Egyptians took shelter from its burning rays and we also left the walls. We would not return to them. We had planted the seed in the mind of the enemy general and we all rested. Those who would remain in the castle knew who they were. They were the wounded knights and the men who were on foot. Only those with good horses would leave for we had a perilous journey ahead of us. The King's remaining standard-bearer would remain in the castle. The standards were rolled and carried by the King's squire. In addition, two of Sir Amaury's wounded men would remain behind. I knew that the act of desertion by the men of Tripoli had a profound effect on Sir Amaury. If nothing else he now knew the bond between warrior and knight; the novice had become a veteran after one battle. In all two hundred and eight of us would be leaving the castle. More would be left in the fort but our number meant we had the best chance of reuniting the King with his city.

The Muslims had a call to prayer many times during the day but we were waiting for dark. Before night fell, the sally port gate was opened and five knights walked their horses out to ensure that there were no enemy sentries close by the patch of dead ground. The King spoke with Sir Hugh; it was a private meeting. I had said all that I had to say to Sir Hugh on the wall. The rest was left unspoken for we were both old soldiers who knew the reality of war. King Baldwin had asked for me and Sir Amaury to flank him. I took it as a mark of respect that he did so. It meant, however, that we would not be riding with our squires and our men. I would only discover if they had survived when we approached Gaza. I could have spoken to them but there would have been little point. Anything I said would be a platitude. I just nodded to Wilfred and gestured towards Edward. His nod in reply was all I needed to know that Wilfred would do all that he could to protect Edward. We led our horses out to the dead ground where we could hear the hustle and bustle of the Egyptian camp. The Bedouin were noisy warriors. The King marched and led his horse like any warrior; his title meant nothing. We did not burden ourselves with spears and lances, therefore swords, axes and maces would have to suffice. We mounted, hidden by the slope where we could hear the Egyptian camp for Darum was in silence as every eye was watching from the walls. Sir Amaury was on the King's left and I was on his right. We heard the first cry for the call to prayers and, raising my sword to signal the move, we spurred our horses. A line of eight knights preceded the King and their job was to clear a path through whatever obstacles we discovered. As we reached the top of the rise, we saw their camp before us. We were approaching from the west and, therefore, we would ride obliquely through their camp. Sir Hugh's advice had been sage and the Muslims were caught completely unawares. They were on their knees and looking, not to the west but the east. As they heard the hooves approaching, they stood and turned. For many, that was their last view for each of us had a weapon drawn. The eight knights had spread out to punch a large hole. There were still one or two Arabs who stood and tried to draw their weapons but the three of us laid about us with our swords and made life easier for those who were following us. Behind us, the knights, men at arms and squires rode in a five-man wide column. We were like a bodkin blade and would slide through the enemy's defences. We needed to delay the Arabs just a little. We had less than seven miles to travel before we would reach Gaza and then another thirteen to Ascalon. Once we crossed the river which lay close to Gaza, then we would be safe.

The river we had to cross to safety was shallow and easily fordable. What we had not counted upon was the fact that the Arabs had taken their horses there to drink and the hooves had muddied the ground. It made it slippery. In addition, they had sentries there and whilst there were few, these were armed and, having heard the clash of steel the twelve of them were ready. As we approached the eight knights were forced to fight them and that slowed us up. I shouted, "Edward, Richard! Protect the King. Sir Amaury, let us help the vanguard."

We ploughed into the Arabs who had surrounded the knights and were trying to hamstring their horses. My sword found the back of one Arab's neck just as he hacked into the leg of Sir James of Tyre. Sir Amaury despatched a second and I slapped Sir James' mount on the rump to encourage the beast to run. Sir Gilles had been pulled from his horse and was being butchered; we could not help him. Sir Amaury and I charged the Arabs. We could not save Sir Gilles' life but we ended the lives of those who were the last obstacle before safety. I saw that our squires, Richard and Edward, had successfully forded the river and we spurred our horses to rejoin them. As we galloped north, I risked glancing over my shoulder. There were eight empty saddles but that was far fewer than I had expected. With luck, we would be in Gaza within an hour and then we could begin to plan for the future.

Gaza was in darkness when we reached the fortress which was a slightly bigger one than Darum. We were now at the fore and I was with the King when he shouted, "Open the gates! It is King Baldwin."

In answer, an arrow thudded into the ground just five paces from the King. "You lie. You are Muslims in disguise. You are Turcopoles! Count Raymond warned us!"

The King shouted, "I speak the truth! I am King Baldwin!"

"The King is dead and his army massacred. Ride away before we unleash such a shower of arrows that all will be slain!"

A second arrow hit the ground even closer and I said, "Let us ride to Ascalon. There you are known and it is just twelve more miles!"

We had lost men and lost a battle but that single event had a profound effect on the King. He had ever been, because of his affliction, a recluse and now it had come back to haunt him. The knights they would have known in Gaza lay dead on the battlefield. The disaster was growing and not diminishing. However, with Gaza behind us, we were able to slow down. The garrison would hold up any pursuit, as they had held us up. The result was that we reached Ascalon just after dawn and the King did not risk his dignity a second time. We waited for the sun to rise completely so that the sentries could see our faces. We were admitted and the first thing that the King did was to draft a document to send to Jerusalem. Who else thought that the King was dead? The castellan of Ascalon and the commanders of the Holy orders were each given one copy and riders were sent to Jerusalem, Acre and the other major fortresses to tell them of Count Raymond's perfidy and the truth about the King. When we left for Jerusalem, two days later, we were escorted by four hundred knights from the Knights Templar and the Hospitallers. We learned as we neared Jerusalem that Count Raymond had attempted to trick his way in but Queen Melisende was too wise and he had headed for home once he heard of our approach.

I was keen to return to my home for I had done all that had been asked of me but King Baldwin asked me to stay for a few days. I think that part of it was security as he had lost many of his household knights and wished to surround himself with a wall of steel and the other part was that he wished to reward both me and Sir Amaury. He held an audience with the two of us and Queen Melisende.

"Both of you have done Jerusalem a great service for had you not come to my aid then I would have been killed." He looked at his mother and nodded. "My mother and I have discussed this at length. Sir Amaury, we grant you the manor of Nablus which is close to us and will allow you to continue your protection." He shook his head, "Sir Geoffrey, who now lies in the desert had no family! Take heed, Sir Amaury! You need children!

"You are too gracious, King Baldwin. I was happy to serve you."

"You did more than serve and with Henri of Chartres now gone I will need a champion who can protect me from the County of Tripoli." Sir Amaury nodded knowing that he was now committed to defending Jerusalem from the north. The King looked at me, "You already have Jericho and that guards us against the east but I am aware that it is a poor manor. I had promised de Lusignan a rich manor northeast of Jericho. Golden Hills is fertile and prosperous. I give it to you for I have made de Lusignan an outlaw."

I knew the manor and the King was right, it was far richer than mine and, in fact, was richer than Sir William's manor of Aqua Bella. It was, however, a poisoned chalice for it lay just a few miles from the mountains which were the domain of the bandits and was often ravaged by Seljuq Turks. Much of the coin I might make would be spent hiring men for there was no castle. It was a fortified hall. Admittedly, like Aqua Bella, it was built into the side of a cliff and so only had one gate needed for protection but unless help came then we would be trapped within. I could not, in all truth, refuse such a gift and so I bowed, "I thank King Baldwin and Queen Melisende."

In addition, Sir Amaury and I were given a chest of coins. Jerusalem was not only a Holy city, but it was also a rich city. The King might lack good knights to fight for him but money was never an issue. As much as I wanted to get home to Sarah, I knew that I would never have a better opportunity to hire more men and so we stayed in the old town while Wilfred and my men scoured the taverns for men who might be worth the hire. Inevitably, there would be some who had been on the disastrous foray into Egypt. They would know, better than any, the dangers my new manor brought. Wilfred would know their value and choose the best that were available.

We had no weaponsmith at our manor although the blacksmith, Raoul, was a good man and tried his best to repair our armour. We had suffered damage and so we sought Balin the Weaponsmith whom I knew to be the best in his trade. Sir William had used Balin once and so we knew that he was a reliable weaponsmith who produced quality metalwork. He was like Hephaestus. He had a workshop with eight anvils and forges. As you approached his workshop, the smell of burning wood seemed to choke you and once inside it looked like a scene from hell. This was a hot land and the weaponsmiths added to that heat. With huge leather aprons, they sweated and hammered at the iron as they beat swords and mail. The noise was painful to the ears but, as we entered and my spurs and livery were recognised then all work ceased. The silence after the banging came as a shock. A huge man took a piece of cloth from one of the small boys who serviced the smiths and, wiping his brow and hands came towards us.

"My lord, master, I pray you come outside so that we may talk." The moment we left the banging and clanging resumed. Balin, I guessed it was he, smiled, "This is a busy time. Knights need mail to be repaired." He looked at my hauberk which was carried by Edward. "And I am guessing you wish yours to be repaired too, my lord."

"Aye, I would." I held out my right arm. "I am Sir Robert of Jericho."

The title made Balin smile, "Then the whole of this city owes you thanks for you saved the life of our king."

"We have only just returned; how did you know?"

"There were those who fled the field first; there always are and they reached here a couple of days before the King." I realised that we had tarried in Ascalon and taken it easy on our way back to the palace. "They may have been harbingers of doom but they told the tale of the knights who saved the King. You wish your mail repaired?"

"I do. Edward."

My squire handed over the two hauberks and Balin laid them out on the table which abutted the buildings. He shook his head, "No offence, my lord, but this is not the best mail I have ever seen."

I had thought it was for it had cost me much coin to have it made however Balin was the best and so I smiled, "I was a man at arms before I was knighted, Balin, and this is the hauberk I first had made."

Nodding he said, "I can repair it but it would not cost much more to buy a new hauberk which is of better construction."

"You have such a one?"

"There were some knights who left for this war and they ordered hauberks before they left." He shook his head, "They anticipated victory and coin! I have three such hauberks. I believe that one will fit you."

"And how much will it cost me?"

He did not answer, "You wish your squire's to be repaired, too?"

Edward did not have a full hauberk for he was not yet fully grown. It was a short one which came to his waist. "I do."

"Then let me have your old mail shirt and I will repair your squire's and give you a new one for four hundred silver pennies."

I heard the sharp intake of breath from Edward. Such a sum would seem like a fortune but I knew that it was a reasonable price. The weaponsmith would be out of pocket unless he could sell the mail. I did not doubt that the knights who had ordered the hauberks had paid a deposit and that had enabled the smith to keep the price at a reasonable amount. I wondered if he knew that the King had rewarded me. I nodded, "Very well. Let me try one on while my squire goes to fetch the coins."

"There is no need, my lord. You can take away the hauberk and send the money later."

I smiled, "I was not always a knight and when I was a man at arms, I paid my debts promptly. I will do so now. Edward."

The weaponsmith shouted, "Yolande, wine for our guest!" He disappeared into his workshop.

Yolande must have been his daughter and she was a pretty maiden. I guessed her mother must have been a local for Balin was a blond-haired Frank and Yolande had his eyes but a dusky skin. She poured me some white wine which had been kept chilled. I took off my baldric and sheathed sword. Balin returned and showed me the hauberk. "Do you see, my lord, how each rink is rivetted to six others? This is strong mail and the iron has carbon in it. This mail is sturdier than the one you wore. It has been oiled and if your squire maintains the oiling then it will last a lifetime."

I laughed, "And here in Jerusalem that may not be long, eh weaponsmith?"

He laughed, "I can see that you are a knight who has the right attitude. Come, my lord, let us see how it fits."

He was a strong man but he strained as he lifted it over my head. Once on, however, it did not feel unduly heavy. After he slipped the coif over my head and fastened the open mittens over my hands the weight seemed evenly distributed.

"Of course, it will fit better once you wear your aketon and arming cap."

I nodded and unsheathed my sword. The open mittens allowed me to grip the sword's hilt with my hand and yet the back was protected by the mail. I stepped away from the half roof which afforded shelter from the sun and I raised the sword above my head. The hauberk seemed the same weight as my former one but I knew it to be stronger. "This is a good hauberk. I will take it."

He beamed for a weaponsmith liked his work to be appreciated. Edward hurried back with the bag of coins. We kept them in bags of five hundred. I would just need to take out one hundred and the smith would have his money. After I had counted it out, I asked, "And how long for Edward's repairs?"

"It will take at least a week, my lord, but I can send it to your manor."

"Good!"

We left Jerusalem two days later. Wilfred had hired six men at arms and four archers. The archers were all English and I knew I was lucky to have them. I had to buy horses but my name and the fact that I had saved the King meant I was not cheated for no-one wished to offend the King's new friend! We headed for Jericho. I was loath to leave my first manor but I knew that Golden Hills was a better hall and that I would need to supervise the new manor. In my time in Jerusalem, I had listened in the taverns where we had eaten and there was much unrest. Nur al-Din had consolidated his hold on Edessa and, it was rumoured, planned on enlarging his fiefdom. I might have a new and richer manor but it would have to be defended.

Sarah and her son, Henry, were delighted to see us. The hug she gave me lasted a little longer than I had expected and she whispered in my ear, "When we heard of the disaster and that the King was dead I feared that you would lie in the desert with him for I know that you have more honour than is good for you."

I let her hug a little longer and then held her at arm's length, "And all went well, my love, for we survived and none of our men was hurt. Others paid the ultimate price but not my men and the King has rewarded me with the manor of Golden Hills."

"But Jericho was my husband's manor and it has been my home since forever."

I nodded, "Golden Hills is a richer manor and, when time allows, I would speak with you about our future for I have given much thought to it. For now, we have new men and horses to accommodate and I daresay Henry will have questions."

She shook her head, "I fear that the next time you go to war you will have to take him with you. He has seen more than twelve summers and has been training to be a warrior."

I remembered the dead squires and pages who had fallen to Egyptian arrows and spears. Henry was lucky that I had left him at home. I nodded, "We will begin his training to be a squire."

It was good to be back in my manor. I had lived with the Warlord and Sir William but that had been in their homes. This hall felt like mine and I found myself touching the walls and the furniture almost as though it was a person. It took most of the day to show the new men their quarters and by the time it was time for the evening meal I felt drained. Edward should have served us but my wife used the servants instead, "Edward is a hero, for he survived Darum and besides, he can tell the tale with you, my husband."

Henry was wrapt as Edward and I gave the sanitized version of the battle. There was little point in upsetting my wife by the graphic description of the death of Henri of Chartres and Sir Gilles. I allowed Edward to describe the battle for he had seen more of it than I had; he had been behind me. I spoke of the treachery of Hugh de Lusignan and the Count of Tripoli. I gave them my views on what had happened but, of course, we did not know the truth for certain. The County of Tripoli lay close to my new hall and I wondered if I might suffer as a result of this gift.

"What happened to Sir Hugh at Darum, Sir Robert?" My wife was kind and the fact that we had skirted around the fate of Sir Hugh made her fear the worst.

I smiled, "Surprisingly the Egyptians lifted the siege not long after the King fled and reached Ascalon. Perhaps there were too many men inside the castle or it may have been that they deemed it unnecessary to reduce it having bloodied the nose of the King. Whatever the reason I am glad for I like Sir Hugh."

Edward and Henry left us and I spoke aloud, my fears, "We cannot win this land over, my love."

She looked surprised and sipped her wine, "What has changed?"

"Nothing and therein lies the root of the trouble. The King of Jerusalem has little power and the other leaders, like the Count of Tripoli, are self-serving. I also wonder about the Military orders. Only the Hospitallers heeded the King's call and most of that company perished. The others? They were not there and I heard, whilst in Jerusalem, that they are just enlarging their own castles. This land can only be Christian if all seek the same ends and they do not."

"Will there be another Crusade to help us?"

"There may well be but that is just more of the same. There will be leaders who will bicker amongst themselves. Until we have a Crusade led by one man who can wield the army into war and defeat the Egyptians and the Seljuq Turks then we are doomed."

She laughed, "You do not paint a hopeful picture."

"I prepare you for the worst. I do not say that it will happen this year or next, but one day we will have to leave this land you call home and return to the west. If you do not then we are doomed to die!"

Her hand went to her mouth. Sarah had been born in this land. Her family had been killed by raiders from the east and so the import of my words was not wasted on her. She was also one of the cleverest women I knew and was eminently practical, "And that is why you are so keen on Golden Hills. You think we can make enough money to buy something in the west."

I nodded. If we lost our manors then we would be penniless. We had to extract every coin we could from Golden Hills in the time we had left.

"And where would we go?"

"Sir William had a manor in Ouistreham and his father has one in Anjou, La Flèche. I did both men good service. When we see that the end is nigh, I shall write to them and ask if there is a manor for me."

She laughed and showed her practicality, "If you wait until then it will be too late. Better to write now."

She was right and the next day I wrote a letter to Sir William. Remarkably the act of writing made me feel much better and my men and I headed to Golden Hills to see my new property. It was not a moment too soon. Even as I arrived, I could sense that something was not right for, although it was a magnificent fortified hall and the fields were filled with animals and crops, there appeared to be few men working the fields. When we dismounted and spoke to the servants, we discovered that the steward was also absent. The man who was in charge was Stephen of Nazareth and his wife Anna. They acted as housekeepers and when I entered the hall, I saw the shamefaced looks on their faces. I noticed that there were neither tapestries nor fine furniture to be seen. I was not noble-born and knew how to read ordinary folk for they were my kind of people. Henry and Edward flanked me; my men at arms were tending to the horses.

"Stephen, where is the steward?" Bluntness seemed to me the way forward.

"Sir Robert, Phillippe of Acre left three days ago. He took the books, the tapestries, the furniture and the chests which had the coins for the taxes."

I worked out that would have been about the time I had discovered I had a new manor. "Who came to tell him that I was the new lord of the manor?"

He looked at me as though I could read his mind, "Lord, it was a servant of the lord who had been promised the manor. It was Hugh de Lusignan's servant, I know not his name but he is a Seljuq Turk. We were sent to the village on an errand and when we returned it was as though locusts had passed through the hall. The horses were all taken and the servants who were the steward's accomplices also left; the ones who remain are the ones who were loyal to the previous lord, Sir Gerard. I swear this is true, my lord."

I believed him and his wife was weeping as though she feared some punishment. I smiled to make them less apprehensive, "And why did you and the others stay here?"

"It is our home, my lord, and what Phillippe of Acre, the steward, did was wrong."

I nodded, "There will be no punishment for you have shown loyalty but my family will be coming to live here and I would have it cleaned from top to bottom."

"What of Phillippe of Acre, lord? Has he got away with this?"

I shook my head, "He has not. There will be a reckoning but first things first. Stephen, organise the cleaning and have food prepared for my men."

"Yes, my lord."

They left happier than they had been when I had entered. "Edward, find some parchment, ink and a quill. I must write to the King."

When he had gone Henry said, "Parchment, Sir Robert?"

"The King will be expecting taxes. I need to tell him why there will be none forthcoming and to warn him about de Lusignan. The King promised this manor to him before we left for the south. I fear that we have not heard the last of de Lusignan."

Although the horses, books and coins had been taken as well as the tapestries and fine furniture they had left farms tools and weapons. In addition, the servants and workers who remained were keen to impress me. I sent Edward to Jerusalem while Henry and my men went to fetch my wife and the furniture from my old hall. I had left my steward in charge and given him the hall for his own. He was happy as he had a large family. We would not need to live in the hall at Jericho in the future. Golden Hills would be my home for as long as the enemies of Jerusalem allowed us to live here.

The first few months were the hardest and I had to eat into the precious fund of coins given to me by the King. His letter was reassuring in that he told me that he expected no taxes for the first year but in a disturbing corollary he said that Hugh de Lusignan had fled to Tripoli. He had not left for Poitou as I had expected! My new men at arms proved to be invaluable. Stephen of Nazareth told me that there were many raids from brigands and bandits. They were a mixture of Turks and deserters. Wilfred and my men at arms went up into the hills to ferret them out. At first, their forays yielded them little reward but after a month they were used to the trails and the land. Leaving the heads of the first four men they caught on spears they brought back the weapons and the animals they had captured. The raids ceased from that moment on although our daily patrols continued. My wife threw herself into making the fortified hall as comfortable and well-furnished as it had once been. The fact that it was far more secure as a building was important and Anna, Stephen's wife, proved to be a right hand my wife had not enjoyed before. That first Christmas was joyous.

It was after Christmas that I put my mind into not only making money but providing us with an escape from the fortified hall. I had seen how strong it was as soon as we had arrived but, as with Aqua Bella, I had seen the fatal flaw. If we were attacked, we would be trapped for there was but one way in and out and the cliff which rose behind it could not be scaled, even by mountain goats. Darum had given me the idea and I went with Edward, Wilfred and Stephen of Nazareth to examine the walls. It took some time but we found what we sought, eventually. The outer wall terminated in the side of a cliff. The masonry had been bonded into the rock. On the north side, however, there was a cleft, a narrow passage that had an open top and was wide enough for one horse and that was all. It was a hundred paces long and led to a dead-end but we realised that the rock between there and the other side of the cliff was only as thick as a man's forearm. We went outside the walls and saw that, like the sally port at Darum, the rock wall was hidden from the road. We set to constructing a gate for the inner section; that was the easy part. We then began to break down the outer wall but when we did so we retained as many large pieces of rock as we could. It took a month to complete the work but, when we had done so we had a crude opening through which a horse and rider could pass. We put the rocks back in the same order and roughly bound them with mortar. We planted creepers in the crevasses so that, by spring, they had taken and by summer covered the wall. If we had to leave in a hurry it would be the work of two men to break down the illusion of a rock wall and we had a strong gate on the inside of the hidden opening. I was satisfied.

With the bandits no longer a problem I had my men ride daily patrols on the road and into the fields to ensure that any enemy would see my men and keep their distance. I also built a stone tower on the clifftop close to the top of the hall. The tower began on the flat roof of the hall and we tied it in to the cliff. Using a ladder, we were able to keep two men there during the hours of daylight, my archers normally, to keep watch on the roads. We had ended the threat of the bandits but we had other enemies. De Lusignan and the men of Tripoli were not to be trusted and Nur al-Din was still a threat.

We were close enough to the road which travelled south down the Jordan valley to have visitors, for we were just four hundred paces from the road. The reassuring sight of armed men on the walls of our hall ensured a steady number of merchants and pilgrims who sought shelter and water on their way south to Jerusalem. From the pilgrims, we learned of the outside world, the west. We learned of the new King of England, Henry son of Matilda, who was being guided by the Warlord. One of them brought a letter, almost eight months after I had sent mine to England. Sir William told me that there were manors to be had in England and that he would be more than happy to have his father give me one. However, he said that if I wished to be close to the place of my birth then Ouistreham could be mine. That was all the reassurance and insurance that I needed. If, as I suspected, life became too dangerous in this land for us then we could leave.

The merchants brought us different information for their news was closer to home. They came from the lands of the Turk and the other Christian counties. Their news was not crystal clear and attributable for it came in the form of rumours, hints and overheard conversations. Sometimes it did not come from the merchants themselves but their servants and guards who chatted with Wilfred and my men. Over that first six months that we were at Golden Hills we learned that Hugh de Lusignan bore me a grudge and had spoken of vengeance. My wife found that rich for he had been the traitor and I had not sought the manor which had been promised to him.

I was a soldier and I understood the reason, "I thwarted his plans and those of the Count of Tripoli. Had we not managed to save the King then the Count would be King and de Lusignan would not only have this rich manor but others too and would, no doubt, have a grander title than merely, knight. Do not fret, my love. Now that we know the fox seeks the hens, we can keep a close watch on the henhouse. Forewarned is forearmed."

We set better watches and my men rode the smaller trails now looking for signs not just of Turks but of Franks. We were vigilant and we were industrious for my new men at arms and archers were not afraid of hard work. When we did not watch the land, we tended to it with my workers. The fact that I would often be found toiling in the vineyard or checking the animals for pests seemed to create a closer bond for all of those who lived on my manor. I told Wilfred that all men would have a bonus at harvest time. I knew it was not necessary but I had been a man at arms and knew how much such acts meant.

My wife had had Henry when she was just sixteen. I had thought I would never father a child of my own but, as high summer approached, my wife discovered that she was with child. I know not why God had made me wait all those years to bless us with a child but I thanked him in the small chapel attached to the hall. Surprisingly, Sarah was quite fearful; Henry's birth had not been easy and when she told me the news her joy was tinged with tears. "If I should die giving birth will you watch over Henry, husband, as well as our new child?"

"You shall not die and I am offended that you ask about Henry. Have I not treated him as I would my own son if I had one?" That dried her tears. "And I will send for a doctor. There is still silver left from the King's gift and I will use it to retain a physician. There are many Greek doctors who came here for pilgrimage and stayed. You shall not stir from the hall until the child is born for I waited many years and fought uncountable battles just waiting for a wife. I thought I would have no child of my own and I will do all in my power to ensure that both the love of my life and my unborn child lives!"

The news reinvigorated me and I went to Jerusalem with Edward and Henry, firstly, to seek a doctor but also to speak with the King. The rumours of vengeance had not merely been about de Lusignan but about the Count of Tripoli. Perhaps the King had heard them himself but it would not hurt for me to speak them to him too. While Edward and Henry found us an inn I went to the King. I had to wait some hours for the King was in great demand. I did not mind waiting for it afforded me the opportunity to speak to the others at court who sought an audience. Some I knew from the flight to Darum while others had heard of me and wished to speak to me. Once more I gained much knowledge. The Warlord had once said that there was no such thing as useless information, there was just knowledge you had not needed, yet!

The King looked tired but his skin looked a little better and, for the first time I saw his hands; they no longer flaked. He looked genuinely pleased to see me. "I hope that Golden Hills prospers, Sir Robert?"

"It does, King Baldwin, and I am pleased that your health is improving."

He beamed at the compliment, "I found a new doctor and he explained that it was nothing to do with smallpox and he gave me a lotion which heals the skin. I wish that I had found him years ago. It is as though my life can begin again!"

"And I, too, seek a doctor, Your Majesty, for my wife is with child."

"I will ask Doctor Basil and see if he knows of another who seeks a lord." He grinned and looked much younger, "You shall not have mine!"

"I just need one who can help my manor and my wife."

"Then I shall do my best but you did not travel all this way to speak to me just for that."

"No, King Baldwin. I have heard rumours that de Lusignan and the Count of Tripoli plot against you and Sir Hugh has sworn vengeance on me."

His face became serious. "I had heard that they were plotting but not of Sir Hugh's wish for vengeance. Tripoli would be King of this land and he is gathering an alliance of other malcontents. He hopes to make a civil war but that will suit none but the Seljuq Turks. Nur al-Din is growing in power. I fear that I may have given you poisoned fruit for Golden Hills would be one of the first to suffer if he chose to make an attack on us."

I felt a chill grip my heart. "But what of Kerak and the other border fortresses?"

"The Templars and Hospitallers will try to block the enemy, but the Turks are mounted and if they can devastate the land then they do not need to fight a battle. If they starve us into submission then their armies can march in and take our fortresses from weakened men. I confess, Sir Robert, it is why I gave you the manor. When you send your crops and animals to market it is Jerusalem which benefits. There are other such manors and all of them lie between us and the Turk." A courtier approached and coughed; my time was up. The King smiled, "I thank you for bringing me this news. I knew that you were loyal already and I am pleased that, this time, I have made a wiser judgement than with de Lusignan. I will have Doctor Basil send you the name of a doctor. Let Roger here know where you stay."

I left the name of our inn with the courtier and then headed for the weaponsmith. Edward and Henry would enjoy some time in the city. They had grown closer while Edward had been training my stepson and I remembered when I had been a young man. It would do them no harm to live a little. Golden Hills was a little isolated and they needed to be as other young men. I had, with me, the last of the King's coins. I had planned on buying something frivolous for my wife but the King's news had disturbed me. I sought out Balin.

He was pleased to see me, "My lord, I hope the mail is satisfactory and that the repairs on your squires' mail met with your approval?"

"They did. I come here to buy weapons. I need arrowheads, spearheads and darts."

He frowned, "You expect an attack and fear you will have to defend your walls?"

The weaponsmith had worked out that I had only asked for missile weapons and that meant defence. "The land I defend is close to the Turk. I would be a foolish knight if I ignored the threat."

We discussed the numbers I would need and I paid him. I still had some coins left and so I went to the market where I found some fine linen which I could afford. The new babe would be swaddled in the finest linen.

The inn was close to the palace and I found our chambers empty. The landlord told me that Edward and Henry had gone to explore the markets. I sat at a table to enjoy a beaker of chilled wine. It was good to sit alone and reflect on how far I had come. I had enjoyed my life as a man at arms. There had been no responsibility for all I had to do was that which Sir William commanded. I had not had to worry about my next meal nor the clothes on my back. All that had changed when I became a knight and suddenly, I had responsibility for others, not least my new family. What should have been a burden was not, it was a joy and I was pleased that Sir William had found happiness with his Rebekah. Perhaps his was the path I ought to tread. He had returned to England when he had seen the dangers he faced here in the Holy Land.

Edward and Henry returned a short while later. I heard them coming down the narrow street which led to the inn for they had been drinking. Henry sounded the worse for wear and I was going to berate him when I remembered that when I had been his age I had been serving with a company of soldiers and had not only been drunk but violently ill. Henry sounded happy that was all. I forced a smile when they entered. Edward looked a little shamefaced when he saw me there. Perhaps he had thought I might be delayed longer at the palace. Henry saw me and he forced a grin, "You are back, Sir Robert."

I nodded, "Aye, come and join me although I think you have had enough to drink. Perhaps we ought to have some food instead, eh?"

Edward looked relieved. I ordered some food. It was a vegetable stew with spiced flatbreads; it would soak up some of the wine and ale they had consumed. I told them what I had learned. It was largely for Edward who was not drunk but had enjoyed the afternoon in Jerusalem. "We will leave for home as soon as we find a doctor for we have much to do." I looked at Henry, "And if you are old enough to have too much to drink then you are old enough to stand a watch. When we return to Golden Hills, I will have a hide vest made for you and we will see if we can find an old helmet to fit."

Henry took that as a reward for his drinking and, at that moment, we were brought closer together. I had not chastised him and I had told him that he was one of my men. He was happy.

We had been to the market and returned to the inn when I spied a stranger waiting outside. He was a stick of a man and looked as though a good feed would not hurt him His hair was unkempt and he had not shaved. He approached me and smiled, "Sir Robert of Jericho?"

"I am."

"Basil of Rhodes sent me. I am a doctor, Michael of Petrion."

"Is that not in Constantinopolis?"

"It is, lord, I was born there and lived close to the docks."

This did not sound like a promising background for the man who would care for my wife and my child.

He saw my look and said, "If I might explain?"

"Aye, but not here in the street. Let us go inside. Edward, you and Henry take our purchases to the room."

I ordered wine and Michael told me his tale. As he told me I studied him closely. His face made me think that he was young and yet, if he was a doctor, how had he gained experience? His clothes were tattered and a little threadbare. Doctors made good money. Why was he poor? I was tempted to give him a coin and send him on his way.

"I might have become a street thief for my mother died when I was young." He shrugged, "She was a whore but I loved her for she was my mother. One of the men who had often paid for her…services, he was fond of her and he took me in. He was a doctor and served the Emperor. I lived in the palace and he trained me as his apprentice. I learned my trade and found I had an aptitude for it." He sipped some of his wine, "To be honest, Sir Robert, I suspect that he had fathered me although he never admitted it. It was easier for his reputation if he made out he did it as an act of Christian kindness. When the Emperor died the new Emperor took on a new physician and so we took ship for Outremer. It was a good trade for the Franks suffered illnesses for which they had no cure. Life might have gone on that way had he not fallen foul of the Count of Tripoli. The Count disagreed with my master's diagnosis and, as he was drunk, had him executed, his money and home were taken from us and I was beaten and thrown into the streets. That was six months since and I have been working my way south from that time. I reached Jerusalem two weeks ago and I came to know Basil. He is a good doctor and I helped him to attend on some of his patients. He was impressed but he does not need another assistant and I think he only took me on out of pity and I need no man's pity. I offer you my services."

He leaned back. I sipped my wine and thought for he posed questions I could not find an answer to. I decided that it would be better to be blunt with him. I liked him for he had an honest face and his story evoked sympathy, especially as it involved one of my enemies, but I would be putting my family in his hands. "I need someone who understands childbirth. I am sorry, Michael of Petrion, but it seems to me that you have little experience in such matters."

He nodded, "Adrian, my master, tended to deal with ailments of the lords and the rich. The wives of the Franks were given to me. I have overseen the pregnancies of seven women and all had successful births. It is why Basil recommended me. I delivered two babies in the palace. He knows my work."

That took me aback. I gestured to his clothes, "The way that you are dressed made me think that you were poor and that was as a result of poor skills."

"This is deliberate, lord. I have better clothes and medical instruments. Basil gave them to me as a reward for my work. I wish to be employed as a doctor but I would not deceive my new master. These are the clothes I wore when Basil found me."

I laughed, "You are a strange one, Michael of Petrion, but I like you and if you would, I would hire you as my doctor."

"I need the work and I will accept your offer but only until the child is born. After that, I may leave for I have a yearning to go to the west. I tire of this land."

"That is an honest answer and is acceptable to me. Can you ride?"

"Aye, I can."

"Then tomorrow return here and we will head back to Golden Hills."

When he returned, he had washed and combed his hair and he had shaved. My wife took to him immediately and after I had told her his story, she was even more under his spell. His appointment was one of the best I ever made and the man never let me down. After I had seen to his needs, I summoned Wilfred. and we made a new rota for the sentries. He, Jacob the Jew, one of the new men, and myself would each command one section of men. One section would be on guard at all times. It meant I would have occasional nights when I did not lie with my wife but, in her condition, that was no bad thing.

We learned much about the Count of Tripoli and his acolyte, Hugh de Lusignan. Michael had seen them when they returned from the abortive attempt to seize the throne and he told me that they then began to recruit mercenaries. "My lord, they did not care about their background and did not hire knights, necessarily. They have the dregs of every port in this land and they have Turks who serve them. It was those men who slew Adrian and beat me. I will not tell you how they killed him." He shivered as he told me. "They are cruel men."

"And do you think they are being gathered to do harm to the King of Jerusalem?"

"I know not but they are not mustered for their company, lord. They were ready to ride when I left and I expected to hear of some deprivations and dire deeds that they had committed. That day is not far off."

I assigned Henry to my watch, that way Edward could also keep an eye on him. Our lands, the fields and the homes of the villagers lay to the west of the cliff. It was a cunningly constructed hall for the rock into which the hall was built could not be assailed from the east. It was impossible even to rain arrows on the walls. I think that was why the builders had been happy with the one entrance and they had hoped that any attacker would tire of an assault. Although I doubted that we would have to endure a siege I knew that the villagers would suffer if we were attacked and my former lord had been a good teacher. You did not abandon your people. When the darts, spearheads and arrows arrived we fletched the darts, fitted the spearheads to ash shafts and my archers made their own arrows. We had a wall with a fighting platform above the gate and I had racks made for the spears and the darts. We also had piles of river stones collected for every man at arms could use a sling. If we were attacked, and it looked increasingly likely that if we were then it would be de Lusignan, then we wanted to keep our foes at bay for as long as possible.

At each change of watch, I spoke with the other two watch commanders. And it was when we spoke that we worked out when we might be attacked. Wilfred was the wisest of my men at arms and we knew each other better than any. One early morning when I relieved him and his men he said, "Nothing happened last night, lord, and that gave me the chance to think. I believe I know when we might be attacked."

I sent the rest of my watch to their places and asked, "When? After the harvest?"

He shook his head, "A little later, lord, when we have the money from the animals and the crops we send to market. Having stolen the last money intended for taxes he knows full well how much he can expect. By waiting until we have collected the money, he will hope to catch us unawares."

"I think you are right but we will still keep a good watch over the harvest."

"Aye, sir. If we drag our eyes away from this hostile land then we will pay the price."

My commitment to keep a watch doubled our work for my men watched and when they were not watching they were protecting the shepherds as they gathered in the sheep or helping my workers harvest the crops. We went to bed each night exhausted. Doctor Michael kept a good watch on my wife who blossomed and bloomed, He knew his business and changed the food that she ate. Sarah told me that he had learned about childbirth before he even trained as a doctor. The whores with whom he was brought up could not afford doctors and were excellent midwives. The one who had brought Michael into the world and now owned the whorehouse had given him her secrets. The result was that my wife looked healthier than anyone else on the manor! He also treated the injuries and wounds sustained by men who had too little sleep. I was happy that Michael had been sent into our lives.

We had collected the harvest in and were in the middle of sorting out the sheep when a messenger came from King Baldwin. He had promised me that he would keep me informed of dangers to my manor and the message, which was oral, said that de Lusignan and his men had left Tripoli and were returning to Poitou. It was said that there was a public falling out between the Count and the traitor. I did not believe it for one moment. From what Michael had told me the Count's punishments for those who fell out with him were Draconian. Had there been a falling out then de Lusignan would be dead. The Count was distancing himself from any potential failure and trying to deceive me that de Lusignan was no longer a threat. Once again it was Michael's unique knowledge which gave me an insight into the mind of my enemy. Wilfred had been right. De Lusignan would be heading south and watching for the moment when my coffers were full. A thought suddenly came to me. Perhaps he knew of my wife's pregnancy and hoped to use that distraction too. Just as I heard the news from the merchants heading south the ones heading north would carry the news to my enemies.

When the messenger had left, I told my men and my workers that we had to be on the alert and keep an even better watch. On the off chance that Wilfred's guess was wrong and that they were coming early, I had every worker armed and they took to the fields wearing leather vests and helmets. It seemed to me a race between my wife giving birth and the enemy coming to take all from us. Fate took a hand and my wife went into labour on the day that we sold the last of our animals. I now had six chests of coins from the sale of cereals, sheep and cattle. That showed how hard we had worked for Stephen of Nazareth had told me that the steward who had fled had only taken one chest. We had increased our yield six-fold. Stephen's wife helped Doctor Michael and my new steward organised the workers. The sheep and cattle we would be keeping were brought within my walls and the villagers told that if they heard the bell in my tower begin to toll, they were to take protection behind my walls and leave their homes immediately. We added larger stones to the weapons on the walls.

I was not on the walls when they came. I had summoned the doctor to my wife's side for the baby was coming. Michael told me that it was coming early and he took that to be a good sign. I had left Henry and Edward to sleep for both were exhausted. Wilfred and his watch were in the tower and on the walls; the six of them would also be tired but they would be on their toes.

Doctor Michael took me by the arm and led me to the door of the bedchamber, "You can do nothing here, my lord, Anna and I can deal with the babe and, to be frank, your presence will merely impinge upon our efforts. Go and have an early breakfast."

"I will leave you but I will go, instead, to my walls and watch." I picked up my mail and baldric before I left the chamber. We walked abroad, even in my hall, mailed. Many knights cannot dress themselves in mail for they have grown up with a squire to attend them. I had been a man at arms and I could dress myself easily. By the time I left the hall and went towards the ladder leading to the fighting platform I saw, in the sky, the first hint of daylight. Every soldier knew that this was always the most dangerous time of day. Attackers, wherever they fought, would try to be in position when the sun rose so that they could take advantage of a gate opened early or a slack sentry who was not vigilant. Even as I climbed the ladder, I heard Wilfred's hiss, "Lord, they come! Rouse the men and I will toll the bell."

I turned and, after leaving my helmet at the foot of the ladder, hurried to the warrior hall. Opening the door, I shouted, "To arms! They come!" I did not bother going to my hall to wake Henry and Edward for, as I left the barracks, the bell sounded. I hurried to the gate where Aaron of Acre stood with Richard of York. They would open the gates to allow in the villagers. I was there because if the gates were threatened then I would have them closed, even if there were villagers who had not made the safety of my home.

Richard peered through the slit we used to inspect visitors and said, "The villagers come, my lord. They have heeded the call quickly!"

"Then open the gate." I drew my sword as they lifted the heavy bar and pulled open the huge gates, as tall as a man on the shoulders of another. Those who lived closest to the walls were there and I saw that they had heeded my commands. The men carried weapons and the women the children. De Lusignan and his men were not concerned with the best pots the village women prized; they were after coins.

As each man passed, I directed him to the walls and the women to the hall. The light was getting better and I saw no enemies before us. It was Wilfred's voice which warned me for he shouted, "Lord, they come!"

I saw the last four villagers. One, an old woman stumbled and her husband stopped to help her. "Begin to close the gates. Leave a gap for me." I ran to the old man for I heard hooves. He had picked up his wife, "Hurry Absalom!"

"Sorry, lord!" The old woman's hand was bleeding and she was distressed but if they could not make the gates then they would be the first casualties. It was eight Seljuq Turks who appeared from the dark of the road leading to the village. My archers sent arrows at them but they held shields above their heads and the darkness made the men and horses fast-moving shadows. I held my sword in two hands as they galloped towards the gate which now showed a sliver of light. The old couple had ten paces to go and if I left then they would die.

Darts joined the arrows and three of the Turks and their horses were hit. Two others wheeled away as arrows hit their shields. Three others, however, came on. I was now committed to defence and I stood with my left foot forward. One of the warriors was ahead of the others and I swung at the head of his horse. My blade hacked through its skull and, as it died, it fell to the left. A spear was hurled from the walls and struck the next wheeling Turk in the back. As his horse baulked before a fallen horse the dying man was thrown from his saddle. I stepped to the side to avoid being run down and then brought my sword across the last Turks neck. The other dead Turk lay at my feet and, sheathing my sword, I pulled the spear from his back. I began to back towards my gate. Franks were now appearing and they wore mail. Unless I managed to get within my gate then I would be at their mercy. I backed away from the last warrior. He must have had a death wish for he dug his heels into his horse's flanks and rode at me with the javelin held in his right hand. I watched an arrow hit his thigh but still, he came on. I wondered if he had been of the ḥaššāšīn cult, the ones who used hashish, for he had a wild look in his eyes. Even as another arrow hit his shoulder and a dart made his horse veer a little he still came on. I had been told, by Sir Hugh in Darum, that the ḥaššāšīn killers, even when in a drugged state, were still cunning warriors. I could take nothing for granted and I braced myself with my spear held in two hands. He let go of the reins as he hurled the spear and then, in a movement so quick that his hands were a blur, he drew his sword. The javelin hit my mail but Balin had been right and it was well made. The head struck my shoulder but did not penetrate. I lunged below his swinging scimitar and rammed the spear into his chest. The speed of his horse and the movement of my hands threw the man at my partly closed gates. His head hit the wood with a sickening thud and his life was ended. I turned and ran. As I squeezed through the gap the gates were slammed shut.

The old man and woman nodded their thanks, "My lord, we owe you our lives!"

"Then repay it, Absalom, and get to my walls. You can hurt those who would have slain your wife!" Pausing only to pick up my helmet I ran up the stairs to join the men on the fighting platform. We had enough men, with the villagers, to fill the wall. My archers were in the tower where they could send their arrows into the attackers. Edward and Henry were with Wilfred. My captain shook his head, "That was foolish, lord. Two old people are not worth your life."

"There you are wrong, Wilfred, but all is well." Just then the sun cleared the cliff and bathed the village and the land to the west in light. I saw the enemy then. The eight who had almost caught us out had been the vanguard. Perhaps they had been selected for their speed, I know not. The men who followed de Lusignan were all mounted. I counted at least fifty of them and I recognised him despite the fact that he wore no livery and his shield was black. Foiled by my vigilance they halted beyond arrow range. This was not formal war and there would be neither discussion nor debate. They would either attack us or move away and, when they dismounted and began to search the houses then I knew that it was the former.

"Wilfred, send half the men, including the night watch, for food. You go with them."

"I should stay here, lord."

"We both know they will not attack yet and, if they do, then we have more than enough men on the walls to deter them. They will need ladders or a ram."

He saw the sense in that. We had often discussed the fact that de Lusignan would know, from the steward who had fled, the layout of the hall; its strengths and its weaknesses. After they had gone, I walked the fighting platform rearranging the order in which men stood. I bolstered the villagers with a man at arms. I pointed out where the darts and spears were but counselled against using them unless they were certain that they would make a kill. Both missiles could be turned against us. I gave advice on what to do when the enemy attacked and, all the time, I watched the village. There was order to their destruction of the homes of my people. They sought ladders and the materials to make them.

Beams were hacked from roofs; there would be a cost to my villagers even if we won.

I rejoined Henry and Edward who stood over the gate. I saw that Henry had his leather helmet, hide hauberk and small buckler. I doubted that he would be able to do much on the wall but as his mother was busy it seemed right to keep him occupied. I picked up one of the bulbous darts. They were front heavy so that when they were thrown, they would hit hard. "We use these but only when you cannot miss. If they climb the ladders then they will do so beneath shields and both a dart and a spear would be useless. Edward can drop a stone and when he hits a shield the warrior may move his arm. Then would be the time to strike but you must hit flesh; an eye or the face would be best." I saw Henry nodding as he took it in.

Soon we heard the sound of hammering. They were building the ladders beyond the village. I was just grateful that we lacked big trees. A ram and an assault on the gate would be disastrous. If they cobbled enough wood together to make an improvised ram it would make life difficult but we might be able to deal with it. At noon I sent the other half for food and Wilfred took command of the walls. I went to see my wife.

Anna was just coming out of the chamber and she held up her hand, "Now is not the time, lord, she is in pain and the contractions are more frequent. You find food and let us battle here in this chamber."

Childbirth was beyond my comprehension and I did as I was ordered. I ate and then told the rest to try to sleep. I knew that it would be impossible but even if they just lay down and closed their eyes, they would be better prepared when we were attacked. I rejoined Wilfred on the walls.

"They will wait until night, my lord. That way our archers will not be able to be as effective." He pointed to the ground below us. "If we had a ditch and bridge, we could have kept them at bay."

"I know and, as we both know, hindsight is always perfect. When would we have found time for such an expenditure of effort? When this is done, we can consider that but we will deal with the attack when it comes. Have a brazier lit in the bailey and then when they attack, we can throw burning faggots down to illuminate them and, if we are lucky, to set fire to their ladders."

"If you are staying here, I will set some men to those tasks. We do not need all of these men on the walls."

I spoke with my men at arms and was pleased that, despite the odds, they seemed in good spirits.

My daughter was born as darkness fell and just as we were filling the walls with all of our men in preparation for an anticipated attack. Stephen and Anna's daughter, Ruth, came for me, "Sir Robert, the baby is coming! Lady Sarah said that you would wish to be there."

I nodded; I did but I was also needed on the walls. Wilfred was close by and he said, "You go, my lord, they have not attacked yet."

I reached the chamber just as the doctor was cutting the cord and the bloody little bundle of a baby was swaddled in my wife's arms. The fact that she was smiling was enough. She and the baby were alive. I kissed my wife and said, "Well?"

"I am sorry, husband, but it is a girl."

I laughed, "I care not for we have a son already and that is Henry! What do we name her?"

My wife moved aside the cloth which bound our daughter so that I could see her piercing blue eyes looking at me, "My mother was Isabelle and I would name her after my mother for she died giving birth to me."

"Then Isabelle she shall be." I turned to the doctor and Anna, "And thank you for delivering both healthy!"

The doctor smiled, "God wanted both to live and it is an honour to serve you both."

Just then Henry burst in. He glanced at his mother and his new sister. He seemed nonplussed. "Yes?"

"Wilfred sent for you, my lord, the attack has begun!"

I smiled, "I will see you soon, my new daughter."

Doctor Michael said, "And I will prepare my instruments for as much as I might wish it, I cannot see this being a battle with no wounds."

I ran from the chamber and I could hear the cries of the enemy as they assaulted the walls. The light from the brazier illuminated the bailey and I saw, in its light, the arrows from my tower as they aimed at men hurrying towards my walls. Wilfred already had men carrying burning faggots to the walls on pitchforks. I donned my helmet. My shield was on the fighting platform. Even as I ascended the ladder, I heard the thud as the first of the ladders was banged against the walls. Reaching the top, I saw the first of the faggots thrown down to the ground. It missed the base of the ladder but by its light, we saw the numbers who were hurrying forward. The Seljuq Turkish archers were sending arrows at my tower and my battlements. Even as we watched, I saw one of my villagers pitch from the walls.

"Men of the Golden Hills, keep your heads down. Archers, get those Turkish archers!" There was little point in wasting arrows on the men in mail. The archers were the greater danger.

With my villagers hidden behind the crenulations, they were relatively safe but it meant I had a mere seventeen of us to face the attack. Five more ladders found the walls. I picked up a rock and went to the wall. An arrow clanged off my helmet. It was not a bodkin but it made my head ring. I dropped the stone and the climbing man at arms cried out as the rock hit his shield. He kept his footing and climbed a little more. I picked up another rock and this time I held it above my head to give greater power. An arrow hit the back of my hand but the mail there protected my flesh. This time when I threw the stone it made the man at arms drop his arm. I think his arm was broken. As he did so Henry killed his first man. The man at arms had his head back and his mouth screaming when the dart hit him in the eye. Even if the dart in the eye did not kill him the fall on to the burning faggot certainly did. I knew he was dead when the smell of burning flesh drifted up and the man did not move. More stones, darts, spears and javelins were thrown and two more ladders were cleared of men but two succeeded. Jacob the Jew had two men with him and two villagers but it was Hugh de Lusignan who followed the man at arms on to my walls. Jacob was a good warrior but Hugh de Lusignan was a knight with a knight's training and weapons. Although Jacob and Alan son of Wilf slew the first man, Sir Hugh backhanded a blow which hacked across Jacob's neck and as blood spurted Alan was knocked from the fighting platform.

"Wilfred, take command here. Edward, with me! Watch my back!" I slipped my shield on to my right arm and shouted, "Absalom and Peter move away from the knight and those men with him!"

De Lusignan now had a foothold and more men would follow him. He had just two men behind him and I heard Wilfred commanding the men with him to concentrate the darts and arrows on the ladder. Sir Hugh had an open space to his right while I had the crenulations; he could strike at any part of me while I could only bring my sword downwards and his shield could block it. I stepped forward and I watched his sword sweep towards my side. He had a long sword and so I ran, risking falling, the last step so that although he hit me it was with the part of the sword which was close to the hilt. The man at arms behind him thrust at my head with his sword but Edward, somehow, manage to deflect it with his sword. Sir Hugh was a knight but I had been a man at arms. I pulled back my head and butted him in the face. He was not expecting the blow and he reeled back. As he did darts were thrown from below us in the bailey. I saw that Wilfred had sent some of the villagers there and they were hurling their darts at the men on the fighting platform. None would be able to kill but their distraction could be invaluable.

The head butt had disorientated Sir Hugh and I took my chance. I brought my sword down across his neck. Although he blocked it with his shield it was a weak block and the blow made him lurch towards the open side of the platform. A dart struck his leg and I laughed, "Not so easy a plum to pick, is it, de Lusignan? The only part of Golden Hills which you shall have will be a patch of ground in the cemetery!" It was the sort of banter I had used as a man at arms and another man at arms would have laughed it off with a retort but Sir Hugh was shaken. His companion tried to step closer to us but Edward's hand darted out and his sword tip took him in the eye for he had an open helmet. As he screamed, I reversed my sword and swung from Sir Hugh's right. He did not expect the blow and my blade rattled against his helmet. He swung at my shoulder but I blocked the blow with my shield and then, realising that more men were already on the fighting platform, I pulled my sword behind me and thrust upwards. The tip entered his neck where his coif protected it but my blade was sharp and it tore through mail into flesh and drove up into his skull. His helmet flew from the top of his head and, as I tore out the sword sideways, his men were splattered with pieces of bone, brain and drops of blood. When Edward slew a shocked man at arms it was all over. Their leader and paymaster was dead and the ones on the platform tried to descend. Less than half made it. No prisoners were taken and the wounded were butchered. Sir Hugh's men were paying the price for their failure.

By the time we had ensured that there were none left in the village and collected the remaining horses, it was dawn. Anna and the women of the village had cooked some food and, after depositing the enemy dead beyond the walls, we ate. The fact that we had only lost one of my hired men was amazing but it was still one man too many. We would bury him and the two villagers first and then dispose of the men who had come to steal the fruits of our hard work. Before we buried Jerome, Alan and Jacob the Jew, I went to speak with my wife and to greet my new daughter. She was asleep and so I tenderly stroked her golden hair.

"She came into the world on an auspicious day."

My wife nodded, "Henry?"

"He did well". I hesitated and then added, "He killed his first man today, Sarah, and that will change him."

"If he turns out like you then I shall not mind. For you are a fierce warrior but the gentlest of men and that is a good combination."

The first two years of Isabelle's life were peaceful and prosperous. We had good harvests and healthy births amongst the animals. Six chests of coins became seven and then eight. We paid our taxes and we were happy. Henry became more skilled and we invested some of the coins we had made into buying the best hauberk for Edward. All of my surviving men at arms now wore a good hauberk and we had hired two more archers. The measure of the peace we enjoyed was that we no longer had to keep watches and our patrols were pleasant rides across my manor.

Isabelle proved to be a delightful handful and, I think, was one of the reasons Michael stayed with us. She enchanted him. The other babes he had delivered had been whisked away from him as soon as they were born but he saw Isabelle each and every day. In addition, he was happy for Stephen and Anna's daughter, Ruth, and he had been smitten by each other. I do not know if it was the fact that she was totally unlike all of the young women amongst whom he had grown up or that God had sent him to woo her but they were married six months after Isabelle was born. It was about that time that Isabelle began to assert herself. Henry, of course, as an elder brother, indulged her and she took advantage of that. Isabelle had the ability to wind any man around her finger. My wife would shake her head but Anna and Ruth would laugh at the precocious little angel with the dancing eyes of a devil. When Michael and Ruth were married in the small chapel we had, then our world seemed idyllic.

Our perfect world ended two years to the day after Isabelle was born. The Seljuq Turks came. There had been raids to the north and south of us for the whole summer. Villages and isolated manors had been destroyed and the people were driven off. Nur al-Din must have had a plan but we had not seen it. Had he simply invaded then King Baldwin and the knights of Jerusalem would have ridden forth and met him in battle but he did not do that. He was bleeding the land to death. Jerusalem was rich because of the pilgrims and because of the land which supported it and Nur al-Din chose to attack the land. It was clever for had he attacked the pilgrims or used an army to invade then the Pope might have invoked another crusade.

The first that we knew was when, just after dawn, horse archers and mounted warriors galloped into the village. This time there was little warning. The archers in my tower rang the bell and used their arrows but it was too little and too late. The villagers who survived were lucky that it was Wilfred who was on duty at the gate for he had a calm head. The eight villagers who survived owed their lives to him. He and the three men with him boldly charged the horsemen and slew two before retiring behind my walls. I was awoken by the screams of the dying. The Seljuq Turks were cruel and the women would be carried off to be used in their camps while the men would be butchered. I joined my men on the walls where we were forced to watch helplessly.

Wilfred was berating himself for having failed to save more villagers but his ideas and plans would save us. Since the attack by de Lusignan, we had built a ditch and added a bridge. In allowing the villagers to be saved he had not been able to raise the bridge. Although it would be hard for the Turks to use ladders, they could build a ram. "I am sorry, my lord, I must be getting old, or soft."

"No Wilfred, none of us could have barred our gates to the people. This was meant to be. Perhaps they will simply take what they can and leave."

Wilfred shook his head and pointed north. "When they raided north of here this summer, they destroyed the halls they found there. They mean to destroy us and that is why they have waited until now. This siege might take a month or so for even if they build a ram it will cost them dearly to take the gate."

Wilfred and I had grown close in the years since I had hired him. I understood him better than any other man for he was me without the spurs; he was more like a brother. I could confide in him. I took him apart so that I could speak quietly, "Then we have to leave and try to get to the coast."

"The coast, lord?"

Nodding I said, "I was happy here but it is now clear that we cannot hold Jerusalem and this land for long. I would take my people, if they are willing, back to Anjou or Normandy. I have been promised a manor there by Sir William and, if he still lives, I would take him up on his offer."

"And if he is dead?"

"Then we have coins enough to buy somewhere. We have not paid our taxes this year and the rest of the coins we have accumulated are here in Golden Hills. I will first speak with my wife and, if she is in agreement, then you can speak with the men. I will not force any to leave this land and all who wish to stay shall be given enough payment for them to be able to choose their own future."

My wife looked fearfully at me. Anna was playing with Isabelle and my walls were manned by my men. We were alone. "But we could leave and go to Jericho! It is a poorer manor but..."

I shook my head. If you wish to stay in this land then we need to find somewhere close to one of the fortresses and that life would not be this one."

She saw the sense in that and tears coursed down her cheeks. "I shall be sad to leave for this is the only world that I have ever known."

"Then I shall introduce you to my world. It is a different one but I believe that you will be happy there." She nodded and I saw her looking around the hall which had seen such joy.

My men at arms and archers were all happy to leave the Holy Land for they were a band of brothers. That evening I stood a watch with them and we heard the noise of banging from the village. The repaired houses were being destroyed to build a ram. We had a week of grace for it would take that time to build one. We had no problem with food for we had within the walls a small flock of sheep and two cattle. We would eat well before we left; if we left, for I needed to speak to the manor workers, Stephen, and the villagers who had escaped the wrath of the Muslims. Leaving my men on the walls I went to speak to the ones who might have to be left.

Aaron was the leader of those who had escaped from the village and, along with Stephen, Doctor Michael and Saul the Shepherd they were the ones I addressed. All had strong personalities. I did not honey my words for that was not my way and they deserved the truth. As the men at arms and archers were on the walls I held the meeting in the warrior hall.

I began by giving them a bald and stark statement. "My family and my men intend to leave the hall before the Turks capture it. We will make our way to the coast and take a ship to the west. If you wish you can come with us either to the west or to safety. But your life here is ended."

I saw Stephen nod and squeeze Anna's hand and Doctor Michael held my gaze and he, too, nodded. He had always expressed a desire to visit the west. Aaron said, "Thank you, lord, but how do you intend to get out of this trap? There is but one gate and the Turks guard it. If we were to try to fight our way out then you and your men might survive but not us."

I smiled, for the first time, "Fear not, Aaron, for we have a back door and we have enough horses to carry all of you with us. I would hope to be ten miles away before the Turks know that we are gone."

Aaron looked dubious but Stephen said, "Sir Robert speaks the truth."

"Then, lord, we have nothing to lose and we will follow you although it breaks my heart to give up this land to Muslims."

In that, I agreed with him. "We will slaughter all of the animals and use the salt to preserve them. We will render down the fat from the cattle and use that to make it harder for the enemy to take our walls!"

With that decided we spent two days ostensibly defending our walls but, in reality, preparing for our departure. We had lots of horses but few saddles. We would have to use the sheepskins as saddles. We took the coins from the chests and I distributed some to my men and to the villagers. The bulk of the coins were placed in leather sacks. And then, two nights after we had made the decision Wilfred, Edward and I went down the narrow cleft to the back door. Over the years growing things had disguised it and I knew, from Aaron's words, that none outside of my men knew of its existence. After opening our gate, we began to remove some of the stones. We did not take out those at the bottom. We were many hundreds of paces from the village and the hammering there would disguise any noise we made. The mortar was a loose mix and we took out three large stones. The growth on the outside wall was a thick barrier. Taking off his mail Edward clambered on Wilfred's shoulders and squeezed himself through the gap. He disappeared and did not return for some time.

When he did return, he had a grin on his face, "The ground outside which leads down to the road is undisturbed. None have been on it for many years. They have no sentries."

"Good, then we leave tomorrow night. Replace the stones."

The trick would be to leave without the enemy knowing. We kept a good watch at night and they would expect to see sentries. During the next day, my men fashioned dummies which would, effectively, keep a watch. They would not fool them during the day but, by then, I hoped we would be gone. I ensured that all ate well and we filled every waterskin we could. During the afternoon, while the work on the ram continued, Wilfred and my men removed the mortar from the rest of the stones. Meanwhile, we poured the fat from the cattle on to the drawbridge. It attracted attention from the Turks and our archers duelled with theirs. I did not think about it until later but the little battle would make them think that we were getting desperate rather than effecting an escape.

As darkness fell, we took our leave of the hall. We had been happy there but we could not remain. Henry would lead his mother's horse for she would need to hold Isabelle. I hoped my daughter would cooperate. Saul the Shepherd knew the land better than any and he and my workers would be the vanguard and lead the way. I would be at the back with my men and archers. We would fight any pursuit although, if we did, I feared it would mean our end. I joined my men as we took apart the stone barrier we had built all those years ago. We laid the stones to the side. It would be a narrow passage and only the taller warriors would need to duck if we chose to ride out. As the sun began to set, we began to cut away the foliage and were rewarded with the most beautiful red sky to the west. It seemed to me a hopeful sign for the future. I walked my horse through the opening. My helmet and shield were on my cantle. My men joined me. In the distance, we could hear the sound of the Turks in their camp. They had not sent all of the women away and we had forced ourselves to ignore the plaintive cries of those who were being abused. We had the ones who were free to consider. Immediately after the village had fallen, we had considered a rescue attempt but the Turks had more than three hundred men. As Wilfred and Aaron pointed out it would be suicide.

Saul and the men walked their horses out. Indeed, everyone but my wife walked and led their horses. Saul nodded to me as he left and I saw him watching the ground. He would choose the path which would make the least noise. We had more than forty people with us and just eighteen soldiers to protect them. The sounds from the village actually helped us for it hardened the resolve and all knew their fate if a noise attracted the attention of the Turks. When the last ones had gone then some of the stones and foliage were replaced to disguise our exit. The foliage would die in a day or two but, by then, I hoped to be safe. Wilfred and I were the last two to lead our horses along the old animal track which led to the road and to the stream. Saul had told us that he had often used it, in times past, to fetch back wandering animals. It was only when we reached the road that we mounted. Saul had halted the column and the men helped the women to mount. We were less than a mile and a half from the village and sound travelled at night. This would be the most crucial time.

To me, the sound of the hooves on the road seemed inordinately loud but Wilfred said, quietly, as I turned around for the umpteenth time, "Lord, it sounds loud because we are close to it. Fear not. It will be dawn at the earliest before they know that we are gone."

He was right but I knew that we had the River Jordan to cross before we reached Nablus. Had I just had my men then the fording of the river would have been child's play but if the Turks caught us on the wrong side of the river then many people would die. We travelled eight miles before I called a halt. We had to conserve the horses and I knew that riding would be hard for all. In addition, Isabelle had begun to wail and my wife could not ride and comfort at the same time.

I had two men ride back half a mile to listen for pursuit and then I summoned my six archers. "I would have you be our scouts. Find the easiest place you can to cross the river and, once you have forded it, dismount and prepare your bows."

"Aye, lord."

I waved over Doctor Michael, Saul, Aaron and Stephen. "When we reach the river, I need the men to form a human and equine chain downstream so that if any of the women or children fall while we are crossing then you can save them."

Michael could read beneath my words, "For you will not be there?"

"No, my men and I will be half a mile behind you so that if we are pursued then we can slow them down. Once we are across the river it is but a short ride to Nablus and that is the fortress of Sir Amaury. There we will find refuge."

We rode on through the darkness until I was aware of the first rays of the sun peering over the hills. By my reckoning, we had travelled twelve miles. That sounded like a long way but we had travelled slowly, it was little more than a warrior's walking pace. If our ruse was discovered then the Turks would cover that distance in an hour. We were closer to safety but, equally, we were still in harm's way. As the sun began to illuminate the land, I saw that the road was above the river and that the land between the river and the road was rocky. I knew why my archers had not headed down to the water. The ground was too rough for inexperienced riders. I had not travelled this road since before Sir William had left. The land to the south and the west I knew but this was too close to the Turkish held land for me to be familiar with it. It was the fourth hour of the day when I saw, far ahead, my archers begin to head down to the river. I touched my cross and said a silent prayer to thank God for our deliverance.

I reined in and donned my helmet, "Let us wait here until the archers have crossed. Karl the Swede and Ralph of Tewksbury, ride back to the rise we just passed and watch for pursuit."

Edward asked, "Surely we are too far from Golden Hills now?"

Wilfred shook his head, "Master Edward, when dawn comes they will see the dummies and know them for what they are. They will send men to inspect the walls and when no arrows fly at them, they will know all. If we are lucky, they will use ladders to gain entry and the cattle fat we used will slow their pursuit but by now they will know that we have fled the henhouse."

I nodded, "And if it was me leading the Turks then while men were scaling the walls, I would send men to find our tracks. They might think we were magicians but they will find our trail and then they will follow."

I saw that my archers had reached the far side and I watched the rest of the men from the manor edge their horses into the water. It was too far away to see details but the water appeared to come to the stirrups of the riders. Some of the women and children rode donkeys and ponies.

They would struggle to cross. In fact, the only way they would be able to do so was if they were led across on a larger horse.

The thoughts were still racing like bees inside my head when Ralph of Tewksbury appeared, shouting, "The Turks! The Turks!" He got no further for his arms were spread like Christ on the cross and he fell from his horse. I knew that he had been slain by Turkish arrows and the fact that Karl the Swede was not there told me of his fate.

We had to buy time. There were nine of us and that was a pathetically small number but I had a wife, daughter and stepson to protect. My life meant nothing compared with theirs. Turning I said, "We charge them. All I wish to do is to hit them hard, turn and then ride to the river!" It says much that none hesitated and, gripping our spears they followed me as I galloped towards the rise. We had rested our horses and all were coursers. We had a chance, albeit a slim one.

The first we saw of them was the spears and that told me that they were not archers. Perhaps the archers had dismounted to loose their arrows but it gave me hope. The first they would see of us would be our helmets and when they saw them, we would be close enough to charge. We reached them just after the high point of the road and we were charging uphill. My spear struck a surprised amir in the chest. He had scale mail and my sharpened spearhead found the gap. I withdrew the spearhead and thrust again at the man behind. I only managed to strike his right shoulder but he tumbled from his horse. From my left, a Turkish arrow thudded into my shield and I knew then that the archers had gone to the right of the horsemen. We would be surrounded but I could do nothing about it.

I shouted, "Wheel right!" It meant exposing our backs to the archers but they would not be able to release their arrows for fear of hitting their own men. We also took the askari by surprise and my spear found the ribs of a warrior who fell from his horse, dragging my spear with him. I had my sword out and was heading for a gap between two Turks when Harold son of Henry fell. There were two arrows in his back. I slashed across the shoulder of an askari and then there was open ground before me. It was rocky and littered with rocks and holes but we were horsemen and not the women and villagers. We knew how to ride.

The valley side dropped alarmingly and I had to lean back to keep my seat but I need have no fear for Remus kept his feet. The drop also saved us from the archers who could no longer see us and the askari were so disrupted that I hoped we had bought enough time. As I reached a flatter part I looked around and saw, to my horror, that I only had Edward, Wilfred, Henry of Dover and Peter the Walker with me. All of the rest must have perished. Arrows fell but we bore charmed lives and they missed. When we reached the river, I decided not to try to ford there. The Turkish archers would easily dispose of us. I headed upstream to where the last of the women were crossing, By the time we reached it there would be just my six archers left and they could give us some cover. I risked a look behind and saw that there were forty men or so pursuing us. We had been lucky. Had it been the whole of the warband then we would have had no chance. Looking ahead I saw that some of the men from the village had joined my archers. The shepherds had slings and Aaron had a bow. They had disobeyed my orders but I was grateful that they had done so. The ground was muddied where my people had crossed and so I passed it and crossed further upstream where it was firmer. I also knew that the river bed would not be as churned up.

As soon as we entered the water we slowed and the Turks began to catch up with us. My archers used their arrows against the horse archers while Saul, the shepherds and Aaron showered the askari. The Turks made the mistake of trying to cross where it was muddy and two paid the price immediately as their horses skidded and the riders were unhorsed. Turkish horse archers were also being struck and I began to hope we might survive. Then Henry of Dover's horse found a hole in the river bed and threw him from the saddle. I wheeled Remus and we returned to help him. An amir with full mail rode at him. Leaving the others to gather Henry's horse and help him out I rode at the amir. He was slightly distracted by Henry and had to change his stroke as I slashed down at his right side. There was a clash of steel and sparks as our blades met. My shield was hit by three arrows and that showed the skill of the archers for had they missed me they might have hit their leader. As I whipped Remus' head around my warhorse snapped at the Turkish mount and it tried to move away. Instead of bringing my sword down I lunged and my sword managed to penetrate under the amir's armpit. It accentuated his fall and he and his horse crashed into the water.

The weight of the horse and his mail ensured that the amir died and I heard Edward shout, "We are clear, lord!"

As I headed across the river, I felt a thud in my back and a shooting pain race down my body. I forced myself to ignore it and when I reached the west bank of the Jordan I turned and saw that the death of the amir and my archers had discouraged the others. They were heading south once more.

Wilfred took charge and shouted, "Edward, take Sir Robert's reins. Peter, ride to the others and have them halt. We need the healer!"

I was about to protest but the pain which coursed through my body was too much and I obeyed. Doctor Michael saved my life. It took him five hours to remove the arrow which was so close to my spine that he feared, at one point, that the arrow might touch my backbone and render me immobile for life. They made a litter and I was carried to Nablus between two horses. Once we reached Nablus then Sir Amaury sought men from Queen Melisende and they sent a column of knights and men at arms to try to recapture Golden Hills. After a week I had recovered enough so that I was able to stand when they returned. Golden Hills was no more. The Turks had destroyed it. The cattle fat had been ignited and the stone walls had crumbled to the ground. None would rebuild it. Even had we wanted to we could not have gone back.

I thought when we reached Caesarea that all of our troubles were over and, indeed, they largely were. We took rooms close to the port and I arranged a passage for all those who wished to leave. Stephen of Nazareth went to buy spices for our new life but, when he returned, it was as though he had seen a ghost.

"What is it?"

"Phillippe of Acre, he is here. I saw him in the market and he has armed men with him. I spoke with some of the stallholders and they said his name is Roger of Poitou but I know him to be Phillippe of Acre."

We were due to leave the next morning but I could not leave this traitor free to enjoy the fruits of his thievery. I took Wilfred, Edward and Stephen with me and headed for the castle. The port was run by the Templar order and I would tell them of the man. Jacques de Hughes was an ambitious knight and, when I was admitted to his court, I could see that he wanted power and using the order to further his status. He told me that Roger of Poitou was a man of some standing and, unless I had proof then he could do nothing.

"If I bring him to you with three witnesses who attest to his identity then will you act?"

"Of course, Sir Robert, for you, too, are a man of standing." He did not wish ripples in his little pond and if there was danger then it would be mine alone.

The three of us still wore mail and we headed for the market. "Stephen, when you spy him then just let me know and find yourself a place of safety. We will apprehend him."

"Watch him, lord, for he is a cunning man and has a secreted blade he keeps in his boot."

We found the man with his four companions as they sat outside a tavern with a jug of wine on the table. I recognised their type immediately. They were the ones who always fled a battle first and they would slit a shield brother's throat as easily as an enemy. Three were Franks and one was a Turk. None wore mail but the three Franks had leather vests. Phillippe of Acre wore the fine clothes of a lord. I knew the story even as I waved Stephen away. When de Lusignan had attacked me and died he had taken the stolen gold and become a different man. I guessed that the four men were ones who had fled after we had thwarted their attempt to take my home.

"Wilfred, take the right and Edward the left. Have a weapon ready in case they do not come easily."

"Aye, lord. Master Edward, if it comes to blows then strike to kill!"

I rested my hand on my rondel dagger for it had a wickedly sharp edge to it and was as long as my forearm. "Phillippe of Acre, I am here to take you to the castellan of this town." We had taken them by surprise and the five of them looked up with guilty looks on their faces.

Phillippe of Acre recovered first and smiled. He had seen my spurs and said, "You are wrong my lord. I am Roger of Poitou recently arrived from St Gilles Croix de Ville."

"You are not for you were seen by Stephen of Nazareth." I gambled and looked at the other four, "And you four attacked my home at Golden Hills! You will be tried for your crimes."

I think that Phillippe of Acre might have tried to bluff his way out of it but the other four stood and reached for weapons, seeing just three of us. I wore gloves and grabbing the dagger hand of one I rammed my own dagger into his ribs. The Turk stabbed at me, seeing just my surcoat and cloak but Balin's mail stopped the blow. I thrust my dagger into his eye. Wilfred had torn open the stomach of the third and the fourth punched Edward to the ground and fled.

Phillippe of Acre still tried to brazen it out. He stood and shouted, "I demand the watch! My men have been attacked and murdered!"

The noise had attracted the city watch and four armed men approached. I helped Edward to his feet. The dead men lying in a widening pool of blood would be difficult to explain. The sergeant shrugged apologetically, "I am sorry, my lord, I am certain that there is an explanation but I must ask you to hand over your weapon and come with me." I handed over the blade.

Stephen of Nazareth had disobeyed me and he suddenly appeared, "Sergeant, I can attest that this man is Phillippe of Acre and he robbed my master, Sir Robert here and King Baldwin of a chest of gold!"

The game was up and Phillippe of Acre's hand suddenly went to his hidden blade. He lunged at my unprotected throat and I would have died had Edward's own blade not torn into the stomach of Phillippe of Acre.

There were now two men lying on the ground, writhing and dying. A passing priest knelt and shook his head after he examined them, "The wounds are mortal."

Phillippe of Acre nodded, "Then hear my confession!" For the other man, it was too late and he expired but Phillippe of Acre made a full confession. After he had died the priest made the sign of the cross and closed his eyes.

The sergeant handed me back my dagger, "I am sorry, my lord. I was just doing my job. We will rid the streets of their bodies and find the other man."

I shook my head, "I fear that he and the gold this man stole will be long gone. But at least this one was brought to justice."

As we watched Caesarea disappear to the east, I felt both sad and hopeful. Most of the villagers and half of my people had stayed at Nablus to serve Sir Amaury but my three men at arms and six archers had come with me. Stephen of Nazareth, his wife and children also came with us as did Doctor Michael and his wife. We took ship to Nissa and there our new life would begin. Wilfred and I stood, with Edward at the stern and we said a silent farewell to the men at arms who had given their lives so that we all had a chance of life. We would have to ensure that we made their sacrifice worthwhile. Our new lives in the west would have to be good ones.

The End

If you enjoyed this story then read more about Sir William, the Warlord and Sir Robert in the Anarchy series of books.

Other books by Griff Hosker

If you enjoyed reading this book, then why not read another one by the author?

Ancient History

The Sword of Cartimandua Series
(Germania and Britannia 50 A.D. – 128 A.D.)
Ulpius Felix- Roman Warrior (prequel)
The Sword of Cartimandua
The Horse Warriors
Invasion Caledonia
Roman Retreat
Revolt of the Red Witch
Druid's Gold
Trajan's Hunters
The Last Frontier
Hero of Rome
Roman Hawk
Roman Treachery
Roman Wall
Roman Courage

The Wolf Warrior series
(Britain in the late 6th Century)
Saxon Dawn
Saxon Revenge
Saxon England
Saxon Blood
Saxon Slayer
Saxon Slaughter
Saxon Bane
Saxon Fall: Rise of the Warlord
Saxon Throne
Saxon Sword

Medieval History

The Dragon Heart Series
Viking Slave
Viking Warrior
Viking Jarl
Viking Kingdom
Viking Wolf
Viking War
Viking Sword
Viking Wrath
Viking Raid
Viking Legend
Viking Vengeance
Viking Dragon
Viking Treasure
Viking Enemy
Viking Witch
Viking Blood
Viking Weregeld
Viking Storm
Viking Warband
Viking Shadow
Viking Legacy
Viking Clan
Viking Bravery

The Norman Genesis Series
Hrolf the Viking
Horseman
The Battle for a Home
Revenge of the Franks
The Land of the Northmen
Ragnvald Hrolfsson
Brothers in Blood
Lord of Rouen
Drekar in the Seine
Duke of Normandy

The Duke and the King

New World Series
Blood on the Blade
Across the Seas
The Savage Wilderness

The Reconquista Chronicles
Castilian Knight

The Aelfraed Series
(Britain and Byzantium 1050 A.D. - 1085 A.D.)
Housecarl
Outlaw
Varangian

The Anarchy Series England 1120-1180
English Knight
Knight of the Empress
Northern Knight
Baron of the North
Earl
King Henry's Champion
The King is Dead
Warlord of the North
Enemy at the Gate
The Fallen Crown
Warlord's War
Kingmaker
Henry II
Crusader
The Welsh Marches
Irish War
Poisonous Plots
The Princes' Revolt
Earl Marshal

**Border Knight
1182-1300**
Sword for Hire
Return of the Knight
Baron's War
Magna Carta
Welsh Wars
Henry III
The Bloody Border
Baron's Crusade
Sentinel of the North

Lord Edward's Archer
Lord Edward's Archer
King in Waiting

**Struggle for a Crown
1360- 1485**
Blood on the Crown
To Murder A King
The Throne
King Henry IV
The Road to Agincourt

Tales of the Sword

Modern History

The Napoleonic Horseman Series
Chasseur a Cheval
Napoleon's Guard
British Light Dragoon
Soldier Spy
1808: The Road to Coruña
Talavera
The Lines of Torres Vedras

The Lucky Jack American Civil War series

Rebel Raiders
Confederate Rangers
The Road to Gettysburg

The British Ace Series
1914
1915 Fokker Scourge
1916 Angels over the Somme
1917 Eagles Fall
1918 We will remember them
From Arctic Snow to Desert Sand
Wings over Persia

Combined Operations series
1940-1945
Commando
Raider
Behind Enemy Lines
Dieppe
Toehold in Europe
Sword Beach
Breakout
The Battle for Antwerp
King Tiger
Beyond the Rhine
Korea
Korean Winter

Other Books
Great Granny's Ghost (Aimed at 9-14-year-old young people)

For more information on all of the books then please visit the author's web site at www.griffhosker.com where there is a link to contact him or visit his Facebook page: GriffHosker@Sword Books